"I Was Just Thinking," Becca Said.

She turned away from him and brushed aside a lingering tear. She had loved him so desperately. "I was thinking about us."

"Does that make you sad?"

"It's just that I loved you so much."

"I loved you too," he said.

"Not the same way. I wanted to spend my life with you. I wanted to share all the expectations, the joys, even the disappointments with you. I wanted to bear your children, Brig. I wanted to love them, to teach them, to comfort them when they cried . . . Don't you see? I wanted to be with you forever!"

Dear Reader:

There is an electricity between two people in love that makes everything they do magic, larger than life. This is what we bring you in SILHOUETTE INTIMATE MOMENTS.

SILHOUETTE INTIMATE MOMENTS are longer, more sensuous romance novels filled with adventure, suspense, glamor or melodrama. These books have an element no one else has tapped: excitement.

We are proud to present the very best romance has to offer from the very best romance writers. In the coming months look for some of your favorite authors such as Elizabeth Lowell, Nora Roberts, Erin St. Claire and Brooke Hastings.

SILHOUETTE INTIMATE MOMENTS are for the woman who wants more than she has ever had before. These books are for you.

Karen Solem
Editor-in-Chief
Silhouette Books

Gypsy Wind

Lisa Jackson

Silhouette Intimate Moments
Published by Silhouette Books New York

America's Publisher of Contemporary Romance

Silhouette Books by Lisa Jackson

A Twist of Fate (SE #118)
Dark Side of the Moon (IM #39)
The Shadow of Time (SE #180)
Tears of Pride (SE #194)
Gypsy Wind (IM #79)

SILHOUETTE BOOKS,
300 E. 42nd St., New York, N.Y. 10017

Copyright © 1984 by Lisa Jackson
Cover artwork copyright © 1984 Lisa Falkenstern

Distributed by Pocket Books

ISBN: 0-671-50743-5

First Silhouette Books printing January, 1985

10 9 8 7 6 5 4 3 2 1

To Chris

Chapter 1

THE SMALL DARK ROOM WAS AIRLESS AND FULL OF THE familiar odors of saddle soap, well-oiled leather, and stale coffee. It began to sway eerily, as if the floorboards were buckling. Becca knew that her knees were beginning to give way, but she couldn't steady herself and she had to clutch the corner of the desk in order to stay on her unsteady feet. Her throat was desert dry, her heart pounding with dread as she stared in horror at the small television set across the room. The delft blue coffee cup slipped from her fingers to splinter into a dozen pieces. A pool of murky brown coffee began to stain the weathered floorboards, but Becca didn't notice.

"No!" she cried aloud, though no one else was in the room. Her free hand flew to the base of her throat. "Dear God, no," she moaned. Tears threatened to pool in her eyes and she leaned more heavily against the desk, brushing against a stack of paperwork which slid noiselessly to the floor. Becca's green eyes never left the black and white image on the television but fastened fearfully on the self-assured newscaster who was tonelessly recounting the untimely death of oil baron Jason Chambers.

Flashes of secret memories flitted through Becca's mind as she listened in numbed silence to the even-featured anchorman. Her oval face paled in fear and apprehension and she felt a very small, very vital part of her past begin to wither and die. As the reporter reconstructed the series of events which had led to the fatal crash, Becca vainly attempted to get a grip on herself. It was impossible. Dry wasted tears, full of the anguish of six lost years, burned at the back of her throat and her breath became as shallow and rapid as her heartbeat. "*No!*" She groaned desperately. "It can't be!" Her small fist clenched with the turmoil of emotions and thudded hollowly against the top of the desk.

Hurried footsteps pounded on the wooden stairs, but Becca didn't notice. She couldn't take her eyes off the screen. The door to the tiny room was thrust open to bang heavily against the wall, and a man of medium height, his face twisted in concern, rushed into the office.

"What the hell?" he asked as he noticed the defeated slump of Becca's shoulders and the stricken, near-dead look in her round eyes. She didn't move. It was as if she hadn't heard his entrance. "Becca?" he called softly, and frowned with worry when she didn't immediately respond. He took in the scene before him and wondered about the broken cup and the brown coffee which was running over a scattered pile of legal documents on the floor. Still Becca's fearful eyes remained glued to the television set. "Becca," Dean repeated, more sharply. "What the hell's going on here? I was on my way up here when I heard you scream—"

Becca cut him off by raising her arm and opening her palm to silence him. Taken aback at his sister's strange behavior, Dean turned his attention to the television for the first time since entering the room. The small black and white set was tuned into the news and the story which held his sister mutely transfixed was about some light plane crash in the Southern Oregon Cascades. No big deal, Dean thought to himself. It happened all the time; a careless pilot got caught in bad weather and went down in the mountains. So what? Dean shifted from one foot to the other and searched Becca's stricken white face, searching for a clue to her odd actions. What was happening here? Becca wasn't one to overreact. If anything, Dean considered his younger sister too even-tempered for her own good. A real cool lady. Becca's poise rarely escaped her, but it sure as hell was gone today.

While still attempting to piece together Becca's strange reaction, Dean leaned over to pick up some of the forgotten legal documents. It was then that the weight of the news story struck him: Only one man could break his sister's cool, self-assured composure, and that man, if given the chance, could cruelly twist Becca's heart to the breaking point. It had happened once before. It could happen again, and this time it would be much worse; this time that man had the power to destroy everything Dean had worked toward for six long years.

Silently Dean's thin lips drew downward and his icy blue eyes slid to the screen to confirm his worst fears. He waited while the sweat collected on his palms. A faded photograph of Jason Chambers was flashed onto the screen and Dean's pulse began to jump. It was true! Jason Chambers, head of one of the largest oil companies in the western United States, was *dead*. Dean swallowed back the bile collecting in the back of his throat.

The news of Jason Chambers' death didn't fully explain Becca's outburst. Dean wiped his hands on his jeans before straightening and then listened to the conclusion of the report. He hoped that the reporter would answer the one burning question in his mind—perhaps there was still a way out of his own dilemma. He was disappointed; the question remained unanswered. Dean's jaw tightened anxiously. When the news turned to the political scene, Dean turned the set off.

Becca slumped into the worn couch near the desk and tears began to run down her soft cheeks. She wiped them hurriedly aside as the shock of the newscast began to wear off and the reality of the situation took hold of her. Her hand, which had been raised protectively over her breasts, slowly lowered.

"Are you all right?" Dean asked, his voice harsh despite his concern. He poured a fresh cup of coffee and handed her the mug.

"I . . . I think so . . ." Becca nodded slowly, but she had to catch her trembling lower lip between her teeth. She accepted the warm mug and let its heat radiate some warmth into her hands. Though the temperature in the stifling office had to be well over eighty degrees, Becca felt chilled to the bone.

The silence in the room was awkward. Dean shifted his weight uncomfortably. He was angry, but he didn't really know whom to blame. It was obvious that Becca was caught in the web of memories of her past, memories of Brig Chambers and his tragic horse. Dean's lips pursed into a thin line as he paced restlessly in front of the desk while Becca stared vacantly at the floor. A silent oath aimed at the man who had caused his sister so much pain entered his mind. Brig Chambers could ruin everything! Dean coughed when he leaned against the windowsill and looked across the spreading acres of Starlight Breeding Farm. Brig Chambers, if he was still alive, had the power to take it all away!

Dean asked the one question hanging between his sister and himself. "Was there anyone with Jason Chambers in that plane?"

Becca closed her eyes as if to shield herself from the doubts in her mind. "I don't know," she whispered raggedly.

Dean frowned and rubbed his hands over his bare forearms. He pushed his straw Stetson back on his head, and his reddish eyebrows drew together. His blue eyes seemed almost condemning. "What did the reporter say?"

"Nothing . . . the accident had only happened a couple of hours ago. No one seemed to be sure exactly what caused the crash . . . or who was in the plane. The reporter didn't seem to know too much." Becca moved her head slowly from side to side, as if to erase her steadily mounting fear.

"The station didn't know who was in the plane?" Dean was skeptical.

"Not yet," she replied grimly.

Dean ran a hand over his unshaven cheek and pressed on. "But surely someone at Chambers Oil would know."

Becca sagged even deeper into the cracked leather cushions and toyed with her single, honey-colored braid. It was difficult to keep her mind on her brother's questions when thoughts of Brig continued to assail her. "The reporter said that there was a rumor suggesting that Jason might have had a couple of passengers with him," Becca admitted in a rough whisper. Hadn't Dean heard the story? Why was he pressuring her?

"Who?" Dean demanded. His blue eyes gleamed in interest.

Becca shrugged and fought against the dread which was making her feel cold and strangely alone.

"No one seems to know for sure; I told you it's only speculation that anyone was with Jason . . . no one at Chambers Oil is talking."

"I'll bet not," Dean muttered, unable to hide the edge of sarcasm in his words. His eyes turned frigid.

"Maybe they just don't know."

"Sure, Becca," he mocked. "You of all people know better than that. If Chambers Oil isn't talking, there's a good reason. You can count on it."

"What do you mean?"

Dean looked his sister squarely in the eyes and the bitterness she saw in his cold gaze made her shudder. His scowl deepened. "What I mean is that we, you and I, don't know if Brig Chambers is alive or dead!"

Becca drew in a long, steadying breath as she met Dean's uncompromising stare. Her brother's harsh words had brought her deepest fear out into the open and she had to press her nails into her palms in order to face what might be the cruel truth. *He can't be dead,* she thought wildly, grasping at any glimmer of hope, but fear crawled steadily through her body, making her blood run cold and wrenching her heart so savagely that it seemed to skip a beat in desperation.

She wouldn't allow the small gleam of hope within her to die. "I think that if Brig had been on the plane, the television station would have known about it."

"How?"

"From the oil company, I guess."

"But they're not talking. Remember?"

"I . . . just don't think that Brig was on the plane." Why didn't she sound convincing?

"But you're not sure, are you?"

"Oh, God, Dean," she whispered into her clasped hands. "I'm not sure of anything right now!" As quickly as her words came out, she regretted them.

"I'm sorry . . . I didn't mean to snap at you; it's not your fault," she confessed wearily. "It's all so confusing." Silent tears once again ran down the elegant slopes of her cheeks.

"What are we going to do?" Dean asked, not moving from his haphazard position against the windowsill. Anxious lines of worry creased his tanned brow.

"I don't know," Becca admitted as she faced a tragedy she had never before considered. *Was it possible? Could Brig really be dead?* Her entire body was shaking as she drew her booted feet onto the edge of the couch and tucked her knees under her chin. As her forehead lowered, she closed her eyes to comfort herself. No matter what had happened, she vowed silently to herself that she would find a way to cope with it.

Dean watched his sister until the anger which had been simmering within him began to boil. His fist crashed onto the windowsill in his frustration. "I told you that we should never have gone back to old man Chambers," he rebuked scornfully. "It was a mistake from the beginning to get involved with that family all over again. Look what a mess we're in!"

"Not now, Dean," Becca said wearily. "Let's not argue about this again."

"We have to talk about it, Becca."

"Why? Can't it wait?"

"No, it can't wait, especially now. I told you that going back to Jason Chambers was a mistake, and I was certainly right, wasn't I?"

"I had no choice," Becca pointed out. "*We* had no choice."

"*Anything* would have been better than this mess you managed to get us into! What the hell are we going to do now?"

Trying futilely to rise above the argument, Becca attempted to pull the pieces of her patience and shattered poise into place. "For God's sake, Dean, Jason Chambers is dead! For all we know, other people might have died in that plane and all you can think about is the fact that we owe Jason Chambers some money."

"*Some money*?" Dean echoed with a brittle laugh. "I wouldn't call fifty thousand dollars 'some money.'"

Becca could feel herself trembling in suppressed fury. "The man is *dead,* Dean. I don't understand what you're worried about—"

"Well, then, I'll enlighten you, dear sister. If Jason Chambers is dead, we're in one helluva mess. I don't pretend to know much about estates and wills or anything that happens when a guy as rich as Jason Chambers kicks the bucket, but any idiot can figure out that all of his assets and liabilities will become part of his estate. You and I and the rest of Starlight Breeding Farm are part of those liabilities." Dean took off his hat and raked his fingers through the sweaty strands of his strawberry-blond hair. "There's only one man who is going to benefit by Jason Chambers' death: his only son, Brig. That is, *if* the bastard is still alive."

"Dean, don't . . ." Becca began. She was visibly trembling when she rose from the couch, but in her anger some of the color had returned to her face and a spark of life lightened her pale green eyes.

"Don't you dare come to the aid of Brig Chambers," Dean warned. "Any praises you might sing in his behalf would sound a little hollow, wouldn't you say?"

"Oh, Dean . . . all of that—"

"That what? Scandal?" Dean suggested ruthlessly.

"I don't want to talk about it."

"Why not? Does the truth hurt too much? Don't you remember what happened at Sequoia Park?"

"Stop it!" Becca shouted irritably. In a more controlled voice, she continued. "That was a long time ago."

"Give me a break, will ya, Becca? Brig Chambers nearly destroyed your reputation as a horse breeder, didn't he? And that doesn't begin to touch what he did to you personally. Even if your memory conveniently fails you, I've still got mine." Dean wiped a dusty layer of sweat from his brow with the back of his hand before striding to the small refrigerator and withdrawing a cold can of beer. He dropped into a chair, popped the tab of the can, and let the spray of cool white foam cascade down the frosty aluminum. After taking a lengthy swallow, he settled back into the chair and cradled the beer in his hands. His cold eyes impaled his sister, but he managed to control his temper. Calmly, he inquired, "You're still carrying a torch for that bastard, aren't you?"

"Of course not."

"I don't believe you." Another long swallow of beer cooled Dean's parched throat.

"Oh, Dean, let's not argue. It's so pointless. What happened between Brig and me is part of the past. He took care of that."

Dean noticed the wistful sigh that accompanied her argument. "Then why did you run back to Brig's father when you needed the loan?"

Becca's full lips pursed. "We've been through this a hundred times. I had no other choice. No bank in the country would loan me ten thousand dollars, much less fifty thousand."

"Exactly. Because Brig Chambers ruined your reputation as a horse breeder." His knowing eyes glittered.

Becca ignored Dean's snide comment. "Jason Chambers was my only chance . . . *our* only chance."

Dean drained his beer and crushed the can in his

fist. He tossed it toward the wastebasket and missed. The can rolled noisily across the floor to stop near the worn couch. "Well, Becca, you had better wake up and face facts. Our 'only chance,' as you refer to old man Chambers, is *dead*. And now, for all we know, his son, or whoever's still alive, practically owns our Thoroughbred. The only thing we've got going in our favor is that no one knows about the loan or the horse. That is right, isn't it? Jason Chambers was the only person who knew about Gypsy Wind?"

"I think so. He's the only one at Chambers Oil who would have been interested."

"Good! I guess we can count ourselves lucky that the local press hasn't shown much interest in her. Maybe we'll get a break yet. If our luck holds, the attorneys for Chambers Oil will be too busy with the rest of the Chambers empire to worry about our note for the fifty grand. Maybe they won't even find it. The old man could have hidden it."

"I doubt that."

"Why? He wanted to avoid the publicity as much as we did."

"That was before he died. I don't know what you're suggesting, Dean, but I don't like it. There's no way we can hide that horse and I wouldn't want to try. The Chambers family has to be advised that the collateral for that note is Gypsy Wind. That's only fair, Dean."

"That's not fair, Becca, it's damned near crazy! How can you even think about being fair with the likes of Chambers? What's going to happen is that we'll lose our horse! The last six years of work will go down the drain! Take my advice and keep quiet about the Gypsy."

"I can't! You know that. Keeping quiet would only make things worse in the long run. Sooner or

later someone in the Chambers family is going to
find the note and realize that we owe that money.
And what about the horse? Even if I wanted to, I
couldn't hide Gypsy. For one thing, she's insured.
Soon she'll start racing. One way or another the
Chambers family is going to find out about her."

Dean muttered an oath to himself. "Okay, Sis, so
where does that leave us? Back at square one? Just
like we were six years ago? What the hell are we
going to do?"

The headache which had been building between
Becca's temples pounded relentlessly against her
eardrums. To relieve some of her tension, she tugged at the leather thong restraining her hair and
pulled the thick golden strands free of their bond.
Absently she rubbed her temples and ran her fingers
through her long, sun-streaked tresses. "I wish I
could answer you, Dean, but I can't. Not right now.
Maybe later—"

Dean ground his teeth together. "We can't wait
until you pull yourself together, damn it! We haven't
got the time!"

"What do you mean?"

"I mean that we have to find out if Brig Chambers
is still alive! You've got to call Chambers Oil—"

"No," Becca blurted. "I . . . can't."

Dean bit his lower lip and shook his hands in the
air. "You have to, Becca. We've got to know if Brig
was a passenger on that plane. We have to know if
he went down with his father."

"*No!*" Becca's face once again drained of color.
Caught in the storm of emotions raging within her,
she dropped her forehead into her palm. "We'll find
out soon enough," she murmured.

"What are you afraid of?"

Becca's green eyes, when she raised them, pleaded
with her brother to understand. "I'm not ready,

Dean. Not yet. I don't know if I'll ever be . . . able
to face the fact that Brig might be dead," she
admitted.

"So I was right. You are still in love with him."
Dean's mouth pulled into a disgusted frown. "Damn
it, Becca, when are you going to realize that Brig
Chambers is the one man responsible for nearly
ruining your life?"

The tears which Becca had been struggling against
began once again to pool, but she held her head
proudly as she faced her reproachful older brother.
Why couldn't Dean understand the pain she was
going through? How could he remain so bitter? Her
voice was low when she replied. "I know better than
anyone what Brig did to me, and it hurt for a very
long time. But I cared for that man, more than
anything in my life . . . and I can't forget that. It's
been over for a long time, but once he was everything to me."

"You're dreaming," Dean said icily.

"Just because it's over doesn't mean it didn't
happen."

"Why are you telling me all of this?" Dean
demanded as he stretched and paced restlessly in the
confining room.

"Because I want you to know how I feel. I was
bitter once and it's probably true that I should hate
Brig Chambers, but I don't. I've tried to and I can't.
And now that he might be dead . . ." her voice
broke under the strain of her churning emotions.

For a moment sorrow and regret flashed in Dean's
opaque blue eyes. It was gone in an instant. "There's
no way I can understand how you still feel anything
for that louse, and I think you had better prepare
yourself: Brig might already be dead. As for Gypsy
Wind, I think we have ourselves one insurmountable
problem." His face softened slightly and for a fleeting moment, through the shimmer of unshed tears,

Becca once again saw her brother as he had been during her childhood, the adolescent whom she had adored. The calloused and bitter man had faded slightly. His expression altered and she could feel him closing her out, just as he had for the past few years. Now, when she needed him most, he was withdrawing from her. "Come on, Sis," he said tonelessly. "Buck up, will you?"

He opened the door to the office, and as quickly as he had burst into the room over the stables, he was gone. Becca heard his boots echoing hollowly against the worn steps. Slowly she followed her brother outside. She stood on the weathered landing at the top of the stairs. Holding her hand over her eyebrows to shade her vision, Becca watched the retreating figure of her brother as he sauntered to his battered pickup, hopped into the cab, engaged the starter, and roared down the dry dirt road, leaving a dusty plume of soil in his wake.

The late afternoon sun was blinding for Northern California at this time of the year, and the wind, when it did come, was measured in arrid gusts blowing northward off Fool's Canyon. The charred odor of a distant forest fire added to the gritty feel of weariness which had settled heavily between Becca's shoulder blades.

He can't be dead, she thought to herself as she remembered the one man who had touched her soul. She could still feel the caress of his fingers as they outlined her cheek or pushed aside an errant lock of her hair. She closed her eyes when the hot wind lifted her hair away from her face, and she imagined Brig's special scent: clean, woodsy, provocatively male. Idly she wondered if he'd changed much in the last six years. Were his eyes still as erotic as they once were? It had been his eyes which had held her in the past and silently held her still. Eyes: stormy gray and omniscient. Eyes that could search out and reach the farthest corners of her mind. Eyes that understood her as no one ever had. Eyes that touched her, embraced her. Eyes which had betrayed her.

"He can't be dead," she whispered to herself as her palm slapped the railing. "If he wasn't alive, I would know it. Somehow I would know it. If he were dead, certainly a part of me would die with him."

Slowly she retraced her steps back into the stuffy office and reached down to pick up the remains of the coffee cup. Her movements were purely mechanical as she straightened the papers and placed them haphazardly on the corner of the desk. She wiped up the coffee, but her mind was elsewhere, lost in thoughts of a happier time, a younger time. Though she sat down at the desk and attempted to concentrate on the figures in the general ledger, she found that the mundane tasks of keeping Starlight Breeding Farm operational seemed vague and unimportant. Images of Brig kept lingering on her mind, vivid pictures of his tanned, angular face and brooding gray eyes. Becca recalled the dimple that accompanied his slightly off-center smile and she couldn't help but remember the way a soft Kentucky rain would curl his thick, chestnut hair.

Deeper images, strong and sensual, warmed her body when she thought of the graceful way he walked, fluid and arrogantly proud. Her cheeks burned when she imagined the way he would groan in contentment when he would first unbutton her blouse to touch her breasts.

"Stop it!" she screamed as she snapped the ledger book closed and pulled herself away from the bittersweet memories of a love that had blossomed only to die. "You're a fool," she muttered to herself as she pushed the chair backward and raced out of the confining room. She had to get away, find a place in the world where traces of Brig's memory wouldn't touch her.

Her boots ground into the gravel as she ran past the main stables, across the parking lot, and through a series of paddocks, far away from the central area of the ranch. She stopped at the final gate and her clear green eyes swept the large paddock, searching for the dark animal who could take her mind off everything else. In a far corner of the field, under the shade of a large sequoia tree, stood Gypsy Wind. Her proud head was turned in Becca's direction, and the flick of her pointed black ears indicated that she had seen the slender blond woman leaning against the fence.

"Come here, Gypsy," Becca called softly.

The horse snorted and stamped her black foreleg impatiently. Then, with a confident toss of her dark head, Gypsy Wind lifted her tail and ran the length of the back fence, turned sharply, and raced back to the tree, resuming her original position. Dark liquid eyes, full of life and challenge, regarded Becca expectantly.

A sad smile touched Becca's lips. "Showing off, are you?" she questioned the horse.

Footsteps crunched on the gravel behind Becca.

"I thought I might find you here," a rough male voice called as a greeting to her.

Becca looked over her shoulder to face the rugged, crowlike features of Ian O'Riley. He was shorter than she, and his leatherish skin hid nothing of his sixty-two years. Becca managed a thin smile for the ex-jockey, but nodded in the direction of the spirited horse. "How did the workout go this morning?"

The bit of straw that Ian had been holding between his teeth shifted to one side of his mouth. "'Bout the same, I'd say."

Becca sighed deeply and cast a rueful glance at the blood-bay filly. As if the horse knew she was the center of attention, she shook her dark head before tossing it menacingly into the air.

"There's no way to calm her down, is there?" Becca asked her trainer.

"It takes time," Ian replied cautiously, but his words were edged in concern. "It's hard to say," he admitted. "She's got the spirit, the 'look of eagles,' if you will . . . but . . ."

"It might be her undoing," Becca surmised grimly.

Ian shrugged his bowed shoulders. "Maybe not."

"But you're worried, aren't you?"

"Of course I'm worried. History sometimes has a way of repeating itself." He noticed the ashen pallor of Becca's skin and thought that he was the cause of her distress. He could have kicked himself for so thoughtlessly bringing up the past. He wanted to caution Becca about the Gypsy, but he had to be careful not to disillusion her. In Ian's estimation, Becca Peters was one of the finest horse breeders in the country, even if her brother was worse than useless. Ian attempted to ease Becca's mind. "Gypsy Wind just needs a little more work, that's all."

Becca wasn't convinced. "She does have Sentimental Lady's temperament."

"The spirit of a winner."

"It was Lady's spirit that was her downfall."

Ian waved dismissively and his face wrinkled with his comfortable smile. "Don't think that way, gal. Leave the worrying to me; that's what you pay me for."

"If I paid you for all the worrying you do, I'd be broke."

Laughter danced in Ian's faded blue eyes and his grizzled face showed his appreciation for Becca's grim sense of humor. "Just leave Gypsy to me. We'll be ready, come next spring."

"Ready for what?"

"Whatever the competition can dish out. Surprise them, we will. Even the colts."

"You think she can keep up with the colts?" Becca was clearly dubious and a cold chill of apprehension touched the back of her neck. The last time she had put a filly against a colt, the result had been a nightmare. Becca had vowed never to repeat her mistake.

"Of course she can. Not only that, she'll outclass the lot of them. Just wait and see. Remember, we have the element of surprise on our side."

"Not much longer. The first time she runs, the press will be there, digging up everything on Sentimental Lady."

"Let them. This time will be different," he promised. Ian gave Becca a hefty pat on the shoulders before he sauntered back toward the brood-mare barn.

Becca's gaze returned to the fiery horse. She wanted to be unbiased when she appraised the blood-bay filly, but Becca couldn't help but compare Gypsy Wind with her full-sister, Sentimental Lady. Gypsy was built similarly to Sentimental Lady, so much so that it was eerie at times. Though slightly shorter than Lady, Gypsy Wind was heavier and stronger. Fortunately, Gypsy's long, graceful legs were stouter than Sentimental Lady's, capable of standing additional weight and stress. Her coloring was identical except that the small, uneven star which Lady had worn so proudly was missing on her sister.

Doubts crowded Becca's tired mind. Maybe she had made a foolish mistake in the breeding of Gypsy Wind. The question haunted her nights. How was she supposed to know that the offspring of Night Dancer and Gypsy Lady would produce another filly, an uncanny likeness of the first?

As she watched the dark horse shy from a fluttering leaf, Becca wondered what Brig would think if he saw Gypsy Wind. She had asked herself the same question a thousand times over and the answer had always been the same. He would be stunned, and afterward, when the initial shock had worn thin, he would be furious to the point of violence. Still, Becca had hoped to someday proudly show off the Gypsy to Brig. New tears burned in Becca's throat as she watched the dark horse and realized that Brig might never see Gypsy Wind. Brig Chambers might already be dead.

Becca let loose of the emotional restraint she had placed upon herself and cried quietly, feeling small and alone. She lowered her head to the upper rail of the fence and let out the sobs of fear and grief that had been building within her. Why had she never swallowed her stubborn pride and told Brig Chambers just how desperately she still loved him? Why had she waited until it was too late?

Chapter 2

THE FIRST GRAY FINGERS OF DAWN FOUND BECCA STILL awake, lying restlessly on the crumpled bedclothes. She snapped off the radio that had been her companion throughout the long night. The endless hours had been torture. There had been no broadcasts during the night to relieve her dread. She was numb from the reality that the only man she had ever loved might be lost to her forever.

The night had seemed endless while she stared vacantly at the luminous numbers on the clock radio, listening above the soft static-ridden music to the sounds of the hot summer night. Even in the early hours before dawn, the mercurial temperature hadn't cooled noticeably, making the night drag on even longer. Though the windows of her room had been open, the lace curtains had remained still, unmoved by even the faintest breath of wind. Trapped in a clammy layer of sweat, Becca had tossed on the bed, impatiently waiting for the dawn. When she had finally dozed, it was only to be reawakened by nightmares of an inferno, a disemboweled Cessna, and the haunting image of Brig's tortured face.

It was nearly six o'clock when her silent vigil ended. The familiar sound of a throbbing engine pierced the solitude as it halted momentarily at the end of the drive. At the sound, Becca rolled out of bed and quickly slipped into a clean pair of jeans and a T-shirt. She pulled on her boots as she ran from her room, flew down the stairs, and raced like a wild-woman to the mailbox.

Her heart was thundering in her chest and her fingers were trembling as she opened the rolled newspaper. Anxiously her eyes swept the headlines, stopping on a blurred photograph of a ragged, weary-looking Brig Chambers. *He's alive,* her willing mind screamed at her while her eyes scanned the article to confirm her prayers. Slowly the fear and dread which had been mounting within her heart began to ebb. "Thank God," Becca whispered in the morning sunlight as she crumpled into a fragile mound at the side of the road and let the tears of joy run freely down her cheeks. "Thank God."

It was several minutes before she could collect herself. She stood up and hastily rubbed the back of her hand over her eyes to stem the uneven flow. A tremendous weight seemed to have been lifted from her shoulders as she half-ran back to the house. She reread the article several times before finally opening the kitchen door. A wistful smile crossed her lips. She still felt sadness at the death of Brig's father, but the relief in knowing that Brig was alive warmed her heart.

The newspaper article indicated that Chambers Oil was not, as yet, making a statement concerning the crash, although the rumor that there had been passengers on the plane was confirmed by a company spokesman. The names of the persons accompanying the oil baron on his tragic journey were being withheld until the next of kin had been notified.

Becca stared at the picture of Brig and wondered how he was. His relationship with his father had been close, if sometimes strained. No doubt Brig was immersed in grief, but she knew that he would survive. It was his way.

The aroma of fresh-perked coffee greeted Becca as she entered the roomy old-fashioned kitchen. "What are you doing up so early?" she asked Dean as she reached for a mug of the steaming black coffee.

"Couldn't sleep," Dean grumbled. He sat at the table, his forehead cradled in his palms. His sandy hair was uncombed and he had two days' worth of stubble on his chin. It looked as if he had slept in his dusty jeans and T-shirt.

"You got in late last night," Becca observed quietly. "I didn't expect to see you till mid-afternoon."

"I guess I've got things on my mind," he replied caustically. He raised his bloodshot eyes to stare at his sister, and in an instant he knew that Brig Chambers was still alive. It was written all over Becca's relieved face. "You got the paper?" he asked gruffly.

Becca nodded, taking a sip from her coffee as she sat down at the small table. Because Dean was being irritable, she purposely goaded him. "Do you want the sports section?"

Dean's eyes darkened. "Not this morning." He reached for the paper and began skimming the front page. Mockingly he added, "I'm glad to see you're back to normal."

"A pity you're not."

"All right, all right, I admit it. I've got one helluva

hangover . . . Jesus Christ, give me a break, will ya?" His eyes moved quickly across the newsprint. "So Brig wasn't in the plane with his father!"

Was Dean relieved or disappointed? Becca couldn't guess. Her brother was becoming more of an enigma with each passing day. "Thank goodness for that," she sighed.

Dean shook his head slowly from side to side, trying to quell the throbbing in his temples and attempting to concentrate. "Okay, so now we know exactly what we're up against, don't we?" His eyes narrowed as he ran his thumb over his chin. "The question is, what are we going to do about it."

"I haven't quite decided—"

Before she could continue, Dean interrupted with a shrug and an exaggerated frown. "Maybe we won't have to worry about it at all."

"What do you mean?"

"I mean that it might be out of our hands already. Once Brig finds out about Gypsy Wind *and* the fifty grand, he might make his own decision, regardless of what we want."

"You think so?"

"What's to prevent him from taking our horse? After all, his old man practically bought her."

"I doubt that Brig would want the filly . . . you know that he gave up anything to do with racing—"

"Because of Sentimental Lady?" Dean asked bluntly. "Don't tell me you're still suffering guilt over her, too."

"No . . ."

"Just because Brig blamed you for—"

"Stop it!" Becca got up from the table and went over to the counter. For something to do, she began cutting thick slices of homemade bread. She didn't want to remember anything about the guilt or the pain she had suffered at Brig's hand; not now, not while she was still bathing in the warmth of the knowledge that he was alive. Realizing that she couldn't duck Dean's probing questions, she addressed the issue in a calmer voice. "I think the best thing to do is to wait, until sometime after the funeral. Then we'll have to talk to the attorneys at Chambers Oil."

"They'll eat you alive."

Becca sighed inaudibly. It was impossible to get through to Dean when his mind was set. Sometimes she wondered why he was so defensive, especially whenever the conversation steered toward Brig. After all, it was she whom Brig had blamed, not Dean. She placed the bread on the table near an open jar of honey. "We can handle the attorneys . . . but if you would prefer to talk to Brig—"

"*What?* Are you out of your mind?" Dean's skin whitened under his deep California tan. "I have *nothing* to say to Chambers!"

Becca assumed that Dean's ashen color and his vehement speech were caused by his hangover and his concern for her. She dismissed his hatred of Brig as entirely her fault. Dean knew how deeply she had been wounded six years ago, and her brother held Brig Chambers solely responsible. Dean had never forgiven Brig for so cruelly and unjustly hurting his sister. But then, Dean never did know the whole story; Becca had shielded him from part of the truth. Patiently, she forced a smile she didn't feel upon her brother. "I'll go and talk to Brig myself."

"Becca!" Dean's voice shook angrily and it made her look up from the slice of bread she was buttering. "Don't do anything you might regret . . . take some time, think things over first."

"I have."

"No, you haven't! You haven't begun to consider all of the consequences of telling Brig about the loan or the horse! Don't you see that it will only dredge up the same problems all over again? Think about

what a field day the press will have when they learn
that *you* and the money you borrowed from Chambers Oil have bred another horse, not just any horse,
mind you, but nearly an exact copy . . . a twin of
Sentimental Lady! It may have been six years,
Becca, but the press won't forget about the controversy at Sequoia Park!" Dean's pale blue eyes were
calculating as they judged Becca's reaction.

"Gypsy Wind is going to race. We can't hide her
or the note."

"I'm not asking you to," Dean hastily agreed as he
noticed just a tremor of hesitation in Becca's voice.
He tried another, more pointed tack. "Just give it
time. Brig Chambers has a lot more problems—
important problems—than he can handle right now.
His father was killed just yesterday. If you bring up
the subject of Gypsy Wind now, it will only burden
him further."

"I don't know . . ."

Dean pressed his point home. "Just give it a little
time, will ya? Of course we'll tell him about the filly,
when the time is right. Once she's proved herself."

"She won't race for another five or six months."

"Well, maybe we'll have sold her by then."

"*Sold her*?" Becca repeated, as if she hadn't heard
her brother correctly. "I'll never sell Gypsy Wind."

Dean's lips pressed into a severe frown. "You may
not have a choice, Becca. Remember, when Brig
Chambers finds that note, for all practical purposes,
he owns that horse."

"Then how can you even suggest that we sell
her?" Becca asked, astounded by her brother's
heartlessness and dishonesty. Sometimes she didn't
think she understood her brother at all. She hadn't
in a long while.

"It might be that the horse is worth more now! For
God's sake, Becca, we can't take a chance that she'll
get hurt when she races. Think about Sentimental

Lady! Do you want us to run into the same problem with Gypsy Wind?"

Becca was horror-struck at the thought. Her stomach lurched uneasily. Dean's chair scraped against the plank floor. He raked his fingers through his hair impatiently. "I don't know what we should do," he admitted. "I just wish that for once you would think with your head instead of your heart!"

Becca's green eyes snapped. "I think I've done well enough for the both of us," she threw back at him. "As for listening to my heart—"

"Save it!" Dean broke in irritably. "When it comes to Brig Chambers, you never have thought straight!"

Before she could disagree, the screen door banged against the porch, announcing Dean's departure.

Ten days had passed and the argument between Becca and Dean was still simmering, unresolved, in the air. Although they hadn't had another out-and-out confrontation, nothing had changed concerning the status of Starlight Breeding Farm and its large outstanding debt to Chambers Oil. In Dean's opinion, no news was good news. To Becca, each day put her more on edge.

Becca had considered calling Brig and trying to explain the situation over the telephone, but just the thought of the fragile connection linking her to him made her palms sweat. What if he wouldn't accept the call? Did he already know about the note? Could he guess about the horse? Was he just waiting patiently for her to make the first move so that he could once again reject her? Though the telephone number of Chambers Oil lingered in her memory, she never quite got up enough nerve to call.

Excuses filled her mind. They were frail, but they sustained her. Brig would be too busy to talk to her, now that he was running the huge conglomerate, or he would be attempting to sort out his own grief. Not only had he lost his father in the plane crash, but also a friend. One of the persons on board the ill-fated plane was Melanie DuBois, a raven-haired model who had often been photographed on the arm of Brig Chambers, heir to the Chambers Oil fortune. Her slightly seductive looks opposed everything about Becca. Melanie had been short for a model, but well proportioned, and her thick, straight ebony hair and dark unwavering eyes had given her a sensual provocative look that seemed to make the covers of slick magazines come to life. Now Melanie, too, was gone. Dead at twenty-six.

On this morning, while packing a few things into an overnight bag, Becca tried not to think of Melanie DuBois or the young woman's rumored romance with Brig. Instead, she attempted to mentally check all of the things she would need for a weekend in Denver. Knowing it might be impossible to get hold of Brig at the office, Becca had vowed to herself that she would go back to the Chambers mountain retreat and find Brig if she had to. She had visited it once before when she was forced to borrow the money for Gypsy Wind from Brig's father. Becca was willing to do anything necessary to keep Gypsy Wind. That was the reason she was packing as if she would have to stay for weeks in the enchanting retreat tucked in the slopes of the Colorado Rockies. Wasn't it?

"I don't suppose there is any way I can talk you out of this." Dean said as he leaned against the doorjamb of Becca's small room.

"No." She shook her head. "You may as well save your breath."

"Then you won't begin to listen to how foolish this is?"

Becca cast him a wistful smile that touched her eyes. "Save your brotherly advice."

"When will you be back?"

"Monday."

Dean's bushy eyebrows furrowed. "So long?"

"Maybe not," she replied evasively. She snapped the leather bag closed. "If I can get everything straightened out this afternoon, I'll be back in the morning."

"Uh-huh," Dean remarked dubiously. "But you might be gone for the entire weekend?"

"That depends."

"On what?"

"Brig's reaction, I suppose," Becca thought aloud. Her heart skipped a beat at the thought of the man whom she had loved so desperately, the man she had once vowed never to see again.

"Then you really are going to tell him about our horse, aren't you?"

"Dean, I *have* to."

"Or you *want* to?"

"Meaning what?"

Dean strode into the room, sat on the edge of the small bed, and eyed his younger sister speculatively. How long had it been since he had seen her look so beautiful? When was the last time she had bothered to wear a dress? Dean couldn't remember. The smart emerald jersey knit was as in vogue today as it had been when Becca had purchased it several years ago, and her sun-streaked dark-blond hair shone with a new radiance as she tossed it carelessly away from her face. Becca looked more alive than she had in months, Dean admitted to himself. "Examine your motive," he suggested with a severe smile. He started to say something else, changed his mind, and shook his head. Instead he murmured, "Whatever it is you're looking for in Denver, I hope you find it."

"You know why I'm going to see Brig," Becca replied calmly. She hoisted her purse over her shoulder, but avoided Dean's intense gaze. Unfortunately, she couldn't hide the incriminating burn on her cheeks.

"Yeah, *I* know," Dean responded cynically, while picking up Becca's bag, "but do *you?*"

The cedar house seemed strangely quiet without the presence of his father to fill the rooms. Though it was still fastidiously clean and the only scent to reach Brig's nostrils was his father's favorite blend of pipe tobacco, the atmosphere in the room seemed . . . dead.

It's only your imagination, he chastised himself as he tried to take his solemn thoughts away from his father. It had been nearly two weeks since the company plane had gone down, and it was time to bury his grief along with the old man.

In the past twelve days Brig had come to feel that his life was on a runaway roller coaster, destined to collide with any number of unknown, intangible obstacles. There had been the funeral arrangements, the will, the stuffy lawyers, the stuffier insurance adjusters, the incredibly tasteless press, and now, unexpectedly, a wildcat strike in the oil fields of Wyoming. It appeared that everyone who remotely knew Jason Chambers had a problem, a problem Brig was supposed to handle.

Damn! Brig ran his fingers under the hair at the base of his head and rubbed the knot of tension that had settled between his shoulder blades. In the last week he hadn't had more than two or three hours sleep at a stretch and he was dog-tired. The last thing in the world he had expected was for his robust father to die and leave him in charge of the corporation.

Brig had worked solely for Chambers Oil for the last six years, and in that time his father had trained him well. Brig had become the best troubleshooter ever on the payroll of Chambers Oil. No problem had seemed insurmountable in the past, and usually Brig flourished with only a few hours of sleep. But not now—not tonight. In the past the problems had come one at a time, or so it seemed in retrospect. But since Jason Chambers' death, the entire company appeared to be falling apart, piece by piece. Somehow, Brig was expected to hold it steadfastly together. A sad smile curved his lips as he now understood that maybe his father had only made running the company seem simple. "I've got to hand it to you, old man," Brig whispered as he held his drink upward in silent salute to his father.

Maybe I'm just not cut out for this, he thought to himself as his lips pulled into a wry grimace. *Maybe I just don't have what it takes to run an oil conglomerate.*

As he sat in his father's favorite worn chair, his elbows rested on the scarred wooden desk, the same desk he remembered from his childhood. Brig took a long swallow from his warm scotch. It was his third drink in the last hour. He rubbed the back of his neck mechanically and rotated his head before tackling the final task of the day. His frown deepened as he stared at the untidy stack of papers banded loosely together in the bottom drawer of the desk. A few moments earlier Brig had discovered that this drawer, and this drawer only, had been kept locked. So this was where Jason Chambers had kept all of his personal records—the transactions that were hidden from the disapproving eyes of the company auditors and the disdainful glare of tax attorneys. Brig had suspected that the papers existed, but he had always figured that they were the old man's business, no one else's concern. He smiled sadly to himself and silently cursed his father for the reckless, carefree lifestyle which had ultimately taken his life. "You miserable son-of-a-bitch," Brig whispered fondly. "How could you do this to me?"

His gray eyes lowered to the first scrap of paper in the stack, a yellowed receipt from a furriers for a sable coat. Brig couldn't help but wonder which one of the dozen or so women his father had dated over the last few years had ended up with the expensive prize. With an oath of disgust, leveled for the most part at himself, Brig tossed the papers back into the drawer, slammed it shut, and locked it. He was too tired to think about his father or the string of women who had attracted Jason Chambers since his wife's death.

"If I had any sense I'd burn those blasted papers and forget about them," he muttered to himself; to open that portion of his father's life seemed an intrusion of the old man's privacy. Unfortunately, the inheritance tax auditors didn't see things from the same perspective. He dimmed the desk lamp, picked up his drink, and walked to the window to draw the shade. Flickering lights in the distance caught his attention and he left the shade open. He narrowed his eyes and squinted to be sure just as the twin beams of light flashed once again. Headlights. Someone was coming. *Who?* Brig's thoughts revolved backward in time to earlier in the afternoon. He was certain he had ordered his secretary to keep his whereabouts under wraps. Hadn't Mona understood him; he didn't want to be disturbed. He needed this weekend alone.

Don't get crazy, he told himself as the car drove up the long gravel road. Brig Chambers couldn't hide, not since he took command of Chambers Oil. If someone wanted to find him badly enough, it wouldn't be hard to do. It didn't take a genius to guess that he would be spending a quiet weekend in Jason's rustic cottage in the mountains. Brig had hoped that the two-hour drive from Denver would discourage most people interested in contacting him. He had the foresight to take the phone off the hook, and he hadn't expected to be interrupted. From the looks of the strong headlights winking through the trees, he'd been wrong. Perhaps it was critical business. He checked his watch. Why else would someone be coming to the cabin at nearly ten o'clock at night?

The car rounded the final curve in the driveway and Brig strained to get a glimpse of the driver. Who the hell was it?

Becca's heart was racing as rapidly as the engine of the rental car she had picked up at the airport. All of the confidence she had gathered at dawn had slowly ebbed with the series of problems she had encountered during the day. It was almost as if she were fated not to meet Brig again. To start off her day the flight had been delayed, then there was a mixup in her hotel reservation, not to mention that the rental car which was supposed to be waiting for her had never been ordered, according to the agency's records. It had taken an extra four hours to get everything straightened out. To top off matters, when she had finally managed to arrive at Chambers Oil, she had been politely but firmly rebuked. The efficient but slightly cool secretary had informed Becca that Brig Chambers was gone for the remainder of the day and wasn't expected back into the office until Monday morning. If no one else could help her, then Becca was out of luck. No, the silver-haired woman had replied to her query, Mr. Chambers hadn't left a telephone number where he could be reached . . . if Becca would kindly leave her name and number, Mr. Chambers was sure to get back to her early next week. Becca had declined. It had seemed imperative at the time that she see Brig in person. Right now, she wasn't so certain.

After cresting the final hill and following the road around an acute turn, Becca stepped lightly on the

brakes of the rented sedan. In front of her, silhouet-
ted against a backdrop of rugged, heavy-scented
pine trees, stood the rustic cedar cabin of Jason
Chambers. Soft light from the paned windows indicated that someone was inside. Becca swallowed
with difficulty as six abandoned years without Brig
stretched before her. After all of the pain, would she
be able to see him . . . or touch him? There was no
doubt in her mind that he was in the house; she only
hoped that he was alone and that he would see her.
The angry years apart from him dampened her
spirits and she wondered fleetingly why she had
decided to come to the lonely cabin to seek him out.
She had even brought her overnight bag with her.
Was it an oversight or had Dean been right all along?

Before the questions which had been nagging at
her could steal all of her determination, Becca
switched off the ignition, opened the car door, and
stepped into the night.

As Brig sipped his scotch he watched the idling car
sitting in the driveway. The engine died and Brig
strained to identify the driver. When the car door
opened and the interior light flashed for a second, he
caught a quick glimpse of a woman stepping from
the car. Brig's jaw tensed. This wasn't just any
woman, but a tall, graceful woman with a soft mane
of golden hair which shimmered in the moonlight.
He didn't catch sight of her face, but he knew
intuitively that she was incredibly beautiful. The
pride with which she carried herself spoke of beauty
and grace. Hazy, distant clouds of memory began to
taunt him, but he savagely thrust aside his cloudy
thoughts of another striking blonde, knowing that
she was lost to him forever. Though she still occu-
pied his dreams, he denied himself conscious
thoughts of her. Why did she still haunt him so? And
why could he remember every elegant line of her
face with such breathtaking clarity? He was a

damned fool when it came to Becca Peters. He always had been.

Brig cocked an interested black eyebrow as he stared voyeuristically at the well-shaped stranger hurrying to the porch. What *woman* would be looking for him in the middle of the night, at this secluded mountain home? An expectant smile lit his face only to withdraw into a suspicious frown when he realized that the gorgeous creature now rapping upon his door was probably another one of his father's mistresses, coming to claim what she considered rightfully hers. Brig drained his drink as he advanced toward the door. He hoped to hell that the blonde wasn't wearing a sable coat.

In the past week Brig had secretly dealt with one of his father's mistresses. Nanette Walters was a calculating bitch who was ready to spill her guts about her relationship with Jason Chambers to any interested gossip columnist for the price of a one-way ticket to the Bahamas. Fortunately, Brig had gotten to her first. The thought of Nanette's aristocratic beauty and easily bought affections soured Brig's stomach and he clenched his jaw in determination as he steeled himself against what would certainly be another cold, expensive demand by one of his father's latest women.

Every muscle in Brig's body had tensed in anticipation by the time he reached the door. The insistent rapping had stilled, but the woman was persistent. Brig hadn't heard her restart the car and leave. He jerked the door open and let the light from the interior of the house spill into the night. The pale lamplight rested on the long, tawny hair of the woman standing on the porch and a familiar scent hung in the night air. Brig felt himself waver. He couldn't see her face; her head was bent over her purse and she was rummaging through it as if she were looking for something. Disgust forced a smile

of contempt to Brig's lips when he understood: The
blonde obviously had her own key to his father's
private retreat.

The stranger lifted her bewitching green eyes and
Brig's breath caught in his throat. Memories of
making love to her in a fragrant field of spring clover
clouded his mind. Was she an illusion? As his
stunned gaze met and entwined with hers, Brig
couldn't help but slip backward in time. It was as if
six long years of his life had suddenly disappeared
into the darkness. He damned himself for the stiff
drinks. *It couldn't be Becca, not after six unforgiving
years.*

"Rebecca?" he whispered, not believing the trick
his mind was playing on him. He must have had
more to drink than he thought. A thousand questions surfaced as he stared at her and just as quickly
those questions escaped, unanswered. It had to be
Rebecca—the resemblance was too perfect for it to
be unreal. What was she doing here, at his father's
private cabin in the middle of the night?

Wasn't it just yesterday when they had made love
in the rain? Couldn't he still taste the warm raindrops on her smooth skin? He closed his eyes for just
a moment—to steady himself—and his dark brows
knitted in the confusion that was cutting him to the
bone. Why the hell couldn't he think straight?

The sound of his disbelieving voice whispering her
name moved Becca to tears. Her answer caught in
her swollen throat. Why hadn't she sought him out
sooner? Why had she waited so long? Was pride that
important?

A wistful smile, full of the memories they had
shared together, touched her lips. He looked so
tired . . . so worried. Her lips trembled when she
realized that he, too, might be vulnerable. He had
always been so strong. Without understanding the

reasons behind her actions, she reached up and touched his rough cheek with her fingertips.

His eyes flew open. They were as she had remembered them: deep-set and steely gray. They touched her as no other eyes had dared. They held her imprisoned in their naked gaze, encouraged rapturous passion.

"Brig," she murmured, her voice raw. "How are you?" Her hand still caressed his cheek.

He studied her for an endless second, but ignored her concerned inquiry. His eyes probed deeply into hers, asking questions she couldn't hope to answer. "What are you doing here, Rebecca?"

"I came to see you."

It was so simple and seemed so honest. For an instant Brig believed her. He needed to trust her. Perhaps it was the look of innocence in her round, verdant eyes, or maybe it was the effect of more than one too many drinks. But that didn't entirely explain his feelings. More than likely it was because, in the past few weeks, he had felt so incredibly alone. Whatever the reason, Brig couldn't resist the look of naive seduction in her eyes. "God, Rebecca, why did you wait so long to come back?"

Chapter 3

HE DIDN'T THINK ABOUT THE PAST AND GAVE LITTLE consideration to the future. Instead, Brig took Becca into his arms and crushed her savagely against him. He couldn't let her vanish as quickly as she had come. His lips captured hers almost brutally, as if he could reclaim in a single kiss what had been lost to him for so long.

Becca's knees weakened in his embrace and she wound her arms possessively around his neck to cling to him in silent desperation. She returned the fever of his kiss with the same passion she felt rising in him. Tears of joy ran unashamedly down her cheeks and lingered on her lips. He tasted the depth of her longing in the salt of her tears.

Becca didn't resist when he lifted her from the porch and carried her inside the cabin. Instead she held him more tightly than before and wondered if she would feel the ecstasy of dying in his arms.

The room into which Brig took Becca was shadowed in darkness. There was the slight hint of an expensive blend of pipe tobacco in the air which reminded Becca of Brig's father and her reason for seeking him out. She knew she should tell Brig about Gypsy Wind now, before things got out of hand. But she couldn't. It felt too right being held by the man she loved. She couldn't tear herself from his embrace.

A thin stream of moonglow pierced through the skylights and gave the room some visibility. As Becca's eyes became adjusted to the darkness, she realized that she was in a bedroom: Brig's bedroom.

Brig walked unerringly to the bed. He dropped Becca on a soft down comforter and let his weight fall against her body. He crushed her to him, holding her fiercely to him. His lips brushed hers in tender kisses flavored with scotch and warm with need. His hands pressed intimately against the muscles of her back and through the light jersey fabric of her dress, Becca could feel the heat of his fingertips. They sparked fires in her she had thought dead and rekindled a passion she had buried long ago.

He tasted just as she remembered and the roughness of his unshaven face reminded her of lazy mornings spent waking up in his arms, arousing desires smoldering from the night. His kisses were the sweetest pleasure she had ever known.

"Rebecca," Brig moaned, tortured by the demons playing in his mind. "Rebecca . . . God, how many nights has it been?" His warm breath fanned her face.

"Since what?" she prodded, her breath torn from her throat.

"Since we made love?"

She swallowed the lump in her throat. "Too many," she admitted. His fingers entwined in the strands of her honey-gold hair. She couldn't read his expression in the darkness, but she could feel his

unchallenged sincerity. Slowly, she touched his lips
and felt the hard angle of his masculine jaw. His
hand reached up and covered hers and he kissed it.

"Why did you wait to come back?" he asked.

"I don't know . . . I was afraid, I suppose."

"Of me?"

"No!" She tried to think, tried to explain what she
felt, but she couldn't.

"You had the right to be." He pulled his head
away from her hand, putting a little distance between them. He let go of her hand and rolled away
from her. Why was she here? Why now?

"Don't!" she cried, refusing to release him. Her
arms wrapped around his back and she whispered
against the back of his neck. "It was my pride. . . .
Let's not talk about it. Not here. Not now."

He tried to disentangle her arms. "Rebecca.
Don't you think we should talk things through?" He
tried to keep his wits about him, attempted to think
logically, but he couldn't. The feel of her breasts
crushed against his back and the warmth of her arms
around his chest made his blood begin to race.

"Please, Brig. Can't we just forget . . . just for a
little while?" Her heart was pounding so loudly she
knew he could hear it. Her breath was barely a
whisper, a small plea in the middle of a clear
mountain night.

"Dear God, woman. Don't you know how you
torture me?" he asked raggedly. Becca let the air out
of her lungs. He was about to deny her, again . . .
she could feel it. "I wish I could forget you," he said
as if she weren't listening. The bed sagged as he
shifted again. He loomed over her in the darkness as
he planted one hand on either side of her body. "Do
you know what you're asking?"

"Yes," she said.

Cold suspicion had begun to form in his mind, but
as he gazed down upon her his doubts fled. The

moonlight caressed her face in its protective radiance and her eyes took on a heavenly silver-green purity that begged him to believe her. As she lay upon the bed staring trustingly at him, he knew her to be the most beautiful and beguiling woman he had ever had the misfortune to meet.

Becca couldn't see the pain in Brig's gray eyes, couldn't hope to read his expression, but she knew that he was gazing down upon her, trying to find the strength to pull away again. That knowledge was a dull silver blade twisting slowly in her heart. He wanted to love her, but was denying himself.

"Why did we let it go sour?" he asked, his fists clenching in the restraint he was holding over his body. Dear God, she was beautiful. His question was rhetorical; he didn't expect an answer.

"We made mistakes . . ."

"Like tonight?" he asked cruelly.

"Does this feel like a mistake to you, Brig?" If only she could look into his eyes. If only he would let her.

"Nothing has ever felt wrong with you," he conceded as he lowered his head and his lips met hers in a kiss that spanned the abyss of the six lonely years separating them. The warmth of his lips filled her and she let them part to encourage more intimacy. Everything felt so right with him; it always had. As his mouth claimed hers it was as if all the doubts and fears she had furtively harbored had disappeared. *He wanted her.* Her heart clamored joyously and her blood began to run in heated rivulets through her veins. The love she had chained deep in the shadowy hollow of her heart became unbound in the knowledge that he wanted her. She wrapped her arms around his neck and enjoyed the comfort of his caress.

His tongue slid familiarly through her teeth, touching hers and mating with it in a passionate dance once forgotten. He explored her mouth, groaning softly in pleasure at her heated response. "I've missed you," he admitted roughly, drawing his head away from hers for a moment. He brushed back the silken strands of her hair and kissed her forehead lightly before letting his lips trail down her cheeks to recapture her mouth. "Let me love you."

The jersey dress buttoned on the shoulders. Brig's fingers slid the pearl-like fasteners through the holes and the soft fabric parted to expose her neck and shoulders. He kissed the white column of her throat, nuzzling gently against her neck. Without thinking she tilted her head, letting her sun-streaked hair fall away from her throat and offering it to him willingly. His moist tongue pressed against her skin and he tasted the bittersweet tang of her perfume—the same scent she had worn in the past. It was a fragrance he would never forget. Once he had been with a woman who was wearing Rebecca's fragrance; he had left that woman before the evening had begun. The perfume had evoked too many unwanted memories and destroyed any possible attraction he may have felt for the poor woman.

But tonight was different. Tonight he would drown in the gentle fragrance of wildflowers that filled his nostrils. Tonight in the dusky bedroom, the scent that clung to Rebecca's hair fired his blood and summoned a passion in him he had thought was lost long ago. No other woman had reached him the way Rebecca had, and he had vowed that none would. No other woman had dared enrage him so dangerously. Her soft moan of pleasure encouraged him. He felt her body trembling beneath his persuasive hands.

With a gentle tug the dress slid lower on her body. Lace from a cream-colored slip partially obscured the swell of her breasts and highlighted the hollow between them. He moved over her and his mouth moistened that gentle rift.

"Brig," she whispered, closing her eyes and letting him touch her soul. His hands slid over the silky fabric of her slip, arousing in her aching breasts a need that seemed to consume her in its fire. The satin fabric teased her nipples into hard, dark points that strained against the lace. His warm lips touched the gossamer cloth and Becca moaned her gratitude as the moist heat of his mouth covered her nipple.

Dizzy sensations of a lost past whirled in her mind. Images of a moonlit night and a cascading waterfall filled her thoughts. "I'll always love you," she had heard him say, but that was long ago, in a time before treachery and deceit had ripped the two of them so ruthlessly apart.

His tongue moistened the lace and his lips teased her breast through the gentle barrier of silk and satin. Slowly, he turned their bodies, pulling her over him so that her breasts would fall against him and he could take more of her into his mouth. He groaned in satisfaction when the strap of her slip slid down her shoulder and her breast became unbound. She wore no bra to encumber her, and as the rosy-tipped breast spilled from the slip, Brig captured it in his lips and let his teeth tease the engorged nipple.

"Please love me," she gasped, praying that he understood her needs were not only physical. She wanted to relive the happiness they had shared. She needed to claim again the time when he was hers.

His hands were warm as they pressed between the slip and her ribcage. So slowly that it seemed pure agony, he pushed the fabric past her hips and onto the floor. He disposed of each piece of her clothing as if it were a useless piece of cloth, used only to impede him in his quest to claim her. When at last she was nude, lying trembling in his arms, he took her hands and guided her to the buttons of his shirt.

With whispering softness he brushed kisses over her eyelids as she opened his shirt and slid her hands under the oxford fabric. Her fingers touched him lightly at first, gently outlining each of the muscles of his chest. His groan of satisfaction as she traced each male nipple made her more bold and she slid the shirt over his shoulders, letting her fingers glide down his arms and trace each hard, lean muscle. When his shirt dropped to the floor he gripped her savagely, pushing her naked breasts against the furry mat of his chest. His lips rained liquid kisses of pulsing fire over the top of her breasts before returning to her mouth. Once more his tongue pushed insistently through her teeth to capture and stroke its feminine counterpart. Becca wanted to blend with him and break the boundary that separated his body from hers. She wanted to become one with him, to feel his heart beat in her blood. An ache, deep and primal, began to burn within her, igniting her blood until she felt it boil in her veins.

Brig had never stopped kissing her and his hands hadn't halted their gentle, possessive exploration of her body, but he had managed to remove his pants. She didn't know the exact moment when he had discarded his clothes, but rather became slowly conscious of the fact that he was naked, lying under her and matching her muscles with the rock-hard flesh of his own. His hands moved in slow circles over her back and his lips left none of her untouched as he caressed her.

She felt herself tremble at the familiarity of his touch, the intimacy of his skin on hers. A flush of arousal tinged her skin and she felt the warm glaze of his sweat mingling with her own.

His hand passed over her thigh and her body arched against him, pleading for more of his touch.

He wrapped his arms around her and rotated both of their bodies on the comforter, so that once again he was leaning over her, looking at her eyes, misty in moonglow.

Words of love threatened to erupt from her dry throat, but before she could utter them, his knee wedged between her thighs and took her breath away in a rush of desire.

"Becca," he moaned into the tawny length of her hair, "are you sure this is what you want . . . really sure?" All of his muscles had become rigid with the restraint he placed upon himself. Beads of sweat, tiny droplets of self-denial, formed on his upper lip as he awaited her response.

In answer, she threaded his dark hair between her fingers and pulled his head down on hers. She kissed him with the fervid desire so long repressed. Six years she had waited for him. Six years she had yearned for his caress.

He groaned in relief as he gently came to her and found that portion of her no other man had touched. She seemed to melt into him, joining him in a pulsating rhythm that they alone had explored in the past and had now rekindled in the darkness of his bedroom.

The sweet, gentle agony began to build in her as she captured every movement of his body. The fire within her burned more savagely with each persuasive stroke of love, until she felt herself erupt. When he felt her release, he exploded with a passion that shook both of them and left him drained of the frustration that had been with him for the past few weeks. He held her tightly, softly pressing his lips to her hair.

"Stay with me tonight," he coaxed.

She sighed in contentment, warm in the cradle of his arms and the luxury of afterglow. It was moments later, when the beating of her heart had

slowed, when the reality of what she had done
brought her brutally back to the present. Brig's
breathing was regular, but he wasn't asleep. When
she attempted to free herself of his embrace, he
tightened his grip on her, imprisoning her against
him.

"Brig . . . I think we should talk," she whispered,
hoping to find the courage to bring up her reasons
for seeking him out. She felt him stiffen.

"Later."

"But there are things that I—"

"Not now, Rebecca! Let's wait, at least until the
morning." Her resolve began to waver. She closed
her eyes and tried to content herself by resting her
head against his chest and listening to the steady
beat of his heart.

The image of a dark horse, racing dangerously
along the ocean's shore, hoofbeats thundering
against the pale sand, formed in her tired mind.
Lather creamed from the horse's shoulders and foam
from the sea clung to the speeding legs. Sentimental
Lady ran with the wind. The image of the horse
compelled Becca—she had to tell Brig all of her
secrets. He had to know about Gypsy Wind.

"Brig, we *have* to talk."

"I said not now!"

"But it's important. Remember Sentimental
Lady?"

"How could I forget?" His voice was coated in
contempt. He made a derisive sound in the back of
his throat. "Let's just leave this conversation until
later."

"I can't."

"We've waited for six years, Becca. One more
night isn't going to make much difference."

"But you don't understand—"

"And I don't want to!" His voice was stern, his

eyes flashed anger. She felt herself tense at his cutting reprimand.

"I just want to talk to you. Don't treat me like a child. It didn't work before, and it won't work now," she whispered.

His voice softened. "Look, Becca, the past couple of weeks have been a little rough. I'm only asking that you put whatever it is you want to talk about on hold—until the morning." He knew what it was she wanted to discuss, but he was too tired to go through the argument of six years past. He didn't want to think about her deception, nor the ensuing scandal, didn't want to be reminded of how deep her betrayal had been. All he wanted was to hold her and remember her as she had been before all of the damned controversy. His arms bound her tightly as he tried to forget the lies and anguish. "If you really want to talk about anything right now, of course I'll listen . . ." Brig pressed his lips to her eyelids and he felt her begin to relax. If only he could concentrate on anything other than that last hellish race.

For the first time that night, Becca realized how much Brig had aged. The years hadn't been kind to him, especially now, right after the death of his father. Her confidence began to waver.

"I want to talk to you about your father."

Brig's arms tightened around her and in the moonlight Becca could see his eyes opening to study her. "What about my father?" he asked.

Becca sighed deeply to herself, but it wasn't a moan of contentment. It was a sigh of acceptance: Brig would never love her, never trust her. She could feel it in the firm manacle of his embrace, read it in the skepticism of his gaze. The tenderness she had once found in him was buried deeply under a mound of suspicion and bitterness. "I owe your father some money."

No response. Her heartbeat was the only noise in the room. The seconds stretched into minutes. Finally he spoke. "Is that why you came here tonight, because of some debt to my father?"

"It was the excuse I used."

His gray eyes held her prisoner. "Was there any other reason?"

"Yes," she whispered.

"What was it?"

"I wanted to see you, touch you . . . feel for myself that you were alive. When I first heard about the plane crash I thought you might be dead." It was impossible to keep her voice even as she relived the nightmare of emotions which had ripped her apart. Even with his powerful arms about her, she could feel her shoulders beginning to shake.

"So you waited nearly two weeks to find me."

"I didn't want to intrude. I knew things would be hectic—the newspapers couldn't leave you alone. I didn't want to take any chance of dredging everything up again, not until I'd talked to you alone."

"About the money?" His voice was cynical in the darkness.

"For one thing."

"What else?"

"I needed to know that you were all right . . ."

"But there's more to it, isn't there?"

She nodded silently, her forehead rubbing the hairs of his chest. All of his muscles stiffened. Her voice was steady when she finally spoke. "I had to borrow the money to breed another horse."

"So you came to the old man? What about the banks?"

"I didn't have enough collateral—the stud fee was a fortune."

"You could have come to me," he offered.

"I don't think so. You made that pretty clear six years ago."

"People change . . ."

"Do they?" She laughed mirthlessly. "It took all of my courage to come to you now. . . . It would have been impossible three years ago. I didn't even want to approach your father, but it was the only solution. Even Dean agreed, although now he's changed his mind."

"Your brother? He was in on this?" The softness in Brig's voice had disappeared and was replaced by disgust. "I would have thought that by this time you would have gotten enough sense to fire that useless bum."

"Dean was there when you weren't," she reminded him, a touch of anger flavoring her words.

"I wasn't there because you shut me out."

"You weren't there because you chose not to be!" she retorted, shifting on the bed and trying to wiggle free of his embrace.

"After all these years, nothing's changed, has it? You're still willing to believe all the lies in the gossip tabloids, aren't you?" He gave her an angry shake and his eyes blazed furiously.

"Dean was there."

"Dean lied."

"Dean lied and the newspapers lied?" she repeated sarcastically. "What kind of a fool do you take me for?"

"A woman who's foolish enough not to be able to sort fact from fiction or truth from lies."

"I didn't come here to argue with you."

"Then why did you come?" His thumbs slid slowly up her ribcage, outlining each delicate bone as it wrapped around her torso. "Did you come here to seduce me?"

"No!"

"No?" His fingers inched upward until they touched the underside of her breast, teasing the sensitive skin.

"I came here to explain about the money—and about Gypsy Wind."

"The horse?"

"Yes—please, don't touch me. I can't think when you touch me."

"Don't think," he persuaded, his lips and tongue stroking the flesh behind her ear. Her breath became ragged as much from desire as from the frustration she was beginning to feel.

"But I want you to know about the money . . . I want you to understand about Gypsy Wind . . . I want . . ."

"You want me."

How could she deny what her body so plainly displayed? Her nipples had hardened, anticipating his soft caress, her skin quivered beneath his touch and the fire in her veins was spreading silently to every part of her body. "Oh, Brig, of course I want you," she said. "I've wanted you for so long . . ."

Desire lowered his voice. "I don't care about the money and I don't give a damn about your horse—"

"But you will. In the morning, when you're sober—"

"I am sober and the only thing I care about is that you're with me. I don't care how you got here, and I'm not all that concerned with why you came. It only matters that you're here, with me, beside me . . . alone. Just let me love you tonight and tomorrow we'll discuss whatever you want to."

"I just wanted you to know why I had to see you."

"It doesn't matter. What matters is that you did." His lips touched her familiarly, softly tracing the line of her jaw, the curve of her neck. His hands gently shaped her breasts, feeling anew the silky flesh beneath his fingertips. He wasn't hurried when his mouth descended to her nipple. It was as if the slow deliberation of the act increased its intensity and meaning. Becca turned her head and groaned into the pillow as his lips molded over her breast.

"Just love me, Brig!" she cried desperately as his hands slid leisurely down her backside to rest on her buttocks.

"I will, Rebecca," he vowed, moving his body over hers and gently parting her legs. "I will."

Chapter 4

Brig had long since fallen asleep, but Becca was restless. She had tried to unwind in the comfort of Brig's embrace, but found it impossible. Continuing doubts plagued her. Though she had tried to tell him about Gypsy Wind, she was sure that she hadn't really gotten through to him. In the morning, when the scotch he had consumed wouldn't cloud his mind, he would see things in a different light. Nothing would change. If anything, the doubts he felt for her would only be reinforced. He wouldn't forget the agony of the past, nor would he be able to rise above his long-festering suspicions of her. The night had only softened the blow slightly. Under the light of a new day his old doubts would resurface.

Becca shuddered as she anticipated his response to the fact that she owed him more than fifty thousand dollars for a horse which would remind him of the tragedy of Sentimental Lady. The fact that Becca had planned Gypsy Wind's conception and bor-

rowed money from Brig's father to have her conceived would feed Brig's gnawing doubts. Becca
closed her eyes and tried to drift off to sleep,
attempted to be lulled by the sound of Brig's rhythmic breathing. But sleep was elusive; her fear kept it
at bay.

Her love for Brig was as deep as it had ever been,
his just as shallow. If Becca had hoped to find a way
back into his heart, she had destroyed it herself.
Gypsy Wind would become the living proof of
Becca's deceit, a reminder of the grim past. Tears of
frustration burned hotly behind Becca's eyes and slid
silently over her cheeks.

Sleep refused to come. Becca was still awake when
the first ghostly rays of dawn crept into the room and
colored it in uneven gray shadows. Slowly she extracted herself from Brig's arms, careful so as not to
disturb him. She reached for a blue terry robe
hanging on a nearby chair and pulled it over her
shivering body. Without the warmth of Brig's arms
around her, the room seemed frigid and sterile. She
rolled up the sleeves of the robe, cinched the tie
around her waist, and walked across the thick, ivory
pile of the carpet to stand at the bay window. After
pulling the heavy folds of cloth around her neck, she
sat on the window ledge and stared vacantly out the
window to watch the sunrise.

The sun crested the horizon and flooded the
mountainside with golden rays that caught in the
dewdrops and reflected in the snow of the higher
elevations. Becca restlessly ran her fingers over the
moisture which had collected on the panes of the
windows. How many nights had she dreamed of
falling back into Brig's arms? How many unanswered prayers had she uttered that she would find a
way back into his heart? And now that she was here,
what could she do to stay in his warm embrace?
Brig's words of the night before came back to taunt

her: *"Why did we let it go so sour?"* If only she knew.
How had something so beautiful turned ugly? Becca
smiled grimly to herself as she reconstructed the
events which had drawn Brig to her only to cruelly
push him away.

The party had been Dean's idea, a way to gain
more national press coverage for his sister and the
filly. Until that night, not much attention had been
given the tall girl from California with the small
stables and what was rumored to be the fastest
Thoroughbred filly ever bred on California soil. The
wiser, more sophisticated breeders in the East had
considered Becca Peters and Starlight Breeding
Farm much the way they did with any new, West
Coast contender: a lot of California hype. Until the
untried filly had proved herself, few gave her much
notice, with the one glaring exception of Brig Chambers.

When Becca had received word that Brig Chambers, himself a horse breeder of considerable reputation, wanted to see Sentimental Lady, she had
agreed and Dean had suggested the party. Dean's
arguments had included the fact that news coverage
would be good business for the Lady as well as
Starlight Breeding Farm. He had also mentioned
that Brig Chambers, part of the elite racing social
set, deserved more than a smile and a handshake for
flying across the continent to see Becca's horse.
Becca had reluctantly agreed.

The celebration had taken place on a private yacht
harbored in San Francisco Bay near Tiburón. The
owner of the yacht, a rich widow of an insurance
broker and friend to the California racing set, had
been more than delighted to host the gala event on
her late husband's gleaming white vessel. Brig
Chambers wasn't often on this side of the continent,

and rarely accepted invitations to posh gatherings, but this night was different.

Becca caught her first glimpse of him when he was ushered through the door by Mrs. Van Clyde. The short woman with the perfectly styled white hair and sparkling blue eyes looked radiant as she escorted Brig through the crowded, smoke-filled salon. He was taller than Becca had imagined . . . with a leanness that Becca hadn't expected from the spoiled son of an oil baron. In his sophisticated black tuxedo, Brig Chambers looked more than a pampered only son of wealth; he seemed *hungry* and *dangerous,* exactly the antithesis of the image he was attempting to portray in his conservative black suit. Becca had heard him referred to as "stuffy"; she didn't believe it for a moment.

Nina Van Clyde, in a swirl of rose-colored chiffon, introduced him to each guest in turn, and though he attempted to give each one his rapt attention, Becca noticed a restlessness in his stance. It wasn't particularly obvious, just a small movement such as the tensing of his jaw, or his thumb rubbing the edge of his first finger, but it clearly stated that he wasn't comfortable. His smile was well-practiced and charming, a brilliant, off-center flash of white against bronze skin, but his eyes never seemed to warm to the intensity of his grin.

Becca studied his movements over the rim of her champagne glass. He reminded her of a caged panther, waiting for an opportunity to escape, watching for just the right prey. He definitely intrigued her, and when his dark head lifted and he met her unguarded stare, the corners of his mouth turned downward in amusement.

After a brief apology to Mrs. Van Clyde, he advanced on Becca, ignoring any of the other guests.

"You're Rebecca Peters," he said coldly.

"And you're Mr. Chambers."

"Brig."

Becca inclined her head slightly, accepting the use of first names. Perhaps he didn't like to become confused with his famous father.

"I guess I should thank you for all this," he stated, cocking his head in the direction of the other guests and the well-filled bar.

"It was my brother's idea."

He seemed to relax a bit, and his gray eyes softened. "You may as well know, I'm not crazy about this sort of thing."

Becca's full lips curved into a smile. "I could tell."

He answered her smile with one of his own. "Shows, does it?"

"Only to the practiced eye."

"Were you watching me that closely?" His eyes traveled over her face, lingered in the depths of her green gaze, before trailing down her body and taking in all of her, the way the sea-blue silk dress draped over one of her shoulders to hug her breasts before falling in soft folds of shimmering fabric to her ankles.

Becca felt the heat of her embarrassment burn her skin. "Of course I was watching you," she admitted. "You're the center of attention."

As if to give credence to her words, several men Becca recognized as San Franciscan breeders came up to Brig and forcefully stole his attention.

Becca wandered through the crowd, politely conversing with several other California breeders. She sipped lightly at her champagne, never once losing her feel for Brig's presence in the room. Presently he was talking with a reporter from a San Francisco newspaper. Though Becca didn't openly stare at him, she knew where he was in the throng of elegantly dressed people dripping in jewels.

The music from a small dance band was nearly drowned in the clink of glasses and chatter of guests. A hazy cloud of cigarette smoke hung in the salon where knots of people congregated while sipping their drinks from the well-stocked bar. Becca was alone for the first time and she took the chance to escape from the stifling room.

Once on the deck, she took in a deep breath of sea air and tried to ignore the muted sounds of the party filtering from the salon. A breeze caressed her face and lifted the wisps of hair that had sprung from their entrapment in a golden braid pinned to the back of her neck. Water lapped against the sides of the slowly moving vessel, and Becca could see the glimmering lights of San Francisco winking brightly in the moonless night.

She leaned her bare forearms against the railing and smiled to herself, glad to be free of the claustrophobic crowd in the main salon. She felt Brig's presence before he spoke.

"I should apologize for the interruption of our conversation," he announced, leaning next to her on the railing. He didn't look at her, but rather concentrated on the distant city lights and the sounds of the night.

"It wasn't your fault," she replied with a sincere smile. "I'm willing to bet it will happen again."

"I don't think so." He sounded sure of himself and his opinions.

"You underestimate the persistence of we Californians, especially the press."

"I'm used to dealing with the press."

"Are you?"

Brig smiled and clasped his hands together. "I've already had the . . . pleasure of meeting a few reporters tonight. Were they your idea?"

Becca shook her head and her smile faded.

"Don't tell me," Brig continued. "Your brother had something to do with that, too."

Becca was intrigued. "How did you know?"

"Lucky guess," was the clipped reply.

"Dean thought the publicity would be good for the stables and Sentimental Lady. I didn't see that it would hurt."

Brig's hand reached out and touched Becca's wrist. He forced her to turn away from the view to look into his eyes. "There's a subject I've been wanting to discuss all night. I'd like to see your horse. She's the reason I'm here."

Becca tried to manage a smile. "I know," she replied, wondering if he was going to release her wrist. He did.

"Then you'll show her to me?"

"Of course. We can drive there tomorrow."

"Why not tonight?" he demanded.

"It's a three-hour drive," she responded before she began to think clearly. Was he serious? "Besides, it's late . . . and then there's the party. Mrs. Van Clyde would be offended if we left. That is what you're suggesting, isn't it?" Becca wasn't really sure she had understood him correctly.

"That's exactly what I'm suggesting."

"I don't know . . ." The night wasn't going as she and Dean had planned.

"Don't worry about Mrs. Van Clyde. I can handle her."

"But my brother . . ." Becca was grasping at straws, but things were moving too fast. There was an arrogant self-assurance to Brig Chambers which unnerved her. And then there was Dean—he had wanted to talk to Brig in private about a job with Chambers Oil.

Brig's smile became cynical. "I'm sure your brother can take care of himself." His hand touched her bare elbow, guiding her toward the door to the salon and the noisy crowd within. "Make your apologies, get your coat and whatever else you brought here, and meet me on the starboard deck."

"What about transportation? We've got to be more than a mile out."

His gray eyes stared at her as they reentered the room and the din of the party made it impossible to converse. Brig leaned over to whisper into her ear. "I've already arranged it. Trust me."

For the first time in Becca's twenty-six years, she wanted to trust a stranger, completely. She found Dean leaning over a well-endowed brunette, and pulled him aside to tell him of the change in their plan. Dean wasn't pleased and had trouble hiding his anger, but he didn't argue with Becca. He couldn't. He was smart enough to realize that Brig Chambers was used to doing things his way. Any argument would fall on deaf ears and only serve to anger the son of one of the wealthiest men in America. Dean could afford to be patient.

A motor launch was waiting and took Brig and Becca over the cold water to the dock, where Brig's car was parked. The drive through the dark night should have taken nearly four hours, but was accomplished in less than three. Becca should have been nervous and restrained with the enigmatic driver of the car, but wasn't. Their conversation flowed naturally and the only fragments of tension in the air were caused by the conflicting emotions within Becca. The man driving so effortlessly through the winding, country roads was a stranger to her, but she felt as if she had known him all of her life. She had never felt so daring, nor so trusting.

His laughter was rich and genuine, yet there was a dangerous glint in his gray eyes that made Becca tremble in anticipation. How many of her thoughts could he read in her smile? She couldn't dismiss the awareness she felt for his masculinity. It was a feeling that entrapped her and sent shudders of expectation skittering down her spine.

Throughout the long drive, she had managed to keep her poise intact and tried to ignore the voice of femininity that begged her to notice Brig Chambers as a man. But as the sleek car began to twist down the rutted lane toward the farm, she felt all of her composure beginning to slip away. The headlights flashed against the white buildings near the paddock and Becca's pulse jumped. The disrepair of the little farm seemed glaring. Perhaps it was better that Brig had come at night. Perhaps he wouldn't notice what was so painfully obvious to her: rusty gutters, wooden fences mended with baling wire, chipped paint which was peeling off the boards of the barns. She swallowed back her embarrassment. It was all worth it. Money that should have gone to renovation and repair was well-spent on Sentimental Lady and her training. Becca knew deep within her heart that all of the money used on the horse would come back a hundredfold once the filly began to race.

Becca attempted to disregard her hammering heart. She was home; that thought should calm her, but it didn't. The fact that she was virtually alone with a stranger, a pampered rich boy of the socially elite, unnerved her. He would walk through the barns and into her life, scrutinizing it under the same standards of the Kentucky breeders. Starlight Breeding Farm was a far cry from the glamorous blue-grass establishments of the East.

The tires ground to a halt on the gravel, and Brig cut the engine. He reached for the handle of the door, but Becca reached out to restrain him. "Wait."

Brig's hand paused over the handle. "Why?" He turned to face her. She could feel his eyes upon her face in the dark interior.

"This isn't . . . I mean, we don't handle things the same way you do."

"Pardon?"

"I mean we don't have the facilities or the staff to . . ."

His fingers touched her shoulder. "I just came here to look at your filly, Rebecca. I'm not here to judge you."

"I know. . . . Oh, damn! *Why* are you here?" The question that had been teasing her for the past week leapt to her lips.

"I told you, I came here—"

"I know, 'to see the horse.' That's what has been bothering me," she admitted. Was it her imagination, or did his fingers tense over her shoulder?

"Why?"

"This doesn't make much sense, at least not to me."

He removed his hand and Becca felt suddenly cold. "What doesn't make sense?"

"The fact that you came here. No one, not even Brig Chambers, flies more than two thousand miles to 'look at a horse,'" she accused. Her words were out before she had a chance to think about them.

Brig leaned back against the leather cushions of the Mercedes and touched her cheek lightly. He hesitated and frowned. "Someone might if he thought the horse was a threat to one of his own."

"Is that why you're here?"

His hand reached out in the darkness and his fingertips caressed her cheek. Becca took in a deep breath and he dropped his hand, as if suddenly realizing the intimacy of the gesture.

"It's one reason," he conceded. His voice seemed deeper. "I have a pretty decent stable of two-year-olds. I'm sure you already know that."

"Who doesn't? Every racing magazine in the country has run at least one article on Winsome."

What kind of game was Brig Chambers playing with
her, Becca wondered. He wasn't being completely
honest, Becca could feel it. She hadn't earned her
reputation at twenty-six without some degree of
insight into the human psyche, and she knew intuitively that there was more to Brig Chambers than
met the eye. He hadn't flown across the United
States to "scope out the competition." The owner of
a Thoroughbred the likes of Winsome didn't waste
valuable time.

"Are we going to look at your Lady?" Brig asked.

"If you level with me."

She could see the gleam of his white teeth in the
darkness as he smiled. "You're not easily fooled, are
you?"

"I hope not," she shot back. "Is that what you're
trying to accomplish?"

"No. But there is another reason why I'm here,"
he allowed. "If I like the looks of Sentimental Lady,
I'm prepared to offer a good price for her."

The bottom dropped out of Becca's heart, and
angry heat rushed through her veins. "She's not for
sale." As quick as a cat, Becca opened the car door,
stepped outside, and slammed the door. She picked
up her skirt and began to march to the house.

Brig had anticipated her move and was beside her
in three swift strides. "Is there a reason why you're
so angry?" he asked as he grabbed her arm and
turned her to face him. In the dim light from a
shadowy moon, he saw the glint of determination in
her wide eyes.

"I loathe deception." She tried to pull her arm
away from the manacle of his grip, but failed. "Let
go of me!"

"I didn't deceive you." His fingers dug into the
soft flesh of her arm.

"Bull! Dean set this up, didn't he? He's wanted to

sell Sentimental Lady from the moment she was born."

"No!"

"Liar!"

Brig's eyes narrowed as he looked down upon her fury. Even enraged, she was gorgeous. "Your brother mentioned that you might be interested in selling —nothing more."

"Well, he was wrong! She's not for sale!"

"That's too bad," he said softly.

"I don't think so." Her anger began to ebb. There was something about him that soothed her rage. She knew he was going to kiss her and she knew she should stop him, but she couldn't. When his head bent and the fingers of his free hand wrapped around her neck to cradle her head, she began to melt inside. And when his lips brushed hers in a tender kiss that promised a night of unbound passion, she had to force herself to pull away from him.

"Was this part of Dean's plan, too?"

His jaw tensed and the corners of his mouth turned down. "Your brother had nothing to do with this."

Her silent green eyes accused him of the lie. He dropped her arm with a sound of disgust. "You don't know the truth when it stares you in the face, do you? I came out here to see your horse, and perhaps offer to purchase her. Period. Yes, it was your brother's suggestion, but I did know a little about Sentimental Lady, and if I hadn't already been interested, I wouldn't have come, and that's the end of it."

He took a step away from her before continuing. "I put up with that ridiculous party and talked to a crowd of people I hope to God I'll never have to face again. And then I arranged for transportation out here, wherever the hell we are. Now you turn paranoid on me. You asked for the truth, Rebecca, and I've given it to you. If anyone's scheming to take your horse away from you, it isn't me!"

"Didn't you just say you planned to buy her?"

"Only if you're willing to sell! I might consider making an offer on her, *if* I like what I see." He stopped his tirade to take in a deep breath. "Look, Rebecca, I don't know what problems you've been having with your brother, and frankly I don't want to get involved in family disputes. If it's too much trouble for me to look at your filly, then forget it. I think I can find my way back to civilization."

He turned on his heel and began to return to the car. "Wait," Becca called. Brig stopped. "If you want to see Sentimental Lady, I'll take you to her." He followed her to the largest of the buildings surrounding the paddocks.

The door creaked when she opened it and there was a restless stirring when Becca flicked on the lights. A few disgruntled snorts greeted her as she passed by the stalls of the awakened horses. Becca murmured soothing words to the animals and stopped at Sentimental Lady's stall. "Come here, girl," she called to the dark filly and made soft clucking sounds in the back of her throat.

Sentimental Lady's nostrils flared and she backed up distrustfully as she eyed Brig. She stamped her foot impatiently and flattened her dark ears against her head. "She doesn't like strangers," Becca explained to Brig before softly coaxing the high-spirited horse to come forward.

Brig's gray eyes never left the horse. He studied the filly from the tip of her velvet-soft nose to her tail. Lady tossed her near-black head and snorted her contempt for the man appraising her.

"Is she as fast as she looks?" Brig asked.

"She's fast." Becca found it impossible to put into words how effortlessly Sentimental Lady ran, how rhythmically her black legs raced, or how fluidly her muscles worked. The horse was a study in grace when she lengthened into her stride.

"Is she sure?"

Becca snapped off the lights and closed the door. "She's strong."

"And big," Brig murmured. He rubbed his thumb pensively over his jawline. "She's one of the tallest fillies I've ever seen. What's her girth?"

"Seventy-five inches."

Brig shook his head and scowled. "Have you had any trouble with her legs?"

Becca was a little defensive. "We've had to watch her ankles."

"She's too big," was Brig's flat, emotionless statement. "Her legs won't be able to carry her the distance."

"Because she's a filly?" Becca shot back.

"Because she's a *big* filly. Her girth is over an inch larger than Winsome's and his legs are stronger."

"You haven't seen her run," Becca whispered as they walked toward the house.

"I'd like to."

"Why? I told you she wasn't for sale."

Becca placed her hand on the doorknob, but Brig took hold of her arm, catching the warm flesh and forcing her to turn and look at him. "I came all this way; I'd like to see her run." His eyes touched hers and in the darkness she could read more than interest for a horse in his gaze. Passion burned deep within him, Becca saw it as clearly as if he had whispered, "I want you." Becca managed to unlock the door and it swung open, inviting them both into the comfort inside.

Her pulse was racing and her lips desert dry. She tried to think calmly, but found it impossible. Her smile trembled with the confusion that was overtaking her. "Sentimental Lady has a workout scheduled

for tomorrow morning . . ." Was he listening? He
was looking at her lips, but Becca doubted if he had
heard a word she said. "You could come and see her
then." She began to retreat into the house, but felt
the muscles in her back press up against the doorjamb. "She . . . runs at six."

His hands captured her bare shoulders. His face
was only inches from hers and his clean scent filled
her nostrils. "It's already after two."

"I know . . ."

His lips pressed hotly against hers and the delicious pressure of his fingers on her shoulders increased. His warm breath fanned her face as he
pulled his head away from hers to look into her eyes.
"I can't go back to the city tonight. It will be nearly
dawn when I get there," he pointed out.

Becca's senses were swimming and she found it
impossible to think clearly. "But . . ." *What was he
asking?*

His fingers touched the hollow of her throat and
her pulse jumped. He gazed down upon her through
heavy-lidded eyes. "Let me stay with you," he
suggested throatily, and softly nuzzled the inviting
column of her neck. She had to fight the urge to
collapse into him.

She pressed her palms against his chest. Her eyes
searched his face. "I find you very attractive," she
admitted.

"Why do I expect the word *but* to preface the rest
of your response?" He smiled, and in the pale light
from an uneven smattering of stars, Becca returned
his grin.

"Because I don't know you . . ."

His fingers toyed with the neckline of her dress,
rimming the silken fabric. "Tell me you don't want
me," he commanded, softly, before pressing a kiss
to her bare skin above the edge of the dress.

"I can't," she conceded breathlessly. Why did she

feel that the edge of her soul was exposed to his knowing gaze?

"Why not?"

"Because I do want you," she replied honestly.

The corners of his mouth quirked.

"But that's not enough."

"There's nothing wrong with physical need."

The stillness of the night seemed to close in on Becca. Brig's touch was warm and inviting. It seemed as if they were alone in the universe: one man and one woman. His lips once again brushed hers, caressing her with a passion she had never known, promising a night of rapture and warmth, if only she would take it. She had been lonely so long. "Physical need is important," she agreed quietly. "But there has to be more."

"What is it you want, Rebecca? Are you waiting to fall in *love*?" he asked contemptuously.

"I'm not *waiting* for anything. It . . . it just has to be right for me."

He took his hands off of her and planted them firmly on either side of her head, bracing himself on the doorjamb. His gray, brooding eyes forced her to hold his unwavering gaze. "I'm not asking for anything you're not willing to give. I would never push you into anything you don't want. Believe it or not, I know that this isn't easy for you."

"Do you?" She wanted to believe him, needed to hear that he understood her.

"Of course I do. It's written all over your face."

"It's not that I'm a prude."

He smiled. "I know. And I'm not looking for a one-night stand. If that's what I wanted, I could have stayed in San Francisco, or New York, for that matter. The truth of the matter is that you intrigue me, Rebecca Peters. Just who are you?" His finger came up to trace her lips. Shivers of anticipation traveled hurriedly down her spine. "I've read about you and your farm out here. A beautiful young woman with an impoverished breeding farm some-how has the brains to breed Night Dancer, one of the greatest racing studs of all time, to a little-known mare called Gypsy Lady and ends up with perhaps the fastest Thoroughbred filly ever bred. I want to know about you, Ms. Peters, all about you."

"And that includes sleeping with me?" she asked. "Are you stupid enough to think that you could possibly understand me by sleeping with me?" She knew she should feel outraged, but she didn't.

"I had no intention of sleeping with you when I came out here. I was only interested in you because of business."

"But?" she coaxed, lifting her elegant eyebrows.

"But you happen to be the most intriguing woman I've ever met." His hand slipped under her head, and he deftly removed the clasp that held her hair restrained. With one quick movement of his fingers, her golden hair spilled down past her shoulders, still wound loosely in a thick braid. "Trust me," he pleaded as his lips met hers in a kiss that was bold rather than tender. His mouth found the moistness of hers and he held her against him hungrily. "Let me love you, Rebecca," he whispered.

"Oh, Brig . . . I . . ." His lips stilled her response and the heat of passion began to race through her veins. She gasped when his hands found the clasp of her dress and the blue silk fabric parted, leaving her upper shoulder bare. His lips were warm and moist where the fabric had once been, and Becca felt her bones beginning to melt. She couldn't think, couldn't stand. Before she swayed against him, Brig reached down and captured her sagging knees with the crook of his arm. He lifted her off of her feet and touched his lips to her forehead as he carried her inside the old farmhouse.

Becca's heart was racing, but she didn't protest as he carefully mounted the stairs. When he hesitated on the landing, she encouraged him by indicating the direction of her room. He didn't turn on the light and Becca's eyes grew accustomed to the shadowy light cast by a cloud-covered moon. Carefully, Brig set her on her feet and let the elegant blue dress slip into a puddle of silk on the floor. His hands moved downward over her body, as if he were memorizing each soft contour of her muscles, every rib in her ribcage. His groan was primal when he cupped her breast and felt the weight of it in his hungry palm. Her answering sigh of expectation fired his blood and his lips, hungry with unsatisfied desire, pressed forcefully against hers. She felt the tip of his tongue press through her teeth to touch the inner reaches of her mouth.

His lips devoured her, spreading a trail of demanding kisses across her cheeks, inside her ear, and down the column of her throat. His tongue touched the delicate bones surrounding the hollow of her throat and drew lazy, wet circles of delicious torment that forced her to cling desperately to him, hoping the sweet agony would never stop.

"Love me," she whispered, her hoarse voice breaking the stillness of the night. She entwined her arms possessively around his neck and let the tips of her fingers delve below his collar. Her eager hands encountered shoulder muscles tense with desire. "Touch me, sweet lady," he pleaded. Deliberately he forced her onto the bed with the weight of his body. The mattress sagged as their combined weight molded together. Impatiently he discarded his clothes, damning the frail barrier holding them apart.

His body was damp with perspiration. The beads of sweat collected on his forehead and ran down his spine. A gentle breeze lifted the curtains and whispered through the pine trees to scent the room, but it did nothing to cool the passion storming between them.

Heated torment inflamed Becca's veins and pounded in her eardrums. The dim light from a pale moon let her see the man she was about to love, let her read the fire in his eyes, let her witness the rising tide of his emotions.

His hands slid possessively over her body, molding his skin to hers. The sweat that clung to his body blended with hers as he moved his torso over hers, claiming her body. Becca moaned when he took her breast into his mouth and teased the nipple with his tongue and teeth. Her fingers dug into the muscles of his back as she gave in to the sweet ecstasy of his caress.

His eyes were glazed in barely restrained passion when he took her face between his hands and stared into her soul. "I want you," he whispered. "Please let me know that you want me."

"Oh, Brig, please . . ." She didn't have to finish; her eyes pleaded with him to take her.

"May this night never end," he whispered savagely before once again molding his swollen lips to hers.

He braced himself so that he could watch her face as he found her. She gasped with satisfaction at the moment they became one, feeling a delirious triumph at the union of their flesh. The ache within her began to ebb and the words of love forming on her lips died as he slowly urged her to sensuous new heights of passion. They moved as one, together in rapturous harmony, blending flesh to flesh, skin to skin, muscle to muscle until the tempo began to quicken and the pressure within Becca's body began to thunder and echo in her heartbeat.

She felt the fires within her begin to flare and Brig's answering shudder of surrender.

"I love you," she whispered, while tears of relief filled her eyes. "I know it's irrational, but I think I love you."

"I know," he murmured, kissing the wet strands of her sun-streaked hair and holding her trembling body as if life itself depended on it.

Chapter 5

WHEN BRIG OPENED HIS EYES, HE NOTICED THAT HIS body was covered in sweat, evidence of his recent nightmare—the vivid and brutal dream that had interrupted his sleep repeatedly during the last six years. The nightmares had become less frequent, but being with Rebecca again had triggered the ugly, painful dream. He lifted his arm to touch her, to find comfort in the softness of her body and to convince himself that his memory of making love to her hadn't been part of the dream, hadn't been conjured by his imagination. His hand touched the crumpled sheets, cold from the morning air. The bed was empty.

Brig's eyes flew open with the realization that she was gone. He lifted his head from the pillow too quickly, and a ton of bricks pressed on his skull in the form of a hangover. Then he saw her—as beautiful as he remembered. It wasn't part of his dream. Rebecca was really here, in his father's cabin in the foothills of the Rockies. She was huddled in his favorite blue robe, her fingers drawing restless circles on the window ledge where she sat as she stared out the window. She appeared absorbed in thought. Pensive lines of worry marred the smooth skin of her forehead. Her honey-blond hair was unruly and tangled as it framed her delicate face. Her green eyes stared, but saw nothing. What was she thinking?

He started to call her name, but withheld the impulse as he recalled the first time he had seen her. Dressed elegantly in shimmering blue silk, her hair coiled regally upon her head, Rebecca had combined beauty with grace. She had been refined and yet seductive.

Brig hadn't fallen in love with her then. It had come much later when the feelings of respect and trust had grown into love. They had worked together side by side, day after day, in the sweat and grime of training a headstrong bay filly to become the racing wonder she was. With Rebecca's fiery Thoroughbred and Brig's money, they had formed a partnership intent on taking the racing world by storm. They planned to shake up the elite world of horse racing with Sentimental Lady, a filly who could outdistance the colts.

At the thought of the elegant horse, Brig's stomach turned over and the taste of guilt rose in the back of his throat. For the first time in his life, Brig had allowed himself to be shortsighted. Perhaps his clear thinking had been clouded with love, but nevertheless it was a poor excuse for letting his emotions override his logic. He had known from the moment he laid eyes upon Sentimental Lady that her legs weren't strong enough to carry the weight. If only he'd used his head instead of trusting a woman with beguiling green eyes!

His nightmares were a surrealistic replay of the

events that had shattered his life. It was always the
same. He was with Rebecca in a crowd of thousands
of cheering people. The track was dry and fast—
Sentimental Lady's favorite. The warm California
sun glistened on the flanks of a blood-bay horse as
she nervously pranced toward the starting gate. The
other horse in the match race, Winsome, had already won top honors as a three-year-old. His list of
victories included two of the three jewels of the
triple crown and now he faced an opponent he had
never previously encountered. Although Sentimental Lady had stormed into the racing world as a
two-year-old, and at three had won all of her starts,
including the Kentucky Oaks, the Black-eyed Susan,
and the Coaching Club American Oaks, she hadn't
raced against the colts. She had shattered several
world records, and was clocked faster than Winsome. The press and the fans demanded a match
race of the two most famous three-year-olds of the
season: Sentimental Lady challenging Winsome.

There was another side to the story, an interesting
twist that headlined the gossip columns. The filly,
renowned favorite of the feminist fans, was bred and
owned by Rebecca Peters, a young woman making
her way in a man's world. The colt belonged to the
stables of Brig Chambers, heir to an oil fortune and
rumored to be romantically involved with Ms. Peters. It was a story the press loved, a story which
extended the bounds of the racing world and included the romantic glitter of the very rich. Pictures
and articles about the famous couple and their rival
horses were flashed in both racing tabloids and
gossip columns alike. Reporters couldn't get enough
information on the horses or their owners. Speculation ran high on the future mating of Sentimental
Lady to Winsome.

As the world saw it, Brig Chambers had it all: a
beautiful, intriguing woman and two of the fastest

horses ever run. Nothing could go wrong, or so he was told. So why then did he argue against the race, and when he finally relented, why did doubt keep filling his mind as he watched a lathered Lady being led into the starting gate? Why was there an uneasy sense of dread? Where was the exhilaration, the excitement? The false sense of security he had felt earlier in the week began to crumble. The race was a mistake—a terrible mistake.

Winsome, veteran of many victories and known for his calm temperament, was led into the starting gate. The crowd roared its approval and Sentimental Lady spooked at the sound. She skittered across the track and shied as her jockey attempted to urge her toward the gate. Nervous sweat lathered her withers and she tossed her head in apprehension.

"She's too nervous," Brig muttered, but his words of concern were lost in the approving roar of the crowd as Sentimental Lady sidestepped into the starting gate. The gate closed and the Lady reared, striking her head. It was too late; the door opened with the ringing of bells and shouts from the crowd. An empty track stretched out before her and Sentimental Lady bolted. Brig yelled at the officials, but his voice was drowned in the jumble of noise from the fans.

"No!" Brig shouted at the jockey, watching the race between colt and filly in silent horror.

Winsome was ahead, but Sentimental Lady seemed to get her footing. She was astride the black colt before the first turn. The speed of the race was incredible and Sentimental Lady finished the first quarter faster than she had ever run. Winsome liked to lead and was known for crushing his opponents early in the race, but Sentimental Lady hung on, holding her own against the powerful black horse.

The blood drained from Brig's face as he watched the horses, racing stride for stride, heartbeat for heartbeat. "This is a mistake," he screamed at Rebecca. "She's not going to make it . . ."

"She will!" Rebecca disagreed, her eyes shining in pride at the way the Lady was running. The crowd seemed to agree, roaring, urging the horses onward in their blinding pace.

"We've got to stop the race!" Brig shouted, shaking Becca.

"It's too late—"

"We've got to! Lady hit her head in the gate. Her stride's off!"

"You're crazy," Becca screamed back at him, but a flash of doubt clouded her green eyes. "Look at her—she's running with the wind!"

Sentimental Lady was a neck ahead of the colt, but he was pushing her, driving her to greater speeds, forcing her to run faster than she ever had.

The horses were halfway down the backstretch, their legs pounding the track furiously, their dark tails trailing behind. Nostrils distended, they ran, neck and neck, stride for stride, eyeball to eyeball. The white fence inside the track hampered Brig's view, but still he saw the misstep as clearly as if he had been astride her rather than on the sidelines.

The blow to the leg came with a sickening snap that Brig imagined rather than heard. It was the brittle crack of bone as nearly twelve hundred pounds of horse came crushing down on fragile legs.

For a moment Brig stood transfixed, watching in sickened dread. "She broke down," he yelled at Rebecca, who had witnessed the fateful step.

Winsome pressed on, and Lady, her spirit and courage refusing to be extinguished, continued to race on her three good legs. The jockey fought desperately to pull her up, knowing that her competitive fires would carry her on and further injure her. Each stride pushed her tremendous weight on the shattered bone, further pulverizing the bone into tiny fragments ground into tissue, dirt, and blood.

Brig didn't see Winsome finish the race. He ran across the track to the site of the injury, where the jockey was trying to calm the frightened animal. The veterinarian arrived and tried to soothe the horse, while attempting to examine the break. The Lady reared and Rebecca, with frightened tears running down her face, softly called to the horse, hoping to somehow forestall the inevitable.

"Good girl. That's my Lady," she said tremulously. "Let the doctor look at you, girl."

The frightened horse reared. Blood was smeared on her regal white star, and her right foreleg was a twisted mass of flesh and bone. The whites of her dark eyes showed the fear and pain.

Rebecca reached for the horse's reins but Sentimental Lady reared again. The injured leg glanced Becca's shoulder, leaving her ivory linen suit stained with blood and her shoulder bruised.

"Get away from her," Brig shouted, pushing Becca away from the terrified horse.

"I can't . . . oh, Lady . . . Lady," Becca called as she backed away. "Calm down, girl, for your own sake . . ."

The veterinarian looked grimly at Brig. He nodded toward Becca. "Get her out of here." He spoke rapidly as he placed a clear, inflatable cast over the horse's damaged leg. It quickly turned scarlet with blood.

"It's all my fault," Becca screamed as Brig put his arms around her shaking shoulders and led her away from her horse.

"Don't blame yourself."

"It's all my fault!" she cried over and over again, hysterical. "She should never have run. I knew it—I knew it. Damn it, Brig, it's all my fault!"

Brig hadn't understood her overwhelming sense of guilt. He dismissed it as an overreaction to a tragic event, until twelve hours later Sentimental Lady was dead and the results of the autopsy proved Becca right. Only then did he understand that she was, indeed, responsible for the courageous horse's death.

Brig rubbed his hands over his eyes and tried to dispel the brutal apparition that destroyed his sleep. How many nights had he lain awake and wondered how he could have prevented the gruesome tragedy; how many days had he tried to find a way to absolve Rebecca of the guilt? How much of the guilt was his? He should never have agreed to the match race; it was a devil's folly. Even if the tragedy hadn't occurred, there was the chance that the beaten horse would never have been the same.

As it was, a beautiful animal had been ruined unnecessarily, a waste due to the poor judgment of humans. If that wasn't enough to torture him, the truth he had learned after Sentimental Lady's death should have kept him away from Rebecca Peters forever. And yet, last night, without thinking of any of the horrors of the past, Brig had made love to her as if the deception had never existed.

Brig wanted to hate her. He wanted to curse her in the darkness and throw her out of his life forever, but he couldn't. As he watched her staring vacantly out the window, the sadness in her eyes touched his soul. How had she ever been caught in such an evil trap? Why had she drugged her own horse in an expensive attempt to quicken Sentimental Lady's speed? His stomach soured at the thought. Why did she seem so innocent and honest, when he knew her to be a liar? She was a dichotomy of a woman, beguiling and treacherous.

"Rebecca?"

Brig's voice called to her from somewhere in the distance.

"Rebecca, are you all right?"

Becca cleared her mind and found herself staring out the bay window of Jason Chambers' mountain cabin. Brig's concerned voice had brought her crashing back to the present. How long had she been daydreaming about a past that was so distant? She cast a quick glance at Brig. He was still in bed, propped up on one elbow and staring intently at her. He seemed anxious and didn't appear to notice that the navy blue comforter had slid to the floor. How long he had been watching her, Becca couldn't guess.

She shivered and wrapped her arms around herself, to build her courage rather than create warmth. "I guess I was just thinking," she replied evasively. She turned her head away from him and hid behind the thick curtain of her hair, where she brushed aside a lingering tear which had formed in the corner of her eye. She had loved him so desperately and the bittersweet memories of their past caught her unprepared to meet his inquisitive gaze.

His dark hair was rumpled and a look of genuine concern rested in his unguarded stare. "What were you thinking about?" he asked. He didn't attempt to hide the worry he felt for her.

Her lips trembled as she attempted a smile. "Us."

"What about *us*?"

Her voice was frail, but she forced her eyes to remain dry as she found his gaze and held it. "I . . . I was thinking about how much love we had, once," she admitted.

"Does that make you sad?"

She had to swallow to keep her tears at bay. He couldn't understand, he never had. She averted her gaze and stared sightlessly out the window. "It's just that I loved you so much," she admitted raggedly.

His brows knit in concentration as he drew his knees beneath his chin and studied her. Why was she here, opening all the old wounds? What did she want? "I loved you too," he said.

"Not the same way." It was a simple statement of fact.

"You're wrong."

"You still don't understand, do you?" she charged, as she whirled to imprison him with her damning green stare. "I wanted to spend the rest of my life with you. I wanted to share all of the expectations, the joys, even the disappointments with you." Her voice caught in the depth of her final admission. "I wanted to bear your children, Brig. I wanted to love them, to teach them, to comfort them when they cried. . . . Dear God, Brig, don't you see? I wanted to be with you forever!"

"And I let you down?"

"I . . . I didn't say that . . ."

His gray eyes challenged her from across the room. The silence was heavy with unspoken accusations from a distant past. With an utter of vexation, Brig fell back against the bed and stared, unseeing, at the exposed beams in the ceiling. "I wanted those things, too," he conceded.

"Just not enough to trust me."

"Oh, Rebecca . . . don't twist the truth." He felt raw from the torture of her words. "I asked you to marry me, or have you conveniently forgotten that, too?"

"I remember," she whispered.

"Then you can recall that *you* were the one who couldn't make a commitment. *You* were the one who had to prove yourself to the world." The rage which had engulfed him six years before began to consume him once again and he had to fight to keep his temper under control. How many times would he let her deceive him? His fingers curled angrily around the bed sheet.

"I needed time."

"I gave you time, damn it!" He sat upright in the bed and his fist crashed into the headboard. "You asked for time, and I gave it to you!" His ghostly gray eyes impaled her, daring her to deny the truth.

"But you couldn't give me your trust, could you?"

"*Do you blame me?*" Pieces of their last argument pierced Brig's mind. His accusations, her violent denials. If only she could have told him the truth! He didn't wait for her to respond to his rhetorical question. Instead he grabbed his clothes and stood beside the bed. He was still naked and Becca could see the tension in all of his rigid muscles. His voice was uneven, but he managed to pull together a little of his composure. "Look, Rebecca, this argument is getting us nowhere. I'm going to take a shower and get cleaned up. I drank a little too much last night and I'm paying for it this morning. When I clear my head, we'll talk."

He turned toward the bathroom, but paused at the door and faced her once again. His voice was softer and his smile wistful. "I'm glad you're here," he admitted, wondering why he felt compelled to explain his feelings to her.

She didn't move from her seat on the window ledge until she heard the sound of running water. Once she knew he was in the shower and she had a few minutes to herself, her tense muscles relaxed and the tears burning at the back of her eyes began to flow in uneven streams down her cheeks. She pinched the edge of her thumb between her teeth and tried not to think about the love they had found, only to lose.

Was it her fault, as Brig insisted, or was it fate which held them so desperately apart? If only she hadn't been so blind when it had come to Sentimental Lady, if only she had listened to Brig's wisdom. Perhaps they would still be together, would have married, and would share a child. Perhaps Sentimental Lady would still be alive. But Becca had been young and hellbent on making a name for herself as a horse breeder. Sentimental Lady had been her ticket to success. How was Becca to know that Brig's prophecies would be proven correct, that Sentimental Lady's legs were too weak for her strong body? Not even her trainer had guessed that the Lady would break down. And how was Becca to know that someone would inject her horse with an illegal steroid, a dangerous drug that alone might have permanently injured her horse? In the end, Becca had not only lost the fastest horse she had ever owned, but also the trust of the one man she loved. Was it her punishment for being overly ambitious, for fighting her way to the top in a man's domain?

Becca stiffened her spine and tried to ignore the unyielding pain in her heart. Perhaps she was over-reacting. Last night Brig hadn't been overly upset when she had tried to explain about the horse; maybe she was blowing the problem out of proportion. But then again, last night Brig had been drinking and was shocked to see her. Everything that had happened between them was somewhat unreal, an unplanned reunion of two lovers suffering from the guilt of the past. This morning things were different. Gone were the excuses of the night, the passion of six lonely years, the feeling of isolation in the mountains. Today, the world would intrude and the mistakes of the past would become blindingly apparent.

She had decided to accept Brig's decision concerning Gypsy Wind and the money. She realized that, legally, she had virtually no say in the matter. If Brig demanded repayment, she would have to sell the

Gypsy. Nothing she owned even approached fifty thousand dollars. However, she would try her damnedest to make Brig understand what the horse meant to her, what Gypsy Wind represented. Before her resolve could waver, she went to her car and grabbed the overnight bag she had stashed in the back seat. She cleaned herself in the guest bath and changed into her favorite forest green slacks and soft ivory blouse. The outfit was a little dressy for the rugged mountains, but this morning Becca wanted to look disturbingly feminine. She wound her hair into a gentle twist and pinned it loosely to the back of her neck before touching a little color to her pale lips and cheeks.

Without consciously listening, she knew the exact moment when the shower spray was turned off. Apprehension rose in her throat. She had to keep busy and hold her thoughts in some sort of order, because like it or not, she knew that she and Brig were about to become embroiled in one of the most important arguments in her life. She planned her defense while putting together a quick breakfast from the sparse contents of the refrigerator. By the time she heard the bedroom door opening, the hasty meal was heated and the aroma of freshly perked coffee mingled with the scent of honey-cured ham to fill the rustic kitchen and dining alcove.

She thought she heard Brig coming, but his foot-steps paused, as if he had entered another room in the house. She waited and then heard him continue toward the kitchen. She was just sliding the eggs onto a plate when he strode past the dining alcove and through the door. She was concentrating on her task and didn't look up.

"What's this?" he asked, just as she set the plates on the table.

"What does it look like? It's breakfast." She turned to face him and found that he wasn't looking at the table. Instead he was staring intently at her, as if he were trying to put together the pieces of a mysterious puzzle. He looked more like the man she remembered from her past. Clad only in jeans and an old plaid work shirt, he seemed younger. His head was still wet from the shower and his jaw cleanly shaven. The slight hint of a musky aftershave brought back provocative memories of living with him in a rambling beach house overlooking the moody Pacific Ocean.

"I'm not talking about the food," he replied cautiously. His eyes turned steely gray. "Your clothes, did you bring them with you?"

Her eyes met his and refused to waver. "Yes."

"Wait a minute. Are you saying that you *intended* to spend the night with me? Don't you have a hotel or something?" When she didn't immediately respond, he grabbed her arm and his fingers tightened painfully. Suspicion clouded his gaze. "Just what's going on here?" he demanded.

"What do you think?"

"I *think* that you planned last night."

"I only planned to find you . . . not seduce you, if that's what you're implying. I didn't even know if you would see me. I had no idea that we would end up making love."

His grip tightened on her arm. "Then why the change of clothes?"

She couldn't help but blush. "I really didn't know where I'd be spending the night. I only guessed that you would be here, and I knew that it was too late to head back to a hotel in Denver."

"And what if you hadn't found me? Did you plan to sleep in the car?" He couldn't hide the sarcasm in his voice.

"I don't know."

"I'm just trying to understand you." He sighed, releasing her arm.

"I tried to explain everything last night, but you wouldn't listen."

"I'm listening now." He crossed his arms over his chest and leaned against the counter.

Becca took a deep breath before she began. "I told you that I owed your father some money . . . fifty thousand dollars to be exact." She watched his reaction, but he didn't move a muscle, stoically waiting for her to continue. "I needed the money to breed a horse."

"And I assume that your mare conceived and now you have yourself a Thoroughbred."

Becca nodded.

"Colt or filly?"

She met his gaze boldly. "Filly. Her name is Gypsy Wind."

Brig's jawline hardened. "You told me that much last night. But you neglected to tell me that she's a full-blooded sister to Sentimental Lady."

Becca hid her surprise. "I tried to tell you everything last night. You weren't interested."

In frustration, Brig raked his fingers through his hair. He shifted his eyes away from Becca for just a minute. "I can't believe that you would be so stupid as to make the same mistake twice, *the same damned mistake!*"

"Gypsy Wind is no mistake."

"Then why are you hiding her?"

"I'm not."

"Come on, Rebecca. Don't deny it. If you'd let out the word that *you* were breeding another horse, a full sister to Sentimental Lady, the press would have been on you like fleas on a dog. That's why you hid her, came to a private source for money."

"I came to your father as a last resort."

"Sure you did," was Brig's contemptuous response. "I bet the old man really ate it up, didn't he? He never could pass up the opportunity to pull one over on the press." The smile that tugged at the corners of Brig's mouth didn't touch his eyes. There was a sullen quality, a bitterness, that made his features seem more angular.

Becca's chin lifted and a defiant glimmer rested in her round eyes. "How did you know that Gypsy Wind is Sentimental Lady's sister?"

"Because I knew there was more to the story than what you admitted last night." His raised palm stilled her protests. "And I admit that I didn't want to discuss anything with you last night, including your horse or the money you owed my father." Brig noticed that the defensive gleam in her eyes wavered. "But you did pique my interest, and after my shower I went into the old man's den. That's where I found this." He extracted a neatly folded document from his back pocket.

"The note," she guessed aloud, staring at the yellowed paper.

"That's right." He tossed the note onto the table and it slid across the polished oak surface to rest next to Becca's mug. The figure of fifty thousand dollars was boldly scrawled on the face of the document; Becca's signature attested its authenticity.

As Becca reached for the paper, Brig's words arrested her. "Check out the back." Becca turned the note over and saw Jason Chambers' notation. *Proceeds to be used for breeding of Night Dancer to Gypsy Lady.*

"When did you plan to tell me about her, Becca?"

"I did—"

"Because my father died! What if he hadn't?" Brig's voice was deadly. "How long would you have waited? Until she began racing?"

"I don't know," she whispered honestly.

Brig reached for a chair, turned it around, and dropped into it. He straddled the seat and rested his arms against the back while his eyes impaled her. "Why don't you tell me all about it," he suggested, ignoring the now-cold breakfast. "We've got all weekend, and I can't wait to hear why you took it upon yourself to flirt with tragedy all over again."

Chapter 6

WHILE BECCA TRIED TO COLLECT HER THOUGHTS, THE
meal was started and finished in suffocating silence.
All of her well-rehearsed speeches, all of her de-
fenses for breeding Gypsy Wind fled under Brig's
stony gaze. The tension in the air was difficult to
ignore, although Brig tried to appear patient, as if he
understood her need for silence.

When they finished breakfast, Brig opened one of
the French doors in the small alcove and quietly
invited Becca to join him on the broad back porch
that ran the length of the cabin. Becca carried her
cup of coffee, cradling the warm ceramic in her
palms as she stepped outside into the brisk mountain
air. She couldn't help but shiver. It was still early in
the morning and a chill hung in the late autumn air.
Becca took a long sip from her coffee, hoping it
would warm her and give her the strength to face
Brig with the truth concerning Gypsy Wind. There
was little doubt in her mind that Brig would be angry

with her and she half-expected him to push her out of his life again and this time keep the horse.

Brig followed Becca onto the porch. He leaned his elbows on the hand-hewn railing and his gray eyes scanned the secluded valley floor. A clear stream curled like a silver snake along a ridge near the edge of the woods. Already the aspens were beginning to lose their golden leaves to the soft wind. Brig's gaze followed the course of the creek and a wistful smile pulled at the corners of his mouth. It was in that stream where he had caught his first native brook trout. He hadn't done it alone. His old man had taught him how to cast and watch for the fish to strike. God, he missed that cuss of a father.

Abruptly Brig brought his wandering thoughts back to the present. He turned to face Rebecca and caught her watching the play of emotions on his face. He had hoped that in the morning light, without the blur of too many drinks, Rebecca Peters would lose her appeal to him, but he had been wrong. Dead wrong. Even the condemning proof of her treachery, the note to his father, couldn't mar her beauty. He supposed that if anything, it had added to her intrigue. Becca had always been a woman of mystique. The six years he had been away from her had given a maturity to her expressive green eyes which made her captivating. He knew that he shouldn't be susceptible to her, that he should outwardly denounce her, but he couldn't. Instead he tried a more subtle approach. "I guess I should apologize for last night."

"Why?" she asked, observing him over the rim of her cup. Dread began to inch up her spine as she wondered which way the conversation was heading.

"It's been a long week. A lot of problems. I didn't expect to see you last night and I had no intention of getting so carried away."

Why was he apologizing for something so right as making love? "It's all right . . . really."

"I didn't think you would come here."

She shook her head and the sun glinted in the golden strands of her hair. "I know. Look, everything's okay."

"Is it?" A muscle began to jump in his jaw. "Is spending the night with a man so easy for you that you can shrug it off?"

Her gaze hardened. "You know better than that."

"Did you plan last night?"

A hint of doubt flickered in her eyes. "I don't really know," she said honestly. "I . . . I don't think so."

"I'm not usually so easily seduced." His voice was cold.

"Neither am I."

For the first time since she had come to him, Brig allowed himself the fleeting luxury of a smile. It was just as she had remembered, slightly off-center and devilishly disarming. "I know," he admitted begrudgingly. He hoisted himself onto the railing and stared at her. His eyes pierced her soul. "Why don't you tell me about your horse."

"She's the most beautiful animal I've ever bred."

"Looks don't count. Remember Kincsem, an ungainly filly who won all fifty-four of the races she entered."

"Gypsy Wind is fast."

"Sentimental Lady was fast."

"But she's stronger than Lady—"

"She'll have to be." Brig's eyes implored her. "Good Lord, Becca. What I can't understand is why you want to put yourself through all of this again. And the horse. Jesus, Becca . . . what about your horse? The minute she begins to race the press will be all over her. And you can bet that they won't

forget about Sentimental Lady, not for a second!
Damn it, the entire nation was affected by Lady's
last race." His voice had increased in volume and he
could feel the splinters of wood imbedding into his
palms as he curled his fingers around the rough wood
of the railing. His eyes were angry as he remembered Sentimental Lady. "I just don't understand
you, Rebecca Peters . . . I don't know what you're
trying to prove." His voice was softer as he added,
"Maybe I never did."

Despite Brig's violent display of emotion, Becca
remained calm. It was imperative that he understand. "Rebreeding Gypsy Lady to Night Dancer
was a logical move," she stated softly. "Hadn't you
ever considered it?"

"Never!"

"Your father understood."

Brig's gray eyes flashed dangerously. "My father
understood only two things in the past few years:
How to make a helluva lot of money and how to
spend it on a pretty face."

"You know that's not true."

Brig laughed humorlessly. "Maybe not, but I can't
understand for the life of me why he agreed to loan
you so much money—just to see it thrown away on
some fiasco."

Becca could feel her anger starting to seethe.
"Gypsy Wind is no fiasco, Brig. She's probably the
best racing filly ever bred."

"You said the same thing about Sentimental
Lady."

"And I believed it."

"You were wrong!"

"I wasn't! She was the best!"

"She broke down, Becca! Don't you remember?
She couldn't take the pressure—she wasn't strong
enough. Her leg snapped! Are you willing to put

another horse through that agony?" Brig's eyes had
turned a stormy gray.

"It won't happen," she whispered with more
conviction than she felt. Something disturbing in
Brig's gaze made her confidence waver.

"You said that before."

Becca's stomach was churning with bitter memories of the Lady and the grueling, treacherous race.
"In that instance, I was mistaken," she admitted
reluctantly.

"And what makes you so sure that this time will be
any different?"

"Gypsy Wind is not Sentimental Lady." Becca's
voice was thin but determined. Brig recognized the
pride and resolve in the tilt of Becca's face.

"You just admitted your mistake with Sentimental
Lady."

"We aren't talking about Lady. If we were, I'd
probably agree with you. But Gypsy Wind is an
entirely different horse."

"A full-blooded sister."

"But she's stronger, Brig, and fast—"

"What about her temperament?" Brig demanded.

For the first time that morning, Becca hedged.
"She's a winner. Ian O'Riley is training her. You
know that he wouldn't bother with a horse if she
didn't have the spirit."

"That was Lady's problem: her spirit. Ian O'Riley
should know better than anyone. After all, as her
trainer, he paid the price."

"For the last time, we are not talking about
Sentimental Lady!"

Brig was pensive as he sat on the railing, his hands
supporting his posture. Becca's large green eyes
were shining as she talked about the filly. She was
proud of Gypsy Wind, sure of her. Brig found
himself wanting to believe Rebecca, to trust her as

he once had. If only he could. Instead he voiced the question uppermost in his mind. "So why did you come here to tell me about her—why now?"

"I wanted you to know. I didn't want you to hear it from someone else."

"But the old man knew. What if my father hadn't died?"

"I would have come to you."

"When? If that horse is as good as you say she is, why didn't you start her as a two-year-old?"

She avoided his gaze for a moment. "I didn't think she was ready. I don't know when I would have come to you." When she looked up and her eyes met his, they were once again steady. "It would have been soon. I wouldn't have allowed her to race until I had told you about her. I just wasn't sure how to approach you. When I found out that Jason had been killed, I knew I had to see you, as much for myself as for the horse. I wanted to know and see with my own eyes that you were all right."

"You knew that much from the papers."

"I wanted to touch you, Brig, to prove to myself that you were unhurt. I *had* to see for myself. Can't you understand that?" Her honesty rang in the clear air and Brig had to fight the urge to take her into his arms and crush her against his chest.

"Now that you're here, what do you expect of me?"

Becca drew in a deep breath, forcing herself to be calm and think clearly. "I want you to let me race the horse. I'm going to be honest with you, Brig, because I really don't know how else to handle this. I don't own a lot in this world, and most of what I do have is mortgaged to the hilt. But I do own Gypsy Wind, and I'd stake my life on the fact that she's the finest two-year-old alive. When she begins to race, I'll be able to repay you, but not before."

"Are you asking me to forget about the note?" His dark eyes watched her, waited for any emotion to appear on her face.

"No. I'm only asking that you hold onto it a little longer. You can't possibly need the money."

"Do you really think I would try to take your horse away from you?"

She swallowed with difficulty. "I hope not."

His eyes clouded. "You never have understood me, have you?"

"I thought I did once." Becca's throat began to tighten as she looked at him. Why did she still love him with every breath of life within her?

"But you were wrong?" he prodded.

"I never thought you would . . . crucify me the way you did."

"Crucify you? What are you talking about?"

She couldn't hide the incredulous tone in her voice. "You tried to destroy me six years ago."

"I had nothing to do with that—"

"Don't deny it, Brig. Almost single-handedly, you ruined my reputation as a horse breeder."

"No one can tarnish another's reputation. What happened to you was a result of *your* own actions," he spat out angrily.

Becca felt the insult twist in her heart like a dull blade. All these years she had hoped that Brig's condemning silence wasn't what the newspapers had made it. Her hands were shaking and she had to set down the cup of coffee for fear of spilling it. "You really thought I drugged Sentimental Lady?" she asked, her voice barely audible in the still mountain air. Her green eyes accused him of the outright lie.

"I think you know who did."

Becca couldn't resist the bait. "I have my own suspicions," she agreed.

"Of course you do. Because it had to be someone who had access to the horse before the race, someone you employed. Unless of course you injected her yourself."

"You don't believe that!" she cried, desperately holding onto a shred of hope that he could still trust her.

"I didn't want to."

"Then how can you even suggest that I would purposely harm my horse?" Bewilderment and the agony of being unjustly accused twisted her features. Brig lifted his body from the railing and stepped toward Becca. He was so close that she could feel the warmth of his breath against her hair.

"Because I think you know who did, Rebecca, and with your silence, you've become an accomplice to a crime too grotesque and inhumane to understand." Her eyes flashed green fire, but he persisted. "Whether you actually injected Sentimental Lady or not, you were responsible for her well-being and should have protected her against the agony she had to suffer."

Becca reacted so quickly, she didn't have time to think about the result of her actions. Her hand shot up and she flexed her wrist just as her palm found Brig's cheek. "You bastard!" she hissed, unable to restrain her anger.

Brig grabbed her wrist and pulled her roughly to him. "I'm only reminding you of what happened."

"You're twisting the truth to suit yourself."

"Why would I do that, Rebecca? It doesn't make any sense."

"Because you knew that she'd been drugged. Weren't you the one who wanted the race stopped just after the horses were out of the gate?"

"Because Lady hit her head."

"Because you had second thoughts!" she accused, the words biting the cold air.

He jerked her savagely, as if he would have liked to shake her until she began seeing things his way.

"Second thoughts?" he repeated, trying to understand her damning stare. His dark eyes narrowed. "What do you mean?"

"I mean that you don't have to lie anymore, Brig. Not with me. There's no one here but you and me, so you may as well confess. Your secret will remain safe. Hasn't it for the last six years?"

The fingers digging roughly into the soft flesh of her upper arms slowly relaxed. A quiet flame of fury burned in Brig's eyes, but the ferocity of his anger ebbed and he slowly released her. His whisper was rough and demanding. "What secret?" he asked. To his credit, he was a consummate actor. The confusion flushing his face seemed genuine.

Rebecca could feel tears pooling in her eyes, but she blinked them back, reminding herself not to trust this man who had passed his guilt on to her.

"What secret?" he asked again. A portion of his anger had returned as he guessed the twisted path of her defense.

She pleaded with him to be honest with her; her eyes begged for the decency of the truth. "You know that I didn't do anything to Sentimental Lady, Brig, and you also know that no one employed by me would have dared to harm that horse. The reason you know it is that you were the one who paid someone to inject her."

"*What?*" he thundered.

"There's no reason to deny it."

"You're out of your mind!"

"Not anymore. I was once, when I thought I could trust you."

His anger faded into uncertainty. "You've actually got yourself believing this, haven't you?"

"It's the only thing that makes any sense—"

"You mean it's the only way you can absolve yourself of the guilt."

Becca's slim shoulders sagged, as if an insurmountable weight had been placed upon her. The reasoning she had hoped would prove false came easily to her lips. "You were the one who had invested all the money in Sentimental Lady's training, and you were the one who received the lion's share of the insurance against her," Becca pointed out. When Brig tried to interrupt, she ignored him, allowing the truth to spill from her in an unbroken wave. "If Sentimental Lady hadn't broken down, but gone on to win that race, you knew that she would be disqualified because of the drugs. They would have shown up in the post-race urine sample. Winsome would have come out the victor. Either way you won. Once again, the stables of Brig Chambers would have come out on top!"

"You scheming little bitch!" he muttered through tightly clenched teeth. "You've got it all figured out, haven't you? It may have taken you six years to come up with an alternative story, but I've got to give you credit, it's a good one."

"Because it's true."

It was difficult to keep his anger in check, especially under the deluge of lies Becca had rained on him, but Brig Chambers was usually a patient man and he forced himself to remain as calm as possible under the circumstances. He told himself to relax and with the exception of a tiny muscle working in the corner of his jaw, he seemed outwardly undisturbed. He watched Rebecca intently. Damn her for her serene beauty, damn her for her quick mind, and damn her for her pride; a pride which couldn't suffer the pain of the naked truth. He hoped that he appeared indifferent when he spoke again.

"You've convinced yourself that this story you've fabricated really happened.

"It did."

"No way. If I wanted Winsome to come out a victor, I wouldn't have spent so much money on the Lady."

"And if you hadn't spent so much time with her, with me, there wouldn't have been all of the hype. The press and the public might not have demanded a match race."

"What good was the race to me? I had the best three-year-old colt of the year. If it was money I was after, I could have sold Winsome to a syndicate and put him out for stud, instead of gambling on another race."

"But he wouldn't have been nearly as valuable."

"What if he had lost?"

"You made sure that he didn't." Her voice was cold and nearly convincing.

"I didn't touch Sentimental Lady—"

"But you know who did," she cut in quickly, sensing his defeat. "You paid them off." Her eyes, lifted to his, were glistening with tears.

For a moment his fists doubled and he slammed one violently against a cedar post supporting the roof of the porch. Startled birds flew out of a nearby bush. He stopped, and restrained his fury before walking back to her. When his hands lifted to touch her chin, they were unsteady, and when his thumbs gently brushed one of her hot tears from her eye, she thought she would crumble against him. She wanted to tell him nothing mattered, that the pain of the past should be forgotten; but pride forbade her.

"Don't twist the truth and let it come between us," he pleaded, his voice as ragged as Becca's own fragile breath. He gently took her into his arms and folded her tightly against his chest. "It's kept us apart too long."

Pressed against him, Becca could hear the steady beat of his heart. She could feel the comfort and strength of his arms around her, shielding her from the pain of the past. She understood his need to be one with her, but she couldn't forget what had held them so desperately apart. Perhaps it was because she had been so young and vulnerable. Maybe she hadn't had the maturity or courage to handle the situation surrounding Sentimental Lady's death.

When Brig's uncompromising silence had condemned her for allowing someone to drug her horse, she should have been more vocal in her denial. When the press had hounded her for the truth, she should have held a press conference to end the brutal conjecture about the accident. If she had, perhaps the newspapers wouldn't have had such a field day with the coverage of the tragic incident. As it was, it had taken months for the story to die down and even after the investigation, when Ian O'Riley had proved by a preponderance of evidence that he made every reasonable effort to protect the horses in his care from any foul deed, the reporters wouldn't give up.

If Becca had been stronger, she might have been able to deny, more vehemently, any knowledge of the crime. As it was, with the death of the great horse and the pain of Brig's accusations, Becca had taken refuge from the public eye. Her brother Dean had helped her piece together her life and slowly she had regained her courage and determination. The gossip had finally quieted. She and Dean had survived, but Brig's brutal insinuations hung over her head like a dark, foreboding cloud.

The worst part of it was that Brig knew she was innocent. He had to. As Becca's tired mind had sifted through the evidence of those last painful days before the race, it became glaringly apparent that Brig Chambers was the one who would most benefit by drugging Sentimental Lady. Only one reasonable solution could be deduced: Brig Chambers paid someone to inject the horse.

In the first few weeks after the race, Becca
thought she would die from the torture of Brig's
deception and accusations. She hadn't been interested in anything in her life when she realized that
Brig, or someone who worked for him, had purposely set her up. Because she had been so devastated by
Brig's ruthlessness, and because she didn't know
how to defend herself, Becca had unwittingly taken
the blame for the deed by her silence. There hadn't
been enough evidence to indict anyone in the crime,
but the scandal and mystery of Sentimental Lady's
accident remained to cripple Rebecca's career. If it
hadn't been for her brother Dean and his care for
her, Becca doubted that she would have ever gathered the courage to return to horse racing and the
life she loved.

As she stood in the shelter of Brig's arms, she
knew that she should hate him, but she was unable.
Her bitterness toward him had softened over the
years, and then, when for a few lonely, wretched
hours she had thought him dead, she finally faced
the painful truth that she still loved him. As she
gazed upward at him, wondering at the confusion in
his brow, she agonized over the fact that he had
treated her so callously. How could he have abused
her? After all, she had held her tongue and when the
press had accused her unjustly, she hadn't defended
herself by smearing his name. Despite the silent rage
and humiliation, she hadn't lowered herself to his
level nor dragged his famous name through the mud.
Meticulously, she had avoided fanning the fires of
gossip as well as steadfastly refusing to give the
columnists the slightest inklings of her side of the
argument. It was no one's business. Her affair with
Brig had been beautiful and intimate. She wasn't
about to tarnish that beauty by making their personal lives public. Her dignity wouldn't allow it. Instead
she had gone home and licked her wounds with the

help of her brother. Dean was right; by all reasonable standards she should loathe Brig Chambers for what he did to her.

Why then did the feel of his arms around her give her strength? Why did the steady beat of his heart reassure her? Why did she secretly long to live in the warmth of his smile?

They stood holding each other in the autumn sunlight, as if by the physical closeness of their bodies they could bridge the black abyss of mistrust which silently held their souls apart. They didn't speak for a few breathless moments, content with only the sound of their hearts beating so closely together and the soft whisper of the cool breeze rushing through the pines.

"I've never stopped loving you," Brig whispered in a moment of condemning weakness. The muscles in his arms tightened around Becca with his confession. He hated himself intensely at that moment. For six years he had ignored his feelings for Rebecca, hidden them from the world and from himself. In one night of revived passion, she had managed to expose his innermost secrets.

Becca's knees sagged. So long she had waited to hear those words of love from this proud man. She had yearned for this moment, and when it was finally hers, she grasped it fleetingly only to release it. The words sounded too hollow, a convenient excuse for a night of passion. "I don't think we should talk about love," she managed to say, though her throat was unreasonably dry.

His hands moved upward to her chin and tilted her face to his. Dark eyes, gray as the early morning fog, gazed into hers. "Why not?"

"Because you and I have different meanings for the word. We always have."

His dark eyebrows drew pensively together. "I suppose you might be right," he reluctantly agreed.

"But I can't believe that you're denying what you feel for me."

"I've always known that I'm attracted to you and I thought that I loved you once . . . sometimes I think I still do."

"But you're not sure?"

She wanted to fall back into his arms and reassure him, to pledge the love she felt welling in her heart, but reason held her words at bay. "I'm just . . . trying not to get caught in the same trap I fell into before."

A fleeting expression of pain crossed his face, but was quickly hidden beneath the hardening of his rugged features. "Is that what I did to you—'trapped you'?" The thin thread of patience in his voice threatened to snap.

"I trapped myself."

"And you're not about to let it happen again."

Her attempt at a frail smile faded. "I try not to repeat my mistakes."

"With the one glaring exception of Gypsy Wind."

Becca pursed her full lips. "If there's one thing I'm sure of in this world, it's that Gypsy Wind is no mistake."

"What about your feelings, Rebecca? Can't you trust them?"

"About horses, yes."

"But not men?" He cocked an angry black brow.

"They're more difficult," she admitted.

He stepped back from her, leaned insolently against the railing, and crossed his arms over his chest. *"They?* I'm not talking about the other men in your life, Rebecca. I'm just trying to sort out how you feel about me . . . about what happened last night."

She drew in an unsteady breath. "That's not easy."

His eyes narrowed and the gray pupils glittered

like newly forged steel. Every muscle in his body tensed. "So what you're attempting to say is that you have become the kind of woman who keeps all of her emotions under tight rein. Everything you do is well thought out in advance."

"I mean that I try not to see the world through rose-colored glasses anymore—"

He cut her off. "So you've become a bitter, calculating woman who works men into her life when it's convenient, or when she needs a favor."

It took every ounce of strength in Becca's heart to rise above the insult. "I hope not."

Again he mocked her as he continued, "The kind of woman who can hop into bed with a man as part of a business deal."

Her face flushed with anger. "Stop it, Brig. I'm not like that. You know it as well as I do."

"I don't think I know you at all. Not anymore. I was hoping that what we did last night meant something more to you than a quick one-night stand."

"It does."

"What?" he demanded. His voice was low, his eyes dangerous, his jaw determined.

"It would be easy for me to excuse what we did last night as an act of love."

"Excuse? For God's sake, woman, I'm too old for excuses!"

"Brig, what I feel for you is very strong and sometimes I delude myself into believing that I still love you," she began hesitantly. "What happened last night happened because of a set of circumstances and the fact that we care for each other—"

"Care for?" he echoed. "What the hell is that supposed to mean? 'Care for' is something you do for an elderly aunt!"

"Don't insult me, Brig. I said that I care for you; it means exactly what it implies."

Brig ran his fingers impatiently through his dark hair. Hot spurts of jealousy clouded his thinking. "Tell me this, Becca, just how many men have you *cared for* in the last six years?"

Becca's eyes flashed dangerously. "Is that what you want to know? Why don't you come straight to the point and ask me how many men I've slept with?"

"One and the same," he threw back.

"Not necessarily."

"Okay, then, how many men have you slept with?" He watched the disbelief and anger contort her even features. Wide eyes accused him of being the bastard he was. The thought of another man kissing those lips or touching her golden hair made his stomach knot.

"That's none of your business, Brig. You gave up all of those possessive rights when you threw me out of your life."

"You walked away."

Her lower lip began to tremble, but she held back her hot angry tears. "I had to, Brig. Because you thought so little of me that you honestly contended that *I* destroyed Sentimental Lady. Even with everything we had shared together, you never trusted me. In my opinion, without trust, there is no love." Her voice cracked, but she continued. "Just who the hell do you think you are? You have no right to ask me about my love life."

"I'm just *someone who cares for you*," he mocked disgustedly.

Becca felt her entire body shake. "You really can be a bastard when you want to be."

"Only when I'm pushed to the limit."

"It's reassuring to know that I bring out the best in you," she tossed out heatedly. She could feel her anger coloring her cheeks. "I think this discussion is over. We don't have much to say to each other, do we?" She pivoted on her heel and started toward the door. As quick as a springing cat, Brig was beside her. His grasp on her arm forced her to spin around and face the rage contorting his chiseled features. His lips were thin, his eyes ruthlessly dark.

"You'd like to run out on me again, wouldn't you? After all, it is what you do best."

"Let's just say that I don't like to waste my time arguing with you. There's no point to it."

"Counterproductive, is it? Not like sleeping with me?"

She slid her eyes disdainfully upward. "Let it go, Brig. We have nothing more to discuss."

Angrily, he jerked on her arm and she lost her balance. She fell against him and her hair came forward in a cloud of honey-colored silk. "I've never met a woman who could infuriate me so," Brig uttered through his clenched teeth. For the most part his anger was leveled at himself for his weakness.

Becca tossed her hair out of her resentful green eyes. "And you've met your share of them, haven't you? What about Melanie DuBois? Didn't she ever 'push you to the limit'?" The minute the jealous implication passed her lips, Becca knew she'd made a grave error in judgment. The rage in Brig's eyes took a new dimension, one of piteous disgust.

"You really know how to hit below the belt." Brig released her as if holding Becca was suddenly repulsive. She rubbed her upper arms in an effort to erase the pain he had caused.

"I'm sorry," she whispered. He had walked away from her, putting precious space between their bodies. "I had no right to say anything about her." Becca detested anything as petty as jealousy, and she realized that her remark about the dead woman was not only childishly petulant, but also deplorable and undignified. She had to make him understand. "Brig—"

He waved off her apology with the back of his hand. "Don't worry about it." His jaw hardened and his lips thinned as he pressed his hands into the back pockets of his jeans.

"I just didn't mean to say anything that mean." Her animosity faded. "I . . . I don't want to argue with you and I don't want our discussions to deteriorate into a verbal battlefield, where we just try and wound each other for the sake of some shallow victory." She took a step toward him, wanting to touch him, but holding her hands at her sides.

His voice was coldy distant. "You didn't wound me, if that's what you're afraid of."

"What I'm afraid of is that I look like a hypocrite." ·

He arched his eyebrows, silently encouraging her to continue.

"I didn't want to discuss my . . . past relationships with men, and then in the next moment I brought up one of the women in your life."

He shrugged. "Forget about it."

"But I know that you and Melanie were close—"

"I was never close to that woman," he cut in sharply.

Becca was taken aback. "But I thought—"

Again he interrupted, this time more harshly. "You thought what the rest of the world thought, what Melanie DuBois wanted the world to think. If you would have had the guts to come to me before my father was killed, before your back was up against the wall, you would have realized that everything in those cheap gossip tabloids was a hoax. A carefully arranged hoax."

"You never publicly denied it."

"Isn't that a little like the pot calling the kettle black? Besides, why would I? Any statement or contradiction I might have made would only have worsened an already bad situation. I decided it just wasn't worth the effort." Brig read the look of doubt on Becca's elegant face. "I can't deny that initially I was attracted to Melanie. Hell, she was a beautiful woman. But it didn't take me long to figure out what she was really after."

Brig paused, but Becca didn't interrupt, afraid to learn more than she wanted to know about the glamorous woman romantically linked to Brig, and yet fascinated with Brig's denials. A severe smile made him appear older than his thirty-five years.

"Anything you read about Melanie DuBois was precisely engineered by Ms. DuBois and that snake she called an agent." Brig leaned more closely to Becca. He withdrew his hands from his pockets and captured her shoulders with the warmth of his fingertips. She felt the muscles in her back begin to relax. "Don't tell me you believe everything you read in the papers." His gaze was coldly cynical.

Becca cocked her head and eyed him speculatively. Her hair fell over his arm. She knew he was referring to her vehement denouncement of the press coverage of Sentimental Lady's last race. "Of course not," she whispered.

"Then trust me. I have never had anything other than a passing interest in Melanie DuBois."

Her wistful smile trembled. "I'm sorry I made that stupid remark and brought her up. It was . . . unkind."

Brig recognized the flicker of doubt that darkened Becca's green eyes. "You still don't believe me, do you?"

"I'm just trying to understand, Brig. If Melanie had no connection with you, why was she in the plane with your father?"

For a moment he returned her confused stare. She seemed so vulnerable, so genuinely perplexed. He brushed aside an errant strand of her blond hair, pausing only slightly to rub it gently between his fingers. "Do you want me to tell you all about Melanie?" he asked softly.

She hesitated only briefly. "No." It wouldn't be fair. Hadn't she just told him that her love life was none of his business? She had no right to his.

"What if I told you it was important to me that you know?" His eyes moved from the lock of hair he had been studying and gazed intently into hers. He pushed the golden strands back into place.

"I'd listen," she sighed.

His intense gray eyes didn't leave hers. "I met Melanie at a cocktail party in Manhattan. It was one of those sophisticated affairs which everyone dreads but still attends."

"Not exactly your cup of tea."

"That's right. But I was forced to go. Business. Melanie was there. After I'd made the proper appearance and taken care of the Chambers Oil business, I got ready to leave. Melanie came up to me and asked me to take her home. I complied."

Becca's throat became dry, but something in his gaze reassured her. A sick feeling took hold of her as she realized she didn't want to hear about the other women in Brig's life. "I understand," she murmured, hoping to close the subject.

"No, you don't."

"I don't want to hear what happened, Brig. It's your business and I don't want to know about any of your affairs."

"Yes, you do," he persisted. "The business deal had gone sour, and I was dead tired from a flight earlier from the Middle East. That night I had no interest in Melanie."

"But there were other nights."

"Not with her."

Becca shook her head. "Brig, just let it alone. The woman is dead and I don't want to hear about it. Not this morning."

"It's important, Rebecca, because I never did sleep with Melanie."

"I find that hard to believe."

"That's understandable. She was a gorgeous woman . . . desirable, I suppose, but I just wasn't interested."

"Why not?"

"There wasn't any chemistry between us. Do you understand that?" His fingers touched her neck, stroking the soft skin familiarly. It was a warm caress shared only by lovers.

"Yes," she admitted. How many times had she dated wonderful, kind, intelligent men and found that she felt no passion for them. It was as if she was cursed to love only Brig. Only Brig had been able to catch her soul. He looked into her eyes as if he could see into the darkest corners of her mind.

"At first I made the mistake of thinking that Melanie was all right. She was a little vain, but I chalked that up to her being a model. We dated casually, but it wasn't anything serious. The papers got wind of it and blew it out of proportion, but I really didn't care. Not until I understood what it was that Melanie really wanted."

"Which was?"

"My father." Brig let the full impact of his statement settle upon her before continuing. "As a model, Melanie was hot, starting to climb toward the pinnacle of her profession. But she wasn't getting any younger, and modeling is a young woman's game. Melanie was smart enough to realize that her career would only last a few short years at best. She liked the good life. Even with the money she earned, she was always in debt. It takes a lot of cash to keep a townhouse in New York, a condo in L.A., and a cabin in Aspen. That woman could spend money faster than the treasury department could print it."

"And so she became romantically involved with your father," Becca guessed with a sickening feeling of disgust.

"More than that. She was pressuring Dad into marrying her."

"But the press . . . why didn't they know? This sounds like something the gossip columnists would get wind of."

"Melanie had to be patient. Dad insisted on it." Brig looked away and squinted against the rising sun. "Patience wasn't Melanie's long suit, but she played her cards right. When she knew I wasn't interested in her, she moved in on Dad. He was probably her target all along. Anyway, Melanie had to wait in line."

Becca understood. "Because he was involved with Nanette Walters."

Brig frowned and shook his head. "I can't for the life of me understand Jason's choice in women, not since Mom died. But there it was. And even though Nanette was just one in a long succession of women, my father cared for her." Brig's hands slid down Becca's spine and he pulled her close to him. "Jason made sure that all the women in his life were . . . comfortable. He gave Nanette her walking papers along with a sizable gift of jewelry."

"Why are you telling me all of this?" she asked, aware of the soft touch of his hands against the small of her back.

"I wish I knew," he admitted, kissing the top of her head.

Chapter 7

NOTHING WAS RESOLVED, AND, FOR THE MOMENT, IT didn't seem to matter. Becca accepted Brig's silent invitation to stay with him for the remainder of the weekend. Upon his suggestion, she donned her jeans and sneakers and they hiked together through the leaf-strewn trails of the lower slopes, holding hands and flushing out a frightened doe and twin fawns who quickly bounded out of sight and into the protection of the dense woods. Brig held her hand warmly in his and with the other, pointed out secret treasures from his boyhood. The abandoned tree house he had unskillfully crafted at twelve was missing more than a few of its floorboards. It looked weathered and discarded in the ancient maple tree. The bend in the path where he had discovered a broken arrowhead was now overgrown. The deep pool in the mountain stream was as crystal clear as it had ever been, though it had been twenty years since he had last caught a native trout in it or swum naked along its bank.

Becca felt that Brig was showing her a secret side to his nature. A dimension she had never before been allowed to see. It warmed her heart to think that he would share his fondest memories with her. She walked with him until her muscles ached, and they laughed into each other's eyes as if they were the only man and woman in the universe. They were alone, male and female, basking in shared affection, afraid to call their feelings love.

When twilight began to darken the hillside, they raced back to the cabin. Becca lost by a miserable margin, and Brig's gray eyes danced with his victory. She pretended wounded anger, but he saw through her ruse and as she attempted to brush past him into the cabin, his hand shot out and captured her waist. Her head tilted backward and her golden hair fell away from her face, framing her twinkling green eyes in tousled, tawny curls. Her cheeks were pink from the cool fresh air and her lips parted into a becoming smile more sensual than any Brig had ever seen.

"You love to win, don't you?" she asked.

"I love to be with you," he responded, his eyes darkening mysteriously.

Her arms entwined around his neck. "I can't think of another place I'd rather be."

"That, Ms. Peters, is an invitation I can't ignore," he replied, tightening his grip on her waist and bending his head to mold her chilled lips to his. She closed her eyes and let the taste of him linger on her lips. She savored every moment she shared with him. Too long she had waited for the intimate pleasure of his touch.

His fingers spanned her waist to grip her possessively. His tongue slid between the serrated edges of her teeth to explore the warmth of her mouth. He groaned when the tip of her tongue found his. The pressure of his mouth against hers hardened with the passion that fired his blood.

When he lifted his head, it was to smile wickedly into her passion-glazed eyes. "Sometimes I wonder if I'll ever get enough of you," he mused against her ear.

"I hope not," she breathed fervently.

They walked into the cabin silently, arms entwined, bodies barely touching. While Brig started the fire, Becca managed to put together hodgepodge sandwiches from the dwindling supply of food in the refrigerator. Together they drank chilled wine, nibbled on the sandwiches, and warmed their bare feet near the glowing embers of the crackling fire. The tangy scent of burning pitch filled the air. Sitting on the floor, her head nestled against Brig's shoulder, Becca felt more at home than she had in years.

She watched him as he finished the last of his wine. The firelight sharpened the lines of his face, but even in the hard light, the charm of his smile was undiminished. The last six years had added a rugged quality to his masculinity. He was as lean as he had ever been and his hair was still near black with only the slightest sprinkling of gray.

He turned his gaze to her and found her staring intently at his profile. His eyelids lowered and his smile became provocative. "You're an interesting woman, Rebecca," he whispered hoarsely. With his finger he traced the line of her jaw and let it lower to the column of her neck. His finger stopped its descent at the hollow of her throat where it began drawing sketchy, lazy circles. "I'm not sure I like what you do to me."

Her eyebrows raised, prompting him onward. She couldn't find her voice, it was lost in the soft swirl of emotions generated by his feather-soft touch.

"I'm not in control when I'm around you, not in complete command of myself."

His fingers found the top button of her blouse, released it, and toyed with the edge of her collar. Becca closed her eyes and she felt her body warming from the inside out, heard the ragged sound of her uneven breathing as he unhooked another button and then another. She had to draw in her breath quickly when his hand slipped under the soft fabric of her bra to lovingly cup a breast.

"Oh, Brig," she sighed, turning her body, twisting in his arms in order to move closer to him. She felt her nipple harden, and moaned in contentment, when his head lowered and he took her breast in his mouth. The soft movements of his tongue and lips comforted her and helped increase the thundering tempo of her heartbeat.

Slowly he undressed her and then when she was naked, he discarded his own clothes. He lowered himself beside her, letting the hard length of his body mold against the soft tissues of hers. His arms wrapped around her, his hands kneaded the soft muscles in her back. "You're mine," he whispered roughly against her neck. His lips warmed a trail of hungry kisses down her throat, over the hill of her breasts, around her navel. "You've always been mine."

The possessive sound of his voice made her blood thunder in her ears and the moist warm heat from his swollen lips ignited her skin. She ached to be a part of him. The void within her yearned to be filled with the depth of his passion. She began to yield with the persuasive touch of his hands on her buttocks.

"Stay with me," he pleaded. Heavy-lidded eyes held hers in a heated gaze that promised a lifetime of love. If only she could believe those eyes.

"Forever," she whispered, pushing aside her

doubts and letting herself become swept up in the tide of rising passion. She felt the weight of his body as he shifted to part her legs and claim once again what had always been his.

Sunday afternoon came far too quickly. Isolated in the cozy mountain cabin, Becca had felt secluded from the rest of the world. She had forced herself to forget the pain of the past and the brutal anger of her argument with Brig concerning Gypsy Wind. Now it was time to face the truth and unwrap the shielding cocoon of false security she had willingly used to cover herself from the pain of past deceits.

From her vantage point in the kitchen, she could look out the window and see Brig. He was sitting on the porch steps, gazing intently across the valley floor. He rested his elbows on his knees and cradled a cup of steaming coffee in his hands. His wavy hair was rumpled, and despite the fact that he had shaved earlier, already there was evidence of his beard darkening his hard jawline. He squinted past the rising fog and his breath misted in the crisp autumn air.

He must have heard her footsteps as she approached. Though he didn't turn his head to look in her direction, he spoke. His eyes remained distant. "You've come to tell me that it's time you left," he stated flatly.

She sat down next to him, wedging her body between his and one of the strong supports for the roof. "We can't hide up here forever." She huddled her arms around her torso. Though wearing a moss-colored bulky knit sweater, the chill in the air made her shiver.

"I suppose not." Again his voice was toneless. He took a long scalding sip of his coffee.

"It would be nice to spend the rest of our lives up

here," she mused aloud while watching the flight of ducks heading southward.

"But impractical."

"And irresponsible."

His mouth quirked downward. "That's right, isn't it? We both have pressing responsibilities."

She tilted her head and studied his features. This morning he seemed suddenly cold and distant. "Is something wrong?"

"What could be wrong?"

"I don't know . . . but you look as if something's bothering you."

"Any guesses as to what it might be?"

Her smile faded. "Gypsy Wind."

"That's a good start." Brig's lips compressed into a tight, uncompromising line.

Becca's heart missed a beat. "What do you want to do with her?"

"Nothing."

"Nothing?" she repeated.

"I don't want you to race her, Becca. I don't want you to go through all of that pain again."

"A race doesn't have to end in pain and death."

"You're tempting fate."

"Don't tell me you believe in that nonsense. I've never thought of you as a man who put stock in fate or destiny, or whatever else you might call it."

"Not usually. But we're not dealing with a usual set of circumstances here." He set his cup down and grabbed her by the shoulders as if he intended to shake some sense into her. "Damn it, Becca. You don't have to prove anything to me or the rest of the world. There's no need to try and purge yourself of this thing."

"I'm not," she argued, her face tilted defiantly. "I'm only attempting to do what any respectable breeder would if he were in my shoes. I'm trying to race the finest filly ever bred."

"Forget it!"

Becca's anger flashed in her eyes like green lightning. Her fingers dug into her ribs. "Just what is it you expect me to do?"

The severity in his gaze faded. "I want you to hang it up," he implored. His fingers were gentle on her shoulders as he tried to persuade her. "Sell Gypsy Wind if you have to, or better yet, keep her, but for God's sake and hers, don't let her race!"

"That's crazy."

"It might be the sanest thing I've ever suggested."

"It's impossible. Gypsy Wind was bred to run."

"She was bred to absolve you of Sentimental Lady's death."

The insult stung, but she didn't let go of her emotions. "There's no point in arguing about this," she stated, attempting to rise. His hands restrained her.

"There's more." His voice was low.

"More to what?"

"I want you to stay with me."

"Oh, Brig," she said, thinking of a thousand reasons to stay. "Don't do this to me. You know I want to stay with you . . ." Tears began to gather behind her eyes.

"But you can't?"

She shook her head painfully, thinking of Starlight Farm, her brother, Dean, and Gypsy Wind. She had worked six long, tedious years to get where she had, with no help from Brig Chambers. In the beauty of one quiet weekend, he expected her to change all of that. "I've got to go home."

He struggled with a weighty decision. His eyes grew dark. "Stay with me. Make your home with me. Be my wife."

The tears that had pooled began to spill from her eyes and her chin trembled. "I wish I could, Brig," she said. "But it's just not possible. You know it as well as I."

"Because of Sentimental Lady."

"Because you lied to the press. You accused me of killing the horse—"

"I knew that you didn't intend to kill her. I never for a moment thought that you intended to hurt her."

"You know that I didn't hurt her."

"But someone who worked for you did."

"Is that what you're doing? Trying to convince me that it was one of the grooms . . . or maybe Ian O'Riley . . . or how about my brother, Dean, or the vet? You know who did it, Brig. Don't point the finger somewhere else. I might have been gullible enough to believe you once, but not any longer."

"Becca, I'm telling you the truth. Why can't you accept that?"

His eyes were steely gray, but clear, his expression exasperated. Becca longed to trust him. She wanted to believe anything he told her. "Maybe because you never came after me."

"Only because you didn't want to see me."

"That's a lie."

"I called, Rebecca. You refused to speak to me."

Becca shook her head, trying to dodge his insulting lies. "You never called. Don't start lying to me, Brig. It's too hard a habit to break."

The pressure on her arms increased. "I did call you, damn it. I talked with your brother once and that old trainer O'Riley a couple of times. I even talked with your cook, or housemaid, or whatever she is."

Doubt replaced her anger. "You talked to Martha? When?"

"I can't remember exactly."

"But she's been gone for over five years."

"I spoke to her about six months after the accident," Brig replied thoughtfully. "It was the second call I'd made."

Becca drew in her breath. "No one told me that you'd phoned."

Brig's eyes narrowed suspiciously. "And that's why you didn't phone me back?"

"I couldn't very well return what I'd never received."

"Then someone—no, make that everyone in your house is lying to you."

"Or you are," she thought aloud.

His fingers carefully cupped her chin. "Why would I? What purpose would it serve. As soon as you go back to California you could check it out."

"I don't know."

"Face it, Becca. Someone is covering up. Probably the same person who drugged Sentimental Lady."

"It just doesn't make any sense. Why would anyone working with me to make Sentimental Lady a winner want to throw the race?"

Brig got up and began pacing on the weathered floorboards of the porch. He ran his fingers thoughtfully through his hair. "I don't know," he said quietly. "Unless someone had it in for you. Did anyone have an ax to grind with you? It could be something that you might think insignificant like . . . an argument over a raise . . . or the firing of a friend."

Becca rested her forehead on her palm and forced her weary mind to go backward in time, past the ugly race. It was futile. She shook her head slowly.

Brig was desperate. He came back to her and forced her eyes to meet the power of his gaze. "You've got to think, Rebecca. Someone deliberately tried to keep us apart, probably for the single reason of keeping the truth of the race secret. As long as we suspected each other, we wouldn't think past our suspicions. We wouldn't be able to find the

real culprit, even if he left a trail of clues a mile
long."

"But the racing commission . . . certainly its investigation would have discovered the truth."

"Not necessarily—not if the culprit were clever.
And remember, the commission was more concerned about Sentimental Lady's recovery than the
drugging. By the time all of the havoc had quieted,
the culprit could have covered his tracks."

She wanted to believe him but couldn't think past
the six lonely years she had spent in the shadow of
that last damning race without Brig's strength or
support. "I don't know," she whispered. "It all
seems so farfetched."

"No more so than your half-baked accusations
that I had something to do with it!"

"But why? Why would anyone want to disqualify
the Lady?"

Brig closed his eyes for a moment and tried to
clear his head. Nothing was making any sense. "I
don't know." His eyes snapped open. "But you
must. Think, Rebecca, think!"

"I have, Brig. For the past six years I've hardly
thought of anything else. And the only logical answer to the question of who injured Sentimental
Lady was you."

"But you don't believe that anymore, do you?"

Her smile was thin. "I don't know what to believe.
But if it's any consolation, I never wanted to think
that you had anything to do with it."

"But you still have doubts."

She looked bravely into his eyes. "No."

For the first time that morning, the hint of a smile
lightened his features. He took her into his arms,
and held her body close to his. The power of his
embrace supported her. "Then you'll stay with me?"

"Not yet," she said, dreading the sound of her
own voice.

The arms around her relaxed and Brig stepped away from her. "Sometimes I don't think I know what you want, lady, but I assume this has something to do with your filly. You still intend to race her, don't you, despite what happened to Sentimental Lady."

"I have to." Couldn't Brig understand? Gypsy Wind had more than mere potential for winning races—she was a champion. Becca would risk her reputation on it.

"No one's holding a gun to your head."

Becca put her hands on her hips and tried a different approach. "Why don't you come to the farm and see first hand what it is that makes Gypsy so special? Come and watch her work out. See for yourself her power, the grace of her movements, the exhilaration in her eyes when she's given her head. Don't judge her before you've seen her."

Brig tossed the idea over in his mind. His work schedule was impossible. He had no time for horses or horse racing. He'd ended that folly six years ago. But Rebecca Peters was another thing altogether. He wanted her. More than he had wanted her six years ago. More than he had ever wanted anything. He saw the look of pride on her face and he noticed the defiant way she stood as if ready to refute anything he might say. Thoughtfully, he rubbed his thumb slowly under his jaw. "What if I disagree with you?"

"You won't." Becca wondered if she looked as determined as she sounded.

Brig cocked his head but didn't argue. "If I do decide to go to California and I think that Gypsy Wind is unsound, will you promise not to race her and give up this foolish dream?"

"Not on your life." Her eyes glittered with fierce determination.

"And you're not afraid that someone might do to her what was done to Sentimental Lady."

"I've been racing horses ever since Sentimental Lady's death. The incident hasn't recurred."

Brig's voice was edged in steel. "Then I guess we're at an impasse."

"Only if you want to be." Her hand reached out and her fingers touched his arm. "Don't shut me out, Brig. Not now. I don't think I'm asking too much of you. Please come and see my horse. Reserve your judgment until then. If you think she's not as fine as I've been telling you, we'll work something out."

"Such as?"

"I'll find a way to repay your loan within the year. Is that fair?"

"I suppose so. Now, what about my proposition? Will you marry me?"

"Give it time, Brig. We both need time to learn to love and trust each other again. Six years is a long time to harbor the kinds of feelings we've had for each other. You can't wash them away in one weekend in the mountains."

"Nor can you prove to the world that you're one of the best Thoroughbred breeders in the country. I was wrong about you, Rebecca. You haven't changed at all. You're still giving me the same flimsy excuse you did the last time I asked you to marry me. I'm not a man who's known for his patience, nor am I the kind of man who gets a kick out of rejection. I've asked you twice to marry me, and I won't do it again."

Becca struggled with her pride. When she spoke her voice was strangely detached and the words of reason seemed distant. "I didn't come to you to try and coerce a marriage proposal from you, Brig, nor did I intend to have another affair with you. All I wanted was to know that you were safe and to tell you about Gypsy Wind. I've done those things and

I've also told you that I intend to repay my note to your father. Business is done. My plane leaves in less than four hours from Denver. I have to go."

His face was a mask of indifference. "Just remember that you made your own choices today. You're the one who will have to live with them."

Chapter 8

THE TRIP BACK TO STARLIGHT BREEDING FARM WAS uneventful, and Becca had to force herself to face the realization that she had no future with Brig Chambers. If ever she had, it was gone. She had thrown it away. Becca knew that Brig cared for her, in his own way, but she also knew that he didn't trust her and probably never would. The best thing to do was to forget about him and concentrate on paying back the debt to him as quickly as possible. She frowned to herself as she unpacked her suitcase. Forgetting about Brig and what they had shared together was more easily said than done. In the last six years she had never once forgotten the tender way in which he would look into her eyes, or his gentle caress.

"Cut it out," she mumbled to herself. The last thing she should do was brood over a future that wasn't meant to be. With forced determination, she pulled on her favorite pair of faded jeans and started toward the paddock. The first order of business was Gypsy Wind.

Becca clenched her teeth together as she thought about training Gypsy Wind to be the best Thoroughbred filly ever raced. She may have already made a monumental mistake by not racing the filly as a two-year-old, and if she were honest with herself it had something to do with Brig and the fact that, at the time, he didn't know about Gypsy Wind. At least the secret was now in the open, and Becca vowed silently to herself that she would find a way to make Gypsy Wind a winner with or without Brig's approval.

She found Ian O'Riley in the tack room. His short fingers were running along the smooth leather reins of a bridle last worn by Sentimental Lady. He turned his attention toward the door when Becca entered.

"I heard you were back," he said with a smile.

"Just got in a couple of hours ago."

Ian's smile faded. "And how did it go . . . with Brig, I mean?"

Becca tossed her blond braid over her shoulder and shrugged. "As well as can be expected, I guess." She took a seat on a scarred wooden chair near the trophy case. The award closest to her was now covered with dust, but Becca recognized it as belonging to Sentimental Lady for her record-breaking win of The New York Racing Association's Acorn Stakes. Absently, Becca rubbed the dust off the trophy.

"What does he think of Gypsy Wind?"

"Not much," Becca admitted. "Oh, Ian, he thinks I was foolish to breed her. He accused me of trying to absolve myself of her death."

"He thinks that's why you did it?"

Becca nodded mutely.

"And he's got you believing it, too."

Becca shook her head and put the trophy back in

the case. "No, of course not, but he did make me question my motives. He even suggested that I didn't race her as a two-year-old because I was afraid of his reaction."

"Nonsense!" Ian's wise blue eyes sparked dangerously. "He knows better than that—or at least he should! Sentimental Lady's legs weren't strong enough, and I'm not about to make the same mistake with Gypsy Wind. That's the trouble with this country! In Europe many Thoroughbreds never set foot on a racetrack until they're three. And when they do, they run on firm but yielding turf.

"Gypsy Wind's legs won't be fully ossified until she's three, and I'm not about to ask her to sprint over a hard, fast track. It's a good way to ruin a damned fine filly!"

Becca smiled at the wiry man's vehemence. "I agree with you."

Ian's gray eyebrows raised. "I know . . . and I'm proud of you for it. It would have been easier to run her this year and make a little extra money. I know you could use it."

"Not if it hurts Gypsy Wind."

Ian's grizzled face widened into a comfortable grin. He winked at Becca fondly. "We'll show them all, you know. Come early next year, when Gypsy Wind begins to race, we'll have ourselves a champion."

"We already do," Becca pointed out.

"Have you given any thought to moving her to Sequoia Park?"

The smile left Becca's face and she blanched. "I was hoping that we could keep her somewhere else."

Ian put a gentle hand on her shoulder. "It holds bad memories for me, too, Becca. But it's the closest to the farm and has the best facilities around. I thought we would start her in a few short races locally before we headed down the state and eventually back East."

"You're right, of course. When would you want to move her?"

"Soon—say, right after the holidays."

Becca felt her uncertainty mount, but denied her fears. "You're the trainer. Whatever you say goes."

Ian paused and shifted the wooden match that was forever in his mouth, a habit he'd acquired since he'd given up cigarettes. "I appreciate that, gal. Not many owners would have stood up for a trainer the way that you did."

It was Becca's turn to be comforting. "Don't be ridiculous. We've been over this a hundred times before. You and I both know that you had nothing to do with what happened to Sentimental Lady. I never doubted it for a minute."

"She was my responsibility."

"And you did everything you could do to protect her."

His wizened blue eyes seemed suddenly old. "It wasn't enough, was it?"

"It's over, Ian. Forget it."

"Can you?"

Becca smiled sadly. "Of course not. But I do try not to brood about it." She stared pointedly at the bridle Ian held in his gnarled hands. "Is there something else that's bothering you?" It wasn't like Ian to be melancholy or to second-guess himself.

Ian shook his gray head.

"How did the workout go this morning?" Becca asked, changing the subject and hoping to lighten the mood of the conversation.

Ian managed a bemused smile. "Gypsy Wind really outdid herself. She wanted to run the entire distance."

"Just like Lady," Becca observed.

"Yeah." Ian replaced the bridle on a rusty hook near a yellowed picture of Sentimental Lady. He stared wistfully at the black and white photograph of the proud filly. "They're a lot alike," he mumbled to himself as he turned toward the door. "Got to run now, the missus doesn't like me late for supper."

"Ian—"

His hand paused over the door handle and he rotated his body so that he could once again face Becca.

"After the race at Sequoia . . ."

Ian pulled his broad-billed cap over his head and nodded to encourage Becca to continue.

Becca's voice was less bold than it had been and her cheeks appeared pinker. "After all the hubbub had died down about the horse, did you ever take a call from Brig . . . a call for me that you never told me about?"

Ian's lips pursed into a frown. "He told you about that, did he?" Ian asked, pulling himself up to his full fifty-four inches. "I figured he would, should have expected it." Ian rubbed the silver stubble on his chin. "Yeah, Missy, he called, more than once if I remember correctly."

"Why didn't you tell me?"

Ian leaned against the door and had trouble meeting Becca's searching gaze. "We thought about it," he admitted.

"*We?*"

"Yeah, Martha, Dean, and I. We considered it, talked a lot about it. More than you might guess. But Dean, well, he insisted that we shouldn't bother you about the fact that Brig kept calling—said that after all you'd been through, you didn't need to talk to him and start the trouble all over again." Ian shifted his weight from one foot to the other.

"Someone should have asked me."

Ian nodded his agreement. "That's what Martha

and I thought, but Dean disagreed. He was absolutely certain that anything Brig might say to you would
only . . . well, open old wounds."

Becca lifted her chin. "I was old enough to care
for myself."

The old man flushed with embarrassment. "I
know, Missy. I know that now, but at the time we
were all a little shaken up. Martha and I, we never
felt comfortable about it."

"Is that why Martha quit so suddenly?"

Ian's faded eyes darkened. "I don't rightly know."
He considered her question. "Maybe it helped her
with her decision to move in with her daughter.
Leastwise, it didn't hurt."

"Did Dean speak with Brig?" Cold suspicion
prompted her question.

Ian thought for a moment and then shrugged his
bowed shoulders. "I can't say for certain—it's been a
long time. No, wait. He must have, 'cause right after
he told me he'd taken care of Brig, we didn't get any
more calls."

"How many calls were there?" Becca's heart was
thudding expectantly. Brig hadn't lied.

"Can't recall. Four—maybe five. Dean was afraid
you might take one yourself."

"So he told me not to answer the phone, in order
that he could 'protect' me from nosy reporters," she
finished for him.

"Is that what he told you?"

Becca nodded, her thoughts swimming. Why
would Dean lie to her? "So Dean was the one who
made the final decision."

"Yeah. Martha and I, we agreed with him."

"Why?"

"He was only looking after you . . ." His statement was nearly an apology.

"I know," Becca sighed, trying to set the old
man's mind at ease. "It's all right."

Ian gave her an affectionate smile before leaving the tack room and shutting the door behind him. Becca bit at her lower lip and stared sightlessly into the trophy case. Why would Dean hide the fact that Brig had called?

Swallowing back the betrayal that was rising in her throat, she tried to give her brother the benefit of the doubt. Surely he had only wanted to protect her, in his own misguided manner. But that had been six years ago. With the passage of time, Becca would have expected him to tell her about the calls. Why not tell her after the shock of the race had worn off? Was he afraid she would relapse into her depression? For a fraction of a second Becca wondered if there were other things that Dean had hidden from her. Was he responsible for the money missing from petty cash? And what about the roofing contractor he had suggested, the bum who had run off with her down payment for a new roof on the stables.

"Stop it," she chided herself. She was becoming paranoid. Though she didn't understand her brother at times, she couldn't forget that he had been the one who had helped her put her life back together when it had been shattered into a thousand pieces six years ago at Sequoia Park.

Still troubled about the fact that Dean had purposely lied to her, Becca left the tack room and tossed aside the fears that were beginning to take hold of her. She made her way upstairs to the office and tried to concentrate on the books. Though she had been gone for little over three days, she knew that the bookkeeping would be far behind, as it was near the end of the month. It was time to start organizing the journal entries for month-end posting. She opened the checkbook and realized that several checks were missing. What was happening? No entries had been made for the missing checks. A new fear began to take hold of her. Was someone at the farm stealing from her? But the checks were worthless without a proper signature: Rebecca's or Dean's.

"Dear God, no," she whispered as the weight of her discovery hit her with the force of a tidal wave. She sat down at the desk, her legs suddenly too weak to support her.

The sound of a pickup roaring down the drive met her ears. She recognized it as belonging to Dean. She waited. It wasn't long before his boots clamored up the stairs and he burst into the room, smelling like a brewery and slightly unsteady on his feet. His boyish grin was slightly lopsided.

Becca thought he looked nervous, but mentally told herself that she was just imagining his anxiety.

"Hi, sis. How was the flight?" he asked casually as he popped the tab on a cold can of beer, took a long swallow, and dropped onto the ripped couch.

"Tiresome, but on schedule," she replied, watching him with new eyes. He settled into the couch, propped the heels of his boots against the corner of the desk, and let his Stetson fall forward. Balancing the can precariously on his stomach between his outstretched fingers, he looked as if he might fall asleep.

His voice was slightly muffled. "And good ole Brig, how was he?"

Becca hesitated only slightly, carefully gauging her brother's reaction. His eyes were shadowed by the hat, but there appeared to be more than idle interest in his gaze. Becca supposed that was to be expected, considering the situation. "Brig was fine."

Her noncommittal response didn't satisfy Dean. "And I suppose you told him about the horse," he said sarcastically.

"You know I did."

His boots hit the floor with a thud, and beer slopped onto his shirt before he could grab the can.

He stood to his full height and looked down upon her with his ruddy face contorted in rage. "God-damn it, Becca! I knew it! You didn't listen to one word of advice I gave you, did you? I don't know what the hell's gotten into you lately!"

"Precisely what I was thinking about you," she snapped back.

"I'm only trying to look out for your best interests," he proclaimed.

"Are you?"

"You know I am." He took another swallow from the beer but it didn't begin to cool the anger in his steely-blue eyes. He shook his head as if to dislodge a bothersome thought. "I knew it," he said, swearing under his breath. "Damn it! I knew that if I let you go to Denver you'd come back here with your mind all turned around."

"If you let me?" she echoed. "I can make my own decisions, Dean, and there's nothing wrong with my mind!"

"Except that you can't think straight whenever you're near Brig Chambers!"

"You and I agreed that Brig had to know about the horse—there was no other way around it."

"We didn't agree to anything. You went running off to Denver with any flimsy excuse to look up Brig again."

"And you decided to tie one on, after taking a few checks from the checkbook."

For a moment Dean was stopped short. Then, with a growl, he dug into his pockets and threw two crumpled checks onto the desk. "I was a little short—"

"Where's the other check?"

"I cashed it. Okay? So sue me!"

"That's not the point."

"Then what is, sis? And what happened while you

were in Denver? Unless I miss my guess, you started to fall in love all over again with that miserable son-of-a-bitch, and then he threw you out on your ear."

Becca rose from the desk. She had to fight to keep her voice from shaking as badly as her hands. "That's not what happened." Her green eyes deepened with her anger.

"Close enough." Dean took a final swallow of beer and drained the can before he crushed it in his fist. "So what did he tell you to do—sell the horse?" Dean's knowing blue gaze bored into Becca's angry emerald eyes.

"We considered several alternatives."

"I'll just bet you did," Dean agreed with a disbelieving smirk.

Becca swallowed back the hot retort that hovered on the end of her tongue. Trading verbal knife wounds with her brother would get her nowhere. "I've decided to keep the horse. I told Brig that we'd pay him back within the year."

"Are you out of your mind? Fifty grand plus interest?" Dean was astounded. "That'll be impossible! Even if Gypsy Wind wins right off the bat, it takes a bundle just to cover her costs. You're going to have to stable her at a track, hire an entire crew, enter her in the events—it will cost us a small fortune."

"She's worth it, Dean."

"How in the world do you think you can pay off Chambers?"

"She'll win."

"Oh God, Becca. Why gamble? Take my advice and sell her!"

"To whom?"

"*Anyone*! Surely someone's interested. You should have listened to me and sold her at Keeneland when she was a yearling. It's going to be a lot tougher now that she's racing age and hasn't even bothered to start!"

"And you know why," Becca charged.

"Because you didn't have the guts to let Brig Chambers know about the horse, that's why. I don't know how you've managed to keep so quiet about her, or why you'd want to. The more you build her up to the press, compare her to Sentimental Lady, the more she's worth!"

Becca's thin patience frayed. "I didn't run her as a two-year-old to avoid injuring her. As for hype about a horse, it's highly overrated. Any owner worth his salt judges an animal by the horse itself— not some press release."

"I don't understand why you're all bent out of shape about it," Dean announced as he threw the twisted empty can into a nearby trash basket.

"And I don't understand why you insist on trying to run my life!"

Dean's flushed face tensed. "Because you need me—or have you forgotten?" He paused for a moment and his face relaxed. "At least, you used to need me. Has that changed?"

"I don't know," she said. "I . . . I just don't like fighting with you. It seems that lately we're at opposite ends of any argument." Despite the tension in the room, she managed a smile. "But you're right about one thing," she conceded. "I did need you and you were there for me. I appreciate that, Dean, and I owe you for it."

"But," he coaxed, reading the puzzled expression on her face and knowing intuitively that she wasn't finished.

"But I don't understand why you didn't tell me about Brig and why you hid the fact that he called me several times."

Dean seemed to pale beneath his California tan. "So he told you about that, did he?"

"And Ian explained what happened."

A startled look darkened his pale eyes but swiftly disappeared. His thin lips pressed into a disgusted line. "Then you realize that I was just trying to protect you."

"From what?"

"*From Chambers!* Becca, look. You've never been able to face the fact that he used you." Becca started to interrupt, but Dean held her words at bay by raising his outstretched fingers. "It's true, damn it. That man can hurt you like nobody else. I don't know what it is about him that turns a rational woman like you into a simpering fool, but he certainly has the touch. He used you in the past; and if you give him another chance, he'll do it again. I don't think he can stop himself, it's inbred in his nature."

"You're being unfair."

"And you're hiding your head in the sand."

Becca ran her fingers through her hair, unfastening the thong which held it tied and letting it fall into loose curls to surround her face. She thought back to the warm moments of love with Brig and the happiness they had shared in the snow-capped Rockies; the passion, the tenderness, the yearning, the pain. Was it only for one short weekend in her life? Was she destined to forever love a man who couldn't return that love? Could Dean be right? Had Brig used her? "No," she whispered shakily, trying to convince herself as much as her brother. "I can't believe that Brig ever used me, or that he ever intentionally hurt me."

"Come off it, Becca!"

"That's the way I see it."

Dean's eyes were earnest, his jaw determined. "And you live with your head in the clouds when it comes to horses and men. You dream of horses that run wild and free and you try to turn men into heroes who bare their souls for the love of a woman —at least, you do in the case of Brig Chambers."

"Now you're trying to stereotype me," she accused.

"Think about it, sis." Dean gave her a knowing smile before striding toward the door.

Becca couldn't let him go until he answered one last nagging question that had been with her ever since she had spoken with Ian in the tack room. "Dean, why did Martha leave the ranch when she did?"

Dean's hand paused over the doorknob. He whirled around to face his sister, his eyes narrowed. "What do you mean?"

"I mean that she left rather suddenly, don't you think? And it's odd that I haven't heard from her since. Not even a card at Christmas. It's always bothered me."

Dean's face froze into a well-practiced smile. "Didn't she say that she left because her daughter needed her?"

"That's what you told me."

"But you don't think that's the reason?" Dean asked, coolly avoiding her penetrating gaze. How close to the truth was she? He was unnerved, but he tried his best not to let it show. Becca was becoming suspicious—all because of Brig Chambers!

"I just wondered if it had anything to do with Brig's phone calls," Becca replied. The tension in the room made it seem stuffy.

"I doubt it, Becca. Martha's kid was sick."

"The eighteen-year-old girl?"

"Right. Uh, Martha went to live with her and that's the end of the story. Maybe she's just too busy to write."

"I don't even know where they moved, do you?"

"No." Dean's voice was brittle. "Look, I've got to run—see you later." Dean pushed open the door and hurried down the stairs. He seemed to be relieved to get out of the office and away from Becca.

An uneasy feeling of suspicion weighed heavily on Becca's mind. She worked long into the evening, but couldn't shake the annoying doubts which plagued her. Why did she have the feeling that Dean wasn't telling her everything? What could he possibly be hiding. Was it, as he so emphatically asserted, that he was interested only in protecting her? Or was there more . . .

Brig sat at his desk and eyed the latest stack of correspondence from the estate attorneys with disgust. It seemed that every day they came up with more questions for him and his staff. The accident which had taken his father's life had happened more than a month ago, and yet Brig had the disquieting feeling that the Last Will and Testament of Jason Chambers was as far from being settled as it had ever been. He tossed the papers aside and rose from the desk.

Behind him, through the large plate-glass window the city of Denver spread until it reached the rugged backdrop of the bold Colorado Rockies. Brig hazarded a glance out the window and into the dusk, but neither the bustling city nor the cathedral peaks held any interest for him. No matter how he tried, he couldn't seem to take his mind off Rebecca Peters and that last weekend they had spent together.

The smoked-glass door to the office opened and Mona, Brig's secretary, entered. "I'm going down to the cafeteria—can I get you anything?" Brig shook his head and managed a tired smile. "How about a cup of coffee?"

"I don't think so."

Mona raised her perfect eyebrows. "It could be a long night. Emery called. He seems to think that the wildcat strike in Wyoming won't be settled for at least a week."

"Arbitration isn't working?"

"Apparently not."

"Great," Brig muttered. "Just what we need."

Mona closed the door softly behind her and leaned against it. She ran nervous fingers over her neatly styled silver hair. She was only thirty-five; the color of her hair was by choice. "Is something bothering you?" she asked, genuinely concerned.

"What do you think?"

"I think you're overworked."

Brig laughed despite himself. Mona had a way of cutting to the core of a problem. "I can,'t disagree with that."

"Then why don't you take some time off?" she suggested. "Or at least take a working vacation and spend some time in your father's cabin." She watched him carefully; he seemed to tense.

"I can't do that. It's impossible."

"I could route all the important calls to you."

"Out of the question," he snapped.

Mona pursed her lips, stung by his hot retort. It wasn't like him. But then, he wasn't himself lately. Not since that weekend he spent alone. Maybe the strain of his father's death affected him more deeply than he admitted. "It was just a suggestion."

"I know it was, Mona," he admitted, and his shoulders slumped. "I didn't mean to shout at you."

"Still, I do think you should consider taking some time off."

"When?"

"As soon as possible—before you really chop somebody's head off."

"Do you think you can handle this office without me?"

She winked slyly at him. "What do you think?"

"I *know* you can."

"I'll remember that the next time I ask for a raise. Now, have you reconsidered my offer—how about some coffee?"

Brig's face broke into an affable grin. "If you insist."

"Well, while I'm still batting a thousand, I really do think you should take a couple of days off. Believe me, this place won't fall apart without you."

"I suppose not," Brig conceded as the pert secretary slipped out of his office and headed for the cafeteria.

Mona had a point. Brig knew he was tense and that his temper was shorter than usual. Maybe it was because he found it nearly impossible to concentrate on his position. The glass-topped desk was littered with work that didn't interest him. Even the wildcat strike in Wyoming seemed grossly unimportant. Chambers Oil was one of the largest oil companies in the United States, with drilling rights throughout the continental U.S. and Alaska. That didn't begin to include the offshore drilling. Who the hell cared about oil in Wyoming? As far as he was concerned, Chambers Oil could write off the entire venture as a tax loss.

Brig rotated his shoulders and tried to smooth away the tension in his neck and back. Who was he kidding? It wasn't his father's estate that kept him awake at nights. Nor was it the strike in Wyoming, or any of the other nagging problems that came with the responsibility of running Chambers Oil. The problem was Rebecca Peters. It always had been, and he didn't doubt for a moment that it always would be.

Though he went through the day-to-day routine of managing his father's company, he couldn't forget the pained look in Rebecca's misty green eyes when he had accused her once again of knowing who drugged Sentimental Lady. Her violent reaction to his charge and her vicious attack against him, claiming that it was he rather than she who had been involved in the crime, was ludicrous. But it still planted a seed of doubt in his mind.

Brig tucked his hands into his back pockets and looked down the twenty-eight floors to the streets of Denver. Was it possible that Becca didn't know her horse had been drugged? Had he been wrong, blinded by evidence that was inaccurate? Even the racing board could level no blame for the crime. Ian O'Riley's reputation as a trainer might have been blemished for carelessness, but the man wasn't found guilty of the act of stimulating the horse artificially.

As he stared, unseeing, out the window he thought about Becca and her initial reaction to the race. She had been afraid and in a turmoil of anguished emotions. He could still hear her pained cries.

"It's all my fault," Becca had screamed, "all mine." Brig had dragged her away from the terror-stricken filly, holding the woman he loved in a binding grip that kept her arms immobilized. Becca had lost a shoe on the track. He hadn't bothered to pick it up.

Could he have misread her self-proclaimed guilt? Could her cries have erupted from the hysteria taking hold of her? Or was it an honest acceptance of blame, only to be denounced when she had finally calmed down and perceived the extent of the crime? He had always known that she would never intentionally hurt her horse; cruelty wasn't a part of Rebecca's nature. But he hadn't doubted that she was covering up for the culprit. Now he wasn't so sure.

Rubbing his temples as if he could erase the

painful memory, he sat down at the desk. There was a soft knock on the door and Mona entered with a steaming cup of coffee.

"Just what the doctor ordered," she chirped as she handed it to her boss.

"What did I do to deserve you?" Brig asked gratefully.

She winked slyly. "Inherited an oil fortune."

Brig took a sip from the steaming mug and smiled fondly at his father's secretary. He had inherited Mona along with the rest of the wealthy trappings of Chambers Oil. "You were right, Mona, I needed this." He held up his cup.

"Was there any doubt?" she quipped before her eyes became somber with genuine concern. She liked Brig Chambers, always had, and she could see that something was eating at him. "I'm right about the fact that you need a vacation, too," she observed.

"I'm not denying it."

"Then promise me that you'll take one."

Brig cracked a smile. "All right, you win. I promise, just as soon as I can get the estate attorneys and tax auditors off my back *and* we somehow settle the strike in Wyoming."

"Good." Mona returned Brig's grin. "I'll keep my fingers crossed," she stated as she walked out of the office.

Chapter 9

THE FIRST BREAK CAME THREE WEEKS LATER. THE season had changed from late summer into early autumn and Brig wondered if the promise of winter had cooled the angry tempers in Wyoming. Whatever the reason, the wildcat strike had been resolved, if only temporarily, and although anger still flared on both sides of the picket line, it seemed that most of the arguments and threats of violence had been settled.

As for his father's estate, it was finally in the lengthy legal process known as probate. Brig and the rest of the staff of Chambers Oil had given the tax attorneys every scrap of information they could find concerning Jason Chambers' vast financial holdings. Brig had reluctantly included the stack of personal notes and receipts he had found in his father's locked desk drawer. Brig had to suppress a wicked grin of satisfaction as he handed the private papers to the young tax attorney and the nervous man's face frowned in disbelief at the unrecorded transactions.

The only intentional omission was the note signed by Rebecca Peters. Brig had substituted it with one of his own in the amount of fifty thousand dollars. He considered the original note to Jason as his personal business. It had nothing to do with the old man's estate. This was one matter which only involved Rebecca and himself.

It had been difficult to concentrate on running the oil company the past few weeks. The mundane tasks had been impossible as his wayward thoughts continued to revolve around Rebecca Peters. He couldn't get her out of his mind, and cursed himself as a fool for his infatuation. In the last six years he had thought himself rid of her, that he had finally expunged her from his mind and soul. One weekend in the Rockies had changed all of that, and he couldn't forget a moment of the quiet solitude at the cabin near Devil's Creek. To add insult to injury, he began picking up horse-racing magazines, hoping to see her name in print and catch a glimpse of her. He was disappointed. He found no mention of a two-year-old filly named Gypsy Wind, nor of the entrancing woman who owned her.

When the call came through that the strike was settled, Brig didn't hesitate. He was certain that his man in Wyoming could handle the tense situation in the oil fields and he knew that Mona was able to run the company with or without him for a few days. He took the secretary's advice and made hurried arrangements to fly to San Francisco. After two vain attempts to reach Becca by phone, he gave up and found some satisfaction in the fact that he would arrive on her doorstep as unexpectedly as she had on his only a few short weeks ago.

Without taking the time to consider his motives,

he drove home, showered, changed, and threw a few clothes into a lightweight suitcase. After a quick glance around his apartment, he tossed his tweed sports jacket over his shoulder and called a cab to take him to the airport. He didn't want to waste any time. He was afraid his common sense might take over and he would cancel his plans. He kept in motion so as not to think about the consequences of his unannounced journey.

Ominous gray clouds darkened the sky over the buildings of Starlight Breeding Farm. It hadn't changed much since the last time Brig had visited. A quick glance at the buildings told him that only the most critically needed repairs had been completed in the last six years. All in all, the grounds were in sad shape. Brig had to grit his teeth together when he noticed the chipped paint on the two-storied farmhouse and the broken hinge on the gate. With a knowledgeable eye, he surveyed the stables. It seemed as if the whitewashed barns were in better shape than the living quarters; a tribute to Rebecca's sense of priority. A windmill supporting several broken blades groaned painfully against a sudden rush of air blowing down the valley. Brittle dry leaves danced in the wind before fluttering to rest against the weathered boards of a sagging wooden fence.

It was glaringly apparent that because of Sentimental Lady's short racing career and the fact that Rebecca hadn't owned another decent Thoroughbred, she wasn't able to make enough money to run the farm properly. That much was evidenced in the overgrown shrubbery, the rusted gutters, and the sagging roofline of the house. It would take a great deal of cash to get the buildings back into shape, money Rebecca was sadly lacking. It was no wonder she had been forced to go to Jason for a loan. No banker in his right mind would loan money to a

has-been horse breeder with only a run-down breeding farm as collateral. Guilt, like a razor-sharp
blade, twisted in his conscience.

Brig made his way up the uneven steps of the
porch and knocked soundly on the door. His face
was set in a grim mask of determination. No matter
what had happened between himself and Rebecca,
he couldn't allow her to live like this! No one
answered his knock. He pressed the doorbell and
wasn't surprised when he didn't hear the sound of a
chime inside the house. After one last loud knock,
he turned toward the stables. Several vehicles
parked near the barns indicated that someone had to
be on the property.

Rather than explore the stables, he decided to
walk through the familiar maze of paddocks surrounding the barns. The first paddock had once held
broodmares. Today it was empty. With the exception
of a few animals, the paddocks were vacant. The last
time Brig had walked through these gates, the
stables had been filled to capacity with exceptional
Thoroughbreds. But many of the horses were only
boarded at Becca's farm, and when the scandal over
Sentimental Lady had cast doubt on Becca's reputation, most of the animals were removed by conscien-
tious owners.

Becca had never recaptured her reputation as
being a responsible, successful horse breeder. A
muscle in the corner of Brig's jaw worked and his
eyes darkened as he wondered how much of
Rebecca's misfortune was his fault. Had he truly, as
she had once claimed, destroyed her reputation and
her business with his unfounded accusations? How
much of her burden was his?

Unconsciously he walked toward the most removed pasture, a corner paddock with the single
sequoia standing guard over it. That particular field,
with its lush grass and slightly raised view of the rest

of the farm, had been Sentimental Lady's home when she hadn't been on the racing circuit.

As Brig neared the paddock he stopped dead in his tracks, barely believing what he saw. The first drops of rain had begun to fall from the darkened sky, but it wasn't the cool water that chilled his blood or made him curse silently to himself. Color drained from his face as he watched the coffee-colored horse lift her black tail and run the length of the far fence. She stopped at the corner, impeded in her efforts to run from the stranger. She stood as far from Brig as was possible, flattened her ebony ears against her head, and snorted disdainfully.

"Sentimental Lady," Brig whispered to himself, leaning against the top rail of the fence and watching the frightened horse intently. "I'll be damned." There was no doubt in his mind that this horse was Gypsy Wind.

He ran an appreciative eye from her shoulders to her tail. She was a near-perfect Thoroughbred, almost a carbon copy of Sentimental Lady. For a fleeting moment Brig thought the two horses were identical, but slowly, as his expert gaze traveled over the horse, he noted the differences. The most obvious was the lack of white markings on Gypsy Wind. Sentimental Lady had been marked with an off-center star; this dark filly bore none. But that wasn't important, at least not to Brig. Coloring didn't make the horse.

The most impressive dissimilarity between the two animals was the slight variation in build and body structure. Both horses were barrel-chested, but Gypsy Wind seemed to be slightly shorter than her sister and her long legs appeared heavier. That didn't necessarily mean that Gypsy Wind's legs were stronger, but Brig hoped they were for the nervous filly's sake.

The shower increased and Brig wondered why Becca would allow her Thoroughbred to stand unattended in the early autumn rain. It wasn't like Becca. She had always been meticulous in her care of Thoroughbreds, a careful breeder cautious for her horses' health. That was what had puzzled Brig and it made it difficult for him to believe that Becca was responsible for harming Sentimental Lady . . . unless she was protecting someone.

Slowly moving along the fence so as not to startle the horse, Brig called to her. She eyed him nervously as he approached. With the same high spirit as her sister, Gypsy Wind tossed her intelligent head and stamped her right foreleg impatiently. *Just like Lady*. The resemblance between the two horses was eerie. Brig felt his stomach knot in apprehension. He couldn't help but remember the last time he had seen Sentimental Lady alive. It was a nightmare that still set his teeth on edge. He remembered it as clearly as if it had just happened.

Sentimental Lady had virtually been lifted into her stall by Ian O'Riley and his assistants. She tried to lie down, but was forced to stay on her feet by a team of four veterinarians. A horse resting on its side for too long might develop paralysis.

Her pain was deadened with ice while the chief veterinarian managed to sedate the frantic animal. She was led to the operating room where she nearly died, but was kept alive by artificial respiration and stimulants. Brig concentrated on the slow expansion and contraction of her chest. He and Rebecca had agreed with the veterinarians. They had no choice but to operate because of the contamination in the dirt-filled wound. Though the anxious horse needed no further trauma, there were no other options to save her.

Brig watched in silent horror as the veterinarian

removed the fragments of chipped bone and tried to repair the severely torn ligaments. After flushing the wound with antibiotics and saline solutions, drains were inserted in the leg. Finally an orthopedist fit a special shoe and cast onto Sentimental Lady's damaged foreleg. At that moment, the operation appeared to be successful.

The agonizing minutes ticked by as Sentimental Lady was eased out of anesthesia. When she regained control of her body she awoke in a frenzy. She struck out and knocked down the veterinarian who was with her. As her hoof kicked against the side of the stall, she broke off her specially constructed shoe. Within minutes, while Ian tried vainly to calm her, the flailing horse had torn her cast to shreds and her hemorrhaging and swelling had increased. Blood splattered against the sides of the stall.

"It's no use," Ian had told Brig. "She was too excited from the race and the pain—they'll never be able to control her again. It's her damned temperament that's killing her!" He turned back to the horse. "Slow down, Lady! Slow down." For his efforts he was rewarded with a kick in the leg.

"Get him out of there!" the veterinarian ordered, and Dean helped Ian from the stall. "I don't think there's anything we can do for her."

The options had run out. All four veterinarians agreed that Sentimental Lady couldn't withstand another operation. Even if she were stable, it would be difficult. In her current state of frenzied pain, it was impossible. An artificial limb was out of the question, as was a supportive sling: Sentimental Lady's high-strung temperament wouldn't allow her to convalesce.

Brig walked back to the waiting room where Rebecca sat with Martha. Her green eyes were shadowed in silent agony as she waited for the prognosis on her horse. Brig took one of her hands in his as he explained the options to Rebecca. Her small shoulders slumped and tears pooled in her eyes.

"But she's so beautiful," she murmured, letting the tears run down her cheeks to fall onto the shoulders of her blood-stained linen suit. "It can't be . . ."

"This is your decision," he said quietly. Martha put a steadying arm over Becca's shoulders.

"I want to see her." Becca rose and walked hesitantly to the other room, where she could observe Lady. One look at the terrified horse and the splintered cast confirmed Brig's tragic opinion. "I can't let her suffer anymore," Becca whispered, closing her eyes against the terrible scene. She lowered her head and in a small voice that was barely audible repeated, "It's all my fault . . ."

Sentimental Lady's death had been the beginning of the end for Rebecca and Brig. He couldn't forget her claims that she had been responsible for the catastrophe, and hadn't fully understood what she meant until the postmortem examination had revealed that there were traces of Dexamethasone in Sentimental Lady's body. Dexamethasone was a steroid which hadn't been used in the surgery. Someone had intentionally drugged the horse and perhaps contributed to her death.

Because of Rebecca's remorse and the guilt she claimed, Brig assumed that she knew of the culprit. The thought that a woman with whom he had shared so much love could betray her horse so cruelly had ripped him apart. He tried to deny her part in the tragedy, but couldn't ignore her own admission of guilt.

The next day, when he read the newspaper reports

of the event, the quote that wouldn't leave him was that of his father as Winsome had galloped home to a hollow victory. "We threw a fast pace at the bitch and she just broke down," Jason Chambers had claimed in the aftermath and shock of the accident. The cold-blooded statement cut Brig to the bone.

That had been six years ago, and with the passage of time, Brig had sworn never to become involved with Rebecca Peters again. And yet, here he was, in the pouring rain, attempting to capture a horse whose similarities to Sentimental Lady made him shudder. He was more of a fool than he would like to admit.

"Come here, Gypsy," he summoned, extending his hand to touch the horse's wet muzzle. "Let me take you inside."

Gypsy Wind stepped backward and shook her head menacingly.

"Come on, girl. Don't you have enough sense to come in out of the rain?" He clucked gently at the nervous filly.

"*Hey! What's going on here?*" an angry voice called over the rising wind. "*You leave that horse alone!*"

Gypsy Wind shied from the noise and Brig whirled around to face Rebecca's brother striding meaningfully toward him. When Brig's cold gray eyes clashed with Dean's watery blue gaze, a moment's hesitation held them apart. A shadow of fear darkened Dean's eyes but quickly disappeared and was replaced with false bravado.

"You're just about the last person I expected to see," Dean announced as he climbed over the fence and reached for Gypsy Wind's halter. She rolled her eyes and paced backward, always just a few feet out of Dean's reach.

"This trip was a spur of the moment decision,"

Brig responded. Dean managed to catch the horse and snapped on the lead rein, giving it a vicious tug.

"Plan on staying long?" Dean asked. He led the filly into the barn and instructed a groom to take care of her.

"I haven't decided yet."

Dean shrugged as if it made no difference to him one way or the other, but his eyes remained cold. "Was Becca expecting you?" he inquired cautiously.

"No."

"Well, you may as well come up to the house and dry off. She and Ian are in town. They should be home any time."

"They left you in charge?" Brig asked pointedly.

Dean's jaw hardened and he slid a furtive glance in Brig's direction. The man had always made him uneasy. Brig Chambers was in a different league than was Dean Peters. Whereas Dean was only comfortable in faded jeans, Chambers was a man who looked at ease in jeans or a tuxedo. Even now, though he was drenched from the sudden downpour, Brig looked as if he owned the world in his tan corduroy pants, dark blue sweater, and tweed sports coat. Easy for him, Dean thought to himself, he did own the world . . . practically. Chambers Oil was worth a fortune! Dean didn't bother to hide the sarcasm in his voice. "Every once in a while, when Ian and Becca have to do something together, they let me run the place."

"I see," Brig stated as if he didn't and added silently to himself, *and you pay them back by leaving Rebecca's prized Thoroughbred unattended in the rain.*

Dean wasn't easily fooled. He could see that Brig was unhappy; it was evidenced in the dark shade of his unfriendly eyes. Dean also realized that it was a bad break having Brig find Gypsy Wind in the rain, but it couldn't have been helped. The forecast had been for sunshine and Dean had gotten wrapped up in the 49ers game on television. He had a lot of money riding on the outcome of the game. The last thing he needed was Brig Chambers nosing around here. Dean couldn't trust Chambers as far as he could throw him and Becca always went a little crazy whenever she was with Brig. *Why the hell had Brig come to the ranch now?* Dean's throat went dry as he considered the note. Maybe Chambers had changed his mind. Maybe he wanted his loan repaid on the spot! How in the world would Becca put her hands on fifty grand?

Dean stopped at the gate near the front of the farmhouse. "You know your way around, let yourself in, make yourself comfortable." He stood on one side of the broken gate, Brig was on the other. "The 49ers are playing on channel seven."

Brig's smile was polite, but it made Dean uncomfortable. There was a barely concealed trace of contempt in Brig's eyes. "I think I'll dry off and then check on the horse."

Dean raised his reddish brows. "Suit yourself," he said while pulling his jacket more tightly around him. "But take my word for it, the Gypsy will be fine. Garth knows how to handle her." With his final remark, Dean turned toward the stables and headed back to the warm office over the tack room where the final quarter of the 49ers game and a welcome can of beer waited for him.

Brig walked into the farmhouse and smiled at the familiar sight. Some of the furniture had been replaced, other pieces rearranged, but for the most part, the interior seemed the same as it was six years ago. He didn't bother with the lights, though the storm outside shadowed the rooms ominously. Mounting the worn steps slowly, he let his fingers slide along the polished surface of the railing. There was no hesitation in his stride when he reached the second floor; he moved directly toward Rebecca's room. At the open door he paused.

A torrent of long-denied memories flooded his senses. He remembered vivid images of a distant past; the smell of violets faintly scenting the air, a blue silk dress slipping noiselessly to the floor, the moonlight reflecting silver light in Rebecca's soft green eyes, and the powerful feeling of harmony he had found when he had taken her body with his. The reflection had an overpowering effect on him. He braced his shoulder against the doorjamb and plunged his fists deep into his pockets while he stared vacantly into the room. He had been a fool to let Rebecca slip away from him, a damned fool too blinded with self-righteousness to see the truth.

After letting the bittersweet memories take their toll on him, he went into the bathroom and towel-dried his hair. He tossed on his jacket and ran back to the barns, his head bent against the wind. Garth had indeed seen to the horse. Once Brig was satisfied that Gypsy Wind was comfortable, he headed back to the house.

Headlights winding up the long drive warned him that Rebecca was returning. An ancient pickup with a trailer in tow ground to a stop against the wet gravel of the parking lot and the driver killed the rumbling engine.

Rebecca emerged from the cab of the truck, wearing a smile and a radiant gleam in her eye when she recognized Brig huddling against the wind. She couldn't hide the happiness she felt just at the sight of him.

"What are you doing in this part of the country?"

she asked, linking her arm through his and leading him toward the house.

Her good mood was infectious. "Looking for you."

She winked at him and wiped a raindrop off her nose. "You always know exactly what to say to me, don't you?"

"Are you telling me that I haven't lost my touch?"

"If you had, it would make my whole life a lot easier."

"Is that right?" He took her hand in his and stuffed it into the warmth of his jacket pocket.

She hesitated just a moment as they climbed the porch stairs. "I've thought about the last time I saw you . . ."

He lifted his dark brows. "That makes two of us."

She was suddenly sober. "I didn't intend to argue with you. The last thing I wanted to do was fight about Gypsy Wind."

"I know."

A sad smile curved her lips as they walked through the door together. "It seems that every time we're together, we end up arguing."

They stepped into the kitchen. "It hasn't always been that way," he reminded her.

She shook her blond hair. It was loose and brushed against her shoulders. "You're wrong . . . even in the beginning we had fights."

"Disagreements," he insisted.

"Okay, disagreements," she responded. Without asking his preference, she set a cup of black coffee on the table and poured one for herself. "Anyway, the point is, I made a vow to myself on the plane back from Denver."

"Sounds serious."

"It was. I told myself that I was going to get over you."

He sat back in the chair, straddling the cane

backing before taking a sip of the coffee. "Well . . . did you?"

She made a disgusted sound in the back of her throat and shook her head. How could he sit there so calmly when she felt as if her insides were being shredded? "Not yet."

"But you intend to?"

"I thought I did . . . right now, I honestly don't know." She stared into the dark coffee in her cup as if she were searching for just the right words to make him understand her feelings. She lifted her eyes to meet his. "But I think it would make things simpler if you and I remained business partners—nothing more."

Brig frowned. "And you're sure that's what you want?"

"I'm not sure of anything right now," she admitted with a sigh.

"Except for Gypsy Wind."

Becca's somber expression lightened. "Have you seen her?"

"When I first got here."

"What do you think?" Becca's breath caught in her throat. How long had she waited for Brig to see the horse?

"She's a beautiful filly," he replied, keeping his tone noncommittal. Looks were one thing; racing temperament and speed were entirely different matters.

"Where did you see her?"

"In Sentimental Lady's paddock."

"This afternoon?" Rebecca seemed surprised. Brig nodded. "I didn't know she was going to be let out," she thought aloud. "Ian didn't mention it to me . . ."

"Where is O'Riley? I thought he was with you."

"I dropped him off at his place—he lives a couple of miles down the road." She answered him correctly, but her mind was back on Gypsy Wind. "Did you talk to Dean?"

"That's how I knew you were with O'Riley."

"So Dean was with Gypsy Wind?"

"He took her inside and had . . . Garth, is that his name?" Becca nodded. "Garth took care of her. I double-checked her a few minutes ago. She looks fine."

"Garth is good with the horses," Becca said, still lost in thought. What was Dean thinking, leaving the Gypsy outside in the windstorm? It was difficult to understand Dean at times.

"What about your brother?" Brig asked.

A startled expression clouded Becca's sculptured features. "Dean?" She shrugged her slim shoulders. "Dean doesn't seem to have much interest in the Thoroughbreds anymore . . ." her voice trailed off as she thought about her brother.

"Why not?"

Becca smiled wistfully. "Who knows? Other interests, I suppose."

"Such as?"

Suddenly defensive, Becca set her mug on the table and gave Brig a look that told him it was really none of his business. "I don't know," she admitted. "People change."

"Do they?" he asked, his voice somewhat husky as he stared at her. He felt the urge to trace the pouty contour of her lips with his finger.

"Of course they do," she replied coldly. "Didn't we?"

"That was different."

"Why?"

"Because of the horse . . ."

"Dean was involved with Sentimental Lady, probably just as close to her as either one of us. It was hard on him."

"I didn't say it wasn't."

She ignored his remark. Angry fire crackled in her eyes. "It might have been more difficult for him than for either of us," she pointed out emphatically.

"I doubt that."

"Of course you do! That's because you weren't here, were you? You were gone, afraid to be associated with a woman whom you thought intentionally harmed her horse. Dean was the one who pulled me up by my bootstraps, Brig. He was the one who made me realize that there was more to life than one horse and one man. All the while you were afraid of ruining *your* reputation, my brother helped me repair mine!"

"I never gave a damn about my reputation!" he shot back angrily. "You know that," he added in a gentler tone.

"I wish I did," she whispered. "When I was younger, I was more confident . . . sure of myself . . . sure of you." A puzzled expression marred the clarity of her beguiling features. "And I was wrong. Now that I'm older, I'm more cautious, I guess. I realize that I can't change the world."

"Unless Gypsy Wind proves herself?"

"Not even then." She smiled sadly. "Don't misunderstand me—Gypsy Wind is important. But I feel that maybe what she represents isn't the most important thing in my life, and what might have been of greater value is gone."

His chair scraped against the floorboards. He stood behind her and let his palms rest on her shoulders as she sat in the chair. "What are you trying to say?"

"That I'm afraid it might be too late for us," she whispered.

His fingers pressed against the soft fabric of her sweater, gently caressing the skin near her collarbones. He felt cold and empty inside. Rebecca's words had vocalized his own fears. "So you think that destiny continues to pull us apart?"

She slowly swept her head from side to side. The fine golden strands of her hair brushed against his lower abdomen, adding fuel to the fires of the desire rising within him. The clean scent of her hair filled his nostrils, and he had difficulty concentrating on her words.

"I don't think destiny or fate has anything to do with it," she answered pensively. "I think it's you and me—constantly at war with each other. It's as if we won't allow ourselves the chance to be together. Our egos keep getting in the way—mine as well as yours."

The line of his jaw hardened. "Are you trying to say that you want me to leave?"

She sighed softly to herself and closed her eyes. "If only it were that simple. It's not." She shut her eyes more tightly so that deep lines furrowed her brow as she concentrated. "I'm glad you're here," she admitted in a hoarse whisper. "There's a very feminine part of me that needs to know you care."

"I always have . . ."

"Have you?" She reached up and covered his hand with her long fingers. "You have a funny way of showing it sometimes."

"We've both made mistakes," he admitted. The warmth from her fingers flowed into his. He lowered his head and kissed her gently on the crook of her neck. The smell of her hair still damp from a sprinkling of raindrops filled his nostrils. It was a clean, earthy scent that brought back memories of their early autumn tryst in the Rocky Mountains.

"And we're going to make more mistakes . . . tonight?" she asked, conscious only of the moist warmth of his lips and the dewy trail they left on her skin.

"Loving you has never been easy."

"Because you can't let yourself, Brig." With all the strength she could muster, she pulled away from his caress and stood on the opposite side of the chair, as if the small piece of furniture could stop his advances and her yearnings. "Love is impossible without trust. And you can't, not to this day, find it in your heart to trust me—"

"That's not true," he ground out, hearing the false sound of his words as they rang hollowly over the noise of the storm.

"Don't bother to lie to me . . . or to yourself! We're past all that, Brig, and I'm too damned old to be playing games."

There was anger in Brig's dark eyes, but also just a hint of amusement, as if he were laughing at himself. His jaw was tense, but the trace of a self-mocking smile lingered on his lips. "You are incredible, you know. And so damned beautiful . . ." he reached his hand toward her cheek, but she turned her head and clutched his fingers in her small fist. Her face was set in lines of earnest determination.

"I don't want to be *incredible*, Brig! And God knows there must be a thousand beautiful women who would die for a chance to hear you say just that to them—"

"But not you?"

Her green eyes flashed in defiance at the suspicious arch of his dark male brows. "I like compliments as well as the next woman. I'd be a fool if I tried to deny it. But what I want from you"—her fingers tightened around his as if to emphasize the depth of her feelings—"what I want from you is trust! I want you to be able to look me in the eyes and see a woman who loves you, who has always loved you—"

"And who put her career before my proposal of marriage."

The words stung, but she took them in stride. "I needed time."

"That's a lame excuse."

"Maybe you're right," she said.

"Would you do anything differently if you could?" he asked through clenched teeth.

"I don't know . . ."

"Would you?" he demanded, his face tense with disbelief.

"Yes, oh yes!"

His muscles relaxed slightly but the doubt didn't leave his face. "How would you change things, Becca?"

The question stood between them like an invisible wall, a wall that had been built with the passage of six long years. Rebecca's voice was barely audible over the sounds of the storm. "I don't think that there would have been many things I would do differently," she admitted.

"What about me?"

She fought against the tears forming in her eyes and smiled. "I've never for a minute regretted that I met you or that . . . I thought I was in love with you." She cleared her throat as she tried to remain calm. "But you have to know, Brig, that if I could, I would turn back the hands of time and somehow find a way to save Sentimental Lady."

The honesty in her eyes twisted his heart. "I know that, Rebecca. I've always known that you wouldn't intentionally hurt anything."

"But—"

"I just thought that you were covering up for someone whom you cared about very much."

"I had no idea who—"

He stepped toward her and folded her into his arms. "I know that now, and I'm sorry that I didn't realize it before this." As his arms tightened around her he realized that she was trembling. His lips moved softly against her hair. "It's all right now," he murmured, hoping to reassure her.

Becca tried to concentrate on the warmth of Brig's arms. She fought against the doubts crowding in her mind, but she couldn't forget his words. "I thought you were covering up for someone whom you cared for . . ." She had been, but it was because she had thought Brig was somehow involved. If not Brig, then who? "Someone you cared for . . ."

She closed her eyes and let her weight fall against Brig, trying to ignore the voice in her mind that continued to remind her that Dean, her own brother, had been acting very suspiciously the past few weeks. Dean had access to Sentimental Lady.

But *why*? What would Dean have had to gain by having the horse disqualified? *Or had he expected her to lose?*

"Becca—is something wrong?"

The familiar sound of Brig's voice brought Becca back to the present. She could feel his heartbeat pounding solidly against her chest. His breath fanned her hair. "Nothing," she lied. She was anxious to escape from her fears and wanted nothing more than the security of Brig's strong arms to support her.

"You're sure?" He was doubtful, and pulled his head away from hers so that he could look into her eyes.

"Oh, Brig—just for once, let's not let the past come between us."

"I've been waiting for an invitation like that all afternoon," he replied with a crooked smile.

With the quickness of a cat, he scooped her off the floor and cradled her gently against him before turning toward the stairs.

"You can argue with me all night long, Ms.

Peters," he stated, as he strode slowly up the staircase. "But you *are* incredible, and beautiful, and enchanting, and . . ."

"And I wouldn't dare argue with you," she admitted with a smile. "I love every minute of this."

"Then let me show you exactly how I feel about you."

"I can't wait . . ."

Chapter 10

BRIG WAS SILENT AS HE CARRIED BECCA INTO THE bedroom. She was hesitant to say anything for fear it might break the gentle peace that had settled quietly between them. Instead she listened to the movement of the restless wind as it passed through the brittle branches of the oak trees near the house. Above the wind she could hear the reassuring sound of Brig's steady heartbeat.

Still carrying her lithely, he crossed the room and set her on her feet near the edge of the bed. His eyes never left hers as he slowly slid the top button of her blouse through the buttonhole. The collar opened. Brig gently touched the hollow of her throat with his index finger. Becca shivered at his touch while he stroked the delicate bone structure. She felt her pulse jump.

Knowing the depth of her response, he concentrated on the next button, slowly parting the blouse to expose the skin below her throat, and when the blouse finally opened, he gently pushed it off her shoulders. Her skin quivered as his finger slowly made a path from her neck to the clasp of her bra. Without moving his eyes from her face he opened the bra and slid it off her shoulders, allowing her breasts to become unbound.

Becca didn't move. She heard her shallow breathing and felt the rapid beat of her heart as she let his hands work their magic on her skin. She expected him to caress a breast; she yearned for him to take one of the aching nipples in his hands and softly massage the bittersweet agony. He didn't. She felt his hands move between her breasts to flatten against her abdomen. The tips of his fingers slid invitingly below the waistband of her jeans. Involuntarily, she sucked in her breath in order to make it easier for him to come to her.

The button was released. The zipper lowered. Her jeans were pushed over her hips to fall at her feet. She was standing nearly naked in the stormy night, with only the fragil barrier of her panties keeping her from being nude. A breeze from the partially opened window lifted her golden hair from her face and contributed to the hardening of her nipples. But it wasn't the wind that made her warm inside, nor was it the impatience of the brewing storm that electrified her nerve endings. It was the passion in the gray eyes of the man undressing her that persuaded her blood to run in heated rivulets through her body.

"Undress me," he whispered, refusing to give in to the urgent longings of his body. He felt the thrill of desire rising in him, but he fought against it, preferring to stretch the torment of unfulfilled passion to the limit.

She obeyed his command by silently moving her hands under his sweater and pushing it over his head. He had to reaffirm his resolve as he looked at her, standing before him with her arms stretched overhead as the sweater passed over his hands. Her breasts fell forward, their dark tips brushing against his abdomen. He gritted his teeth against the over-powering urge to kick off his jeans and take her in a frantic union of flesh that would be as savage as it was delicious. Rather than give in to his male urge to conquer and dominate, he waited. Every muscle tensed with his restraint, but the pain was worth the prize. He had to swallow when her fingers touched him lightly as they worked with the belt buckle and finally dropped his pants to the floor. He felt the trickle of sweat begin to run down his spine, though the room was cold. Her eyes had clouded with the same passion controlling his body.

She groaned as he kneeled and softly kissed her abdomen. Her weight fell against him and she trembled at his touch when he slipped the lacy underwear down her thighs and over her calves. His fingers ran up the inside of her leg as he raised himself to his full height and gathered her into his arms before pressing against her and forcing her onto the bed with the weight of his body.

"I want to make love to you," he whispered into her hair. "I want to make love to you and never stop."

"Then do, Brig, please make love to me." Her eyes reached for his in the darkness, promising vows she couldn't possibly keep.

He studied her face, lost in the complex beauty of a woman who was intelligent and kind, strong yet vulnerable, wise though young. How could he have ever doubted her? Why had he been such a fool as to cast away six years they could have shared together?

He lowered his head and his lips pressed against hers with all of the pain and torment warring within him. He took her face in his hands as if he had to be sure that she wouldn't disappear. Her lips parted

willingly and his tongue found the delicious pleas-
ures of her moist mouth. He groaned in surrender
when her fingers dug into the solid muscles of his
back.

"These last few weeks have been torturous," he
confided when he finally lifted his head. "I tried to
stay away—Lord knows, I tried, but I couldn't.
You're just too damned mystifying and I can't seem
to get enough of you."

"I hope you never can," she admitted, but before
she could say anything else, his fingers caressed her
breast, cupping it in his palm, feeling the soft,
malleable weight before taking it gently in his
mouth. She sighed with the pleasure he evoked as he
stroked and suckled the nipple with his tongue and
lips. The pressure of his mouth made her arch
against him, hoping to fill the space between his lips
with her breast. She was satisfied in the knowledge
that the pleasure she was receiving was given back in
kind.

She wound her fingers in his hair, cradling his face
against her as if giving comfort. His hands slid lower
as did his lips. Her blood pounded in her eardrums
as his tongue leisurely rimmed her navel while his
hands parted her legs and massaged her buttocks.
"You're beautiful," he whispered against her silky
skin. "I want you . . ."

"Then love me, Brig," she pleaded, "love me."
Her needs were more than physical. Even though
her body longed for all of him, it was her heart and
her mind that had to have him. Her soul was crying
for him to be one with her and share a lifetime
together.

He moved over her, and she could feel each of his
strong hard muscles against her own. Her breasts
flattened with the weight of him, the coiling desire
deep within her beginning to unwind in expectation.

"I want you, Brig. I want you more than I ever have," she admitted roughly.

He shifted, parting her legs with his own. Her feet curled against his calves and rubbed against the hair .on his legs as he became one with her. His lips claimed hers as their bodies joined and she felt the pulse of his blood when he started his unhurried movements of union. Her body responded, pushing against his in the heated tide of sexual fulfillment. Their tongues danced and joined until he pulled his head away from hers and stared into the depths of her eyes as if he were looking for her soul.

The coupling became stronger, their bodies surging together as one. She tasted the salt of his sweat on her tongue and heard the rapid beating of his heart. She groaned in contentment as the tempo increased. His eyes remained open, watching her reaction, and when he felt her quaking shudder of release and saw the glimmer of satisfaction in her velvet green eyes, he let go of the bonds he had placed upon himself and let his passion consume him in one violent burst of liquid fire. He groaned as he sagged against her, letting his weight press her into the mattress.

"Oh, God, Rebecca," he murmured. "I *do* love you." His fingers twined in her hair and his breathing slowed. "You are incredible—whether you believe it or not."

Several minutes later, after his breathing had slowed, he rolled to her side. His arms held her tightly against him and she felt secure and warm, pressed into the hard muscles of his chest.

"Why is it that we never fight in bed?" she finally asked.

"Because we have more important things to do," he teased.

"Be serious."

"I am. Why would we fight in bed? What would be the point?" He smiled and kissed the top of her head, smelling the perfume in her tousled curls.

"What's the point when we're *not* in bed?"

He lifted his shoulders. "I don't know. Boredom?" He looked down at her and she recognized a familiar devilish twinkle lurking in his eyes.

"I doubt that . . ."

"So do I, Ms. Peters . . . so do I." He kissed her lightly on the lips before tracing their pouty curve with the tip of his finger. "Speaking of boredom," he began in a low drawl, "I've got several theories on how to avoid it."

"Do you?" She arched an elegant eyebrow as if she disbelieved him.

A wicked smile allowed just the flash of even white teeth against his dark skin. "Several," he assured her while his eyes moved lazily down the length of her naked body. He looked as if he were studying it for flaws. Satisfied that there were none, he met her gaze squarely. "Would you like a demonstration?"

"That depends."

"On what?"

Provocatively she rimmed her lips with her tongue. "On whom you're going to test your theories."

His finger slid down the curve of her jaw. "You'll do—if you're interested."

"What do you think?" She laughed, her green eyes dancing mischievously.

He grabbed her wrists playfully and pinned them to her sides. His face was only inches from hers in the gathering darkness. "I think, Rebecca, that you're a tease, an *incredible,* gorgeous, and wanton *tease. And* I think I know just how to handle you." Dangerous fires of renewed passion flared in his cool gray eyes.

"Idle threats," she mocked.

"We'll see about that, Becca. Before tonight is over, I'll have you begging for more," he growled theatrically.

"Save me," she taunted.

"You don't know when to give up, do you?"

"Sometimes I wish I did," she sighed, the merriment ebbing from her gaze.

"Don't ever give up, Rebecca," he chided. "It's one of the most wonderful things about you—that spirit of yours. It's as unbeaten and proud as the horses you race."

"Are you serious?"

"About you? Yes!" He released her wrists and kissed her forehead. "I was a fool to ever let you get away from me." He lowered his head and kissed the slope of her shoulder. "It won't happen again."

She felt her skin quiver with his low words of possession. When his lips claimed hers, she was ready and hungrily accepted everything he offered her. She returned his passion with renewed fervor, giving herself body and soul.

His hands moved over her skin, gently kneading her muscles and reigniting the fires of desire deep within her. His lips roved restlessly down her neck, across her shoulder, to stop in the hollow between her breasts. He pushed the soft flesh against his cheeks before he took one nipple and then the other between his lips.

Rebecca sighed and thought she would die in the ecstasy of his embrace. When he shifted his weight and parted her willing legs with his knee, she molded her body against his in an effort to get closer to him . . . become one with him. "That's it, Becca, let go," he encouraged by whispering against the shell of her ear. "Just love me, sweet lady," he coaxed as he entered her and began his gentle rhythmic movements.

His hands began to move in slow, sensual circles over her breasts while he slowly fanned the fires of her love until they were white hot and she groaned in frustration. When he knew that she was ready, he increased his movements against her. They found each other at the same moment, each inspiring the other to the brink of ecstasy in an explosive rush of energy that held them together until at last they were satisfied and the animal growls that came from Brig's lips were moans of contentment.

It was much later that Becca awoke from a drowsy sleep and tried to slip out of the bed unnoticed by Brig.

"Where do you think you're going?" he asked groggily, holding her against him and frustrating her attempts at escape.

"I want to check on Gypsy Wind."

"I told you she was fine." Brig ran his hand over his eyes in an effort to awaken.

"I know, I know. But that was several hours ago and the storm's gotten worse. She may be frightened."

"Is that what you're worried about?" Brig asked, propping himself on one elbow. "Or are you afraid that your brother might have let her out again?"

Becca ignored the pointed remark about Dean. It only served to reinforce her fears. "I'm worried about the horse, Brig. She's high-spirited."

"To the point that a storm would spook her?"

Becca extracted herself reluctantly from Brig's embrace. "I'm not sure . . . I just want to check." She slipped off the bed and began dressing in the dark.

Brig snapped on the bedside lamp and smiled lazily as he watched her struggle into her clothes. "I'll come with you."

"You don't have to."

"Sure I do." He straightened from the bed and

began pulling on his pants. "That's what I came here for—to look at your wonder horse."

A stab of pain pierced Becca's heart, but she ignored it. What did she expect—words of love at every turn in the conversation? For someone who had vowed to keep Brig Chambers out of her heart, she was certainly thinking like a woman in love.

Gypsy Wind stood in the far corner of her stall, eyeing Brig suspiciously and ignoring Becca's cajoling efforts to get the filly to come forward. Not even the enticement of an apple would lure the high-spirited horse. Instead she paced nervously between one side of the stall and the other, never getting close enough for Becca to touch her.

"She's got a mind of her own," Brig stated while he watched the anxious filly.

Becca couldn't disagree. "I've noticed," she commented dryly.

"What does O'Riley have to say about her?"

"He worries a lot," Becca admitted almost to herself, as she clucked softly to the horse. "And he tries not to let on, but I'm sure he has some reservations about her."

"Because of her similarities to Sentimental Lady?"

Becca nodded. "Her temperament."

"A legitimate complaint, I'd venture."

Trying not to sound defensive, Becca replied, "Sentimental Lady's spirit wasn't all bad, Brig. She was bound to be a good horse, but her spirit made her great."

"And killed her." The words hung in the air.

"Sentimental Lady's spirit didn't kill her, Brig . . . *someone* did! If she hadn't been injected, she might not have misstepped, or she might not have continued to run . . . or she might have been able to come out of the anesthesia—"

"But she didn't!" His face had hardened as he

judged Gypsy Wind on the merits of her sister. "And you and I . . . we let our pride get in our way. We should have figured this out long ago. We should never have let it come between us for this long."

"I don't know what we could have done to save Sentimental Lady."

"Maybe we couldn't, but the least we could have done was trusted one another enough to find the culprit."

"But—"

He turned to face her and his eyes glittered like forged steel. "I'm not blaming you—I was as much at fault as anyone. I assumed that you had something to do with it because you kept telling me that it was all your fault. I shouldn't have listened to you, should have followed my instincts instead. God, Becca, I knew you couldn't have done it, but I thought that you knew who did! That was what really got to me—that you'd protect some bum who killed your horse."

"I didn't."

"I know that now." Brig's eyebrows had pulled together as he concentrated. "We have to figure this thing out, Becca, if you really plan to race Gypsy Wind. Otherwise the same thing could happen all over again."

"I don't think anyone would want to hurt the Gypsy—"

"Just like you didn't think anyone would want to hurt Sentimental Lady," he charged.

"That was different—"

"How?"

"Different horses, different circumstances . . . I don't know."

"That's just the point; until we understand the motive behind the drugging of Sentimental Lady, we'll never be certain that Gypsy Wind is safe. And we'll never be able to comprehend the motive until we find out who was behind it."

"But that might be impossible."

"Not really. Ian O'Riley should know exactly who had access to the horse and who didn't." Brig pulled pensively on his lower lip, as if he were attempting to visualize exactly what had happened to Sentimental Lady, as if by thinking deeply enough, he could reconstruct the events leading up to the tragedy.

Becca touched his arm lightly. "Brig, be reasonable—you're talking about six years ago! You can't expect Ian to remember every person who had access to the horse." Becca was incredulous and her wide green eyes reflected her feelings.

"I think you're underestimating your trainer. I'm sure he gave the California Horse Racing Board the name of every person near the horse in those last few hours before the race. The board surely has the records . . ."

"But that list probably includes the names of grooms who have left us. I have no idea how to reach them. And what about security guards at the track, other trainers . . . what could you possibly expect to find that the board overlooked?"

Brig's smile was grim, his jawline determined. "I doubt that the board overlooked anything that was reported. What I'm looking for was probably never brought to their attention."

Becca shook her head at the folly of his idea. "What can you possibly hope to find?"

"I don't know—maybe nothing. But there's a slim chance that we can dig up some shred of evidence that might shed some light on Lady's death."

"It's been too long."

Brig had started toward the door, but stopped dead in his tracks. "Don't you *want* to find out what happened?"

"Of course, but I think it's too late. All we would do is stir up the entire mess all over again. The only thing we would accomplish would be getting the press all riled up. Sentimental Lady's picture, along with yours and mine, would be thrown in front of the public again."

"That's going to happen anyway. Once the press gets wind of the fact that you've bred a sister to Sentimental Lady, they're going to be breathing down your neck so fast it will make your head swim. My investigation isn't going to change the attitude of the media."

Becca had reached up to switch off the lights, but hesitated when she felt Brig's hand on her shoulder. She turned to face him, but couldn't hide the worry in her eyes. "What is it?" he asked gently. "What makes you afraid?"

"I'm not afraid—"

"But something isn't right, Becca." His face was softened by concern for her.

"What do you mean?"

"I mean that there are a few things that just don't add up."

She drew in a deep breath and tried to mask the ever increasing dread. "Such as?"

"Such as the fact that, for the most part, you held your silence after the tragedy."

"I told you why. I thought you were involved."

"*Thought*. Past tense. You don't anymore?"

She shook her head and snapped off the lights, hoping that Brig wouldn't notice that her hands were unsteady. "No."

Becca pushed the door open with her shoulder and walked outside. She hoped that Brig would change the subject, because of the unnamed fear growing stronger within her. The wind had quieted to occasional chilly gusts that seemed to rip through Becca's light jacket and pierce her heart.

"What made you change your mind?" Brig asked after he had secured the door to the barn.

"Pardon me?"

"About my guilt—what changed your mind?"

Becca shrugged and hoped to appear indifferent. "I guess I knew it all along. It was just an easy excuse to justify your . . . change in attitude . . ."

He put his arm around her shoulder and forced her to face him. The darkness was broken only by the security lights surrounding the barns. "Rebecca, I'm sorry—God, I'm sorry. I made a horribly unjust decision about you and I've regretted it ever since. It was my mistake." He crushed her against his chest and Becca felt the burn of tears behind her eyes.

"It's all over now," she whispered, clinging to him and aware of soft drops of rain on her cheeks and hair. It felt so right, standing in the darkness, unconscious of the chill in the air, holding Brig.

"It will never be 'all over,'" he said. "But maybe we can heal the wounds by finding out what happened to Lady."

She stiffened. "I think that's impossible . . ."

"Nothing is. I shouldn't have to tell you that. You found a way to breed Gypsy Wind when all the cards were stacked against you."

"That was only possible because of your father."

"I know, and that's another one of the pieces of the puzzle that doesn't seem to fit."

"What do you mean?"

"I told you that things didn't add up and I mentioned your silence."

"Yes?"

"Well, another thing that won't seem to quit nagging me is the fact that you didn't race Gypsy Wind as a two-year-old."

"Ian and I thought it best, because of her legs—I told you all that, and what in the world does it have to do with your father?"

"Dad is just one other thing that doesn't make any sense."

"What do you mean?"

"I can understand him loaning you some money—but not that much. When my father gave or loaned something to a pretty young woman, he usually expected something in return."

"He did—repayment of the loan with interest."

Brig shook his head as if trying to dislodge a wayward thought. "Not good enough, Rebecca. Jason must have wanted something else."

"I think you're grasping at straws," Becca whispered, but the feeling of dread that had been with her for the past few days increased.

"Do you remember what Jason said after the race between Winsome and Sentimental Lady?"

"I know. But he was upset, we all were."

Brig raked his fingers through his hair and noticed it was wet from the rain. He ignored the cool water running under his collar. He watched Becca's reaction when he repeated his father's damning words: "We threw a fast pace at the bitch and she just broke down."

Becca shuddered. "He didn't know what he was saying—"

"A handy excuse . . ."

Placing her palm to her forehead, Becca tried to close out the painful memories taking hold of her. "Don't, Brig . . . let's not dredge it all up again. What's the point?"

He took her by the shoulders and shook her until she met his eyes. "You're going to have to face everything if you really intend to race Gypsy Wind, Rebecca. You won't be able to hide here at Starlight Breeding Farm and expect the reporters to respect your privacy. All the old wounds are going to be reopened and examined with a microscope."

"You still think I had something to do with it," she accused, near hysteria. The rain, Brig's dark eyes, the haunting memories all began to unnerve her.

"No, dear one, no. But I have to know why you would go to my father for money after he said what he did."

"I had no choice. There was no other way. Dean suggested your father and I picked up on it . . ."

"Your brother?"

Becca hastened to explain. She had to make Brig understand. "Originally it was Dean's idea, but when I really decided to go through with it and approach Jason, Dean tried to talk me out of it. He told me I was crazy to consider the idea, that he had only been joking when he mentioned your father as a possible source of money."

"And yet he was the first to consider Jason. Interesting. I didn't think he knew Dad."

"He didn't."

"You're sure of that?" Brig's eyes narrowed as he witnessed Rebecca's face drain of its natural color.

"I . . . I can't be sure, but I think that if Dean had ever met your father, Jason's name would have come up in conversation at some point in time . . . and I don't remember that it did."

"Did they ever have the opportunity to meet?"

"Who knows?" Rebecca replied, trying to concentrate on the elusive past. "I suppose it was possible when Sentimental Lady was racing . . . there were a lot of parties. You remember."

"Then there was a chance that Dean met my father?"

"They could have . . . but so what?"

In the distant mountains a loud clap of thunder disturbed the silence. Brig chose to ignore her question. "We'd better get inside," he suggested, letting his eyes rove restlessly over her face. He kissed her cheek, catching a drop of rain with his tongue. "If you're lucky, I might consent to drying off your body . . ."

Rebecca managed a weak, but playful smile. "You're insufferable," she whispered, "and you've got to catch me first." She pulled out of his embrace and took off for the house at a dead run, as if the devil himself were pursuing her. When Brig caught up with her, they were both breathless and laughing. He captured her face in his hands and kissed her with all the passion he felt rising within him.

Becca closed her eyes and melted against him, conscious only of the warmth of his lips touching hers and the cool trickle of raindrops against her neck.

She was too obliviously happy to notice the menacing shadow standing in the window of the office, staring down at her with furious blue eyes.

Chapter 11

THE WEEK PASSED TOO QUICKLY FOR BRIG AND IT seemed over before it had really begun. During the days he worked with Rebecca, Ian O'Riley, and Gypsy Wind. He saw, for himself, the potential of the bay filly, but also the danger. Someone had drugged a horse such as this once before. Wouldn't they be likely to do it again? If only he knew who had been involved and what the motive had been. Seeds of suspicion had sprouted in his mind, but he kept silent about his theory until it could be proved one way or another.

Dean had made himself scarce for the duration of Brig's visit. There had always been some excuse as to Dean's whereabouts, but it only strengthened Brig's suspicions. Rebecca's brother was never around the farm, with the one exception of mealtime. Otherwise, Dean was on errands into town, or fixing a broken fence in some distant field, or just plain nowhere to be found. When Brig had questioned

Becca about her brother, she had seemed unconcerned. Dean had always been his own boss and Rebecca rarely kept up on his whereabouts, as long as he carried his weight around the farm. The week that Brig had visited, Dean had done more than his share. He hadn't worked this hard in several years. Becca thought the entire situation odd, but chalked it up to the fact that Dean had never been comfortable around the wealth and power represented by Brig Chambers.

For Rebecca the week had flown by with the speed of an eagle in flight. She had felt ten years younger basking in the happiness of working day to day with Gypsy Wind and Brig and making love to him long into the cold autumn nights. She found herself wishing that this precious time with Brig would never end, that he would stay with her forever. Her love and respect for him had grown with each passing day and she no longer tried to fight the inevitable.

Rebecca had come to understand her love and she realized that it would never die, nor could it be ignored. She would have to accept the fact that she loved him, had always loved him, and probably always would continue to love him. Though their paths might take different courses in life, the depth of her feelings for him would never diminish. Not with time. Not with distance. Her love surmounted all obstacles, and if it could never be returned with the intensity of her feelings, she could accept that. She would take Brig on whatever terms he offered. She was resigned to her fate of loving him, and content in the knowledge that he cared very deeply for her.

What bothered her was the time apart from him. When Sunday evening came, and she finally faced the fact that he would be leaving within a few short hours, she wanted to scream at him to stay, plead with him to content himself for a few more days with her, beg him to love her . . . just one more night.

Instead, she donned what she hoped was a cheery expression and put together an unforgettable meal while he talked to Ian O'Riley. She could watch them from the kitchen window. A tall, dark-haired man with laughing gray eyes hunched over the fence as he listened to the stooped form of the grizzled old jockey. She really didn't understand why, but the scene, set before the weathered receiving barn, brought tears to her eyes. Hastily, she wiped them away with the back of her hand. She had promised herself that she wouldn't give way to the sadness she felt knowing that Brig would be gone within a few hours, and it was a vow she intended to keep. She didn't want to play on his emotions, or appear as just another weepy female. Her pride wouldn't allow it.

She heard Dean's pickup before it came into view. He had been away from the farm for the afternoon and Becca hadn't expected him to return until later in the evening. Since Brig had arrived at the farm, Dean had avoided him. Dean got out of the truck, nodded curtly toward the two men who had witnessed his noisy entrance, and then headed toward the house. The back door opened to close with a thud as Dean came into the kitchen. He tossed his hat onto a hook near the door and scowled.

"I thought Chambers was leaving," he grumbled.

"He is, but he decided to take a later flight."

"Great." Dean's sarcasm was too caustic to ignore.

After seasoning the salmon with lemon butter, Becca put it into the oven and wiped her hands on her apron. "Has Brig's stay here interfered with your life, Dean?" she asked with a forced smile. "I don't see how. You've made a point of steering clear of him."

"He makes me uncomfortable."

"Why?"

"He throws his weight around too much. This is *our* farm. Why doesn't he just leave and take care of his damned oil company? You'd think he'd have more than enough to handle without coming around here and sticking his nose in where it doesn't belong."

"Brig's only trying to help."

"The hell he is," Dean cursed with an impudent snarl. "I'll tell you what he's done, Becca: He's managed to turn this entire operation around until we don't know whether we're coming or going—"

"What are you talking about?" Dean wasn't making any sense whatsoever.

"Just look at yourself, Becca! You're dancing around with a satisfied gleam in your eye, wearing aprons and smiles like some stereotyped housewife in those fifties movies!" He stared at her fresh apron and her recently curled hair in disgust. "You're a Thoroughbred-horse breeder, Becca, not some silly woman who can't think twice without asking for a man's advice!"

An embarrassed flush crept up Becca's neck and her eyes sparked dangerously. "I haven't neglected my responsibilities, if that's what you're suggesting. I've been working with Gypsy Wind every day."

"When you're not mooning over Brig."

"Brig is helping me, Dean, and I'm not going to apologize for that! Neither am I going to deny that I care for Brig."

"And you've changed, sis. You let Brig Chambers get under your skin again. I never thought you'd be so stupid!"

"You're acting like a threatened child. What is it about Brig that intimidates you?"

Dean rose to the challenge and his icy blue eyes narrowed thoughtfully. "I'm not threatened, Becca, I'm just worried—about you. I don't want to see you hurt again, that's all. I was with you the last time. Remember? I know what Brig Chambers can do to you if he wants to," Dean warned with a well-practiced frown.

"The past is gone . . ."

"Until you start resurrecting it by breeding a horse like Sentimental Lady and then add insult to injury by getting involved with Brig Chambers all over again. You're not asking for trouble, Becca, you're begging for it!"

Becca's small fists clenched. "I think you're wrong."

"Time will tell . . ."

Brig entered the room noiselessly and the conversation dissolved. If he had heard the tail end of the argument, he gave no indication of it, nor did he comment on the deadly look in Becca's green eyes and the telltale blush on her cheeks. He strode across the room to lean against a counter near Rebecca. After casting her a lazy, I'm-on-your-side wink, he crossed his arms over his chest and smiled tightly at Dean. Brig seemed relaxed and comfortable, except for the glitter of expectation in his stormy gray eyes.

Dean took a chair and shifted his weight uneasily under the power of Brig's silent stare. Becca could feel the tension electrifying the air of the small country kitchen. Ian O'Riley sauntered into the room and seemed to notice the undercurrents of strained energy. The wooden match between his teeth moved quickly back and forth in his mouth.

"Brig asked me to stay for dinner," Ian remarked to Rebecca. "Said he wanted to talk about the horse . . . but if it's too much bother . . ."

"Nonsense. We'd love to have you," Becca replied quickly, destroying the old man's attempt at escape. Becca thought the conversation would be less strained with Ian involved.

Ian cast Becca a rueful glance before motioning toward the hallway. "I'll just give the missus a jingle. You know, check it out with the boss." His light attempt at humor did nothing to relieve the tension in the room. He shrugged his bowed shoulders and exited as quickly as he had entered, glad for his excuse to find the telephone in the hall.

"Haven't seen much of you around," Brig observed, looking pointedly at Dean.

"Been busy, I guess," Dean retorted as he half-stood and swung the chair around in order to straddle it backward. He rested his forearms on the chair back, and Becca wondered if her brother felt shielded with the tiny spokes of polished maple between himself and Brig.

Brig nodded as if he understood. "There is a lot of work around this place," he agreed complacently. Too complacently. Becca could sense the fight brewing in the air.

"I can handle it."

The affable smile on Brig's face faded. "Ian mentioned that it was your decision not to tell Rebecca that I had called her several times after Sentimental Lady's death."

Defensively, Dean managed a strained smile. "Is that what he said?"

Becca's breath caught in her throat.

"Uh-huh. And I suppose that woman . . . what was her name?" Brig squinted as if he were trying to remember something elusive.

"Martha?" Becca whispered.

"Right. Martha—she would confirm Ian's story, no doubt."

Dean seemed to pale slightly under his deep California tan. Becca's fingernails dug into her palms. *What was Brig doing?* It was as if he and Dean were playing some slow-motion game which they alone could understand. With a dismissive shrug of his broad shoulders, Dean answered. "I suppose she might."

"*If* I could find her," Brig added with a twisted smile. "Do you have any idea where she is?"

"Of course not!" Dean snapped angrily.

Brig's dark brows cocked in disbelief. "No one knows where she is?"

Before Becca could explain, Dean answered. "I suppose she's with her daughter somewhere. We really don't know. She doesn't work here anymore."

"But weren't you involved with that girl . . . Martha's daughter, Jackie?"

It was Becca's turn to be shocked. Dean had been involved with Martha's daughter? What did that mean?

"We dated a couple of times. No big deal. What's this all about, Chambers? What does Jackie have to do with anything?"

"Nothing really." Brig took an apple from the counter and began to polish it against his jeans. Dean's nerves were stretched to the breaking point. His blue eyes darted nervously around the room. "I just wanted you to admit that you told Martha not to let Becca know that I called."

"I already told you that much!" Dean's eyes flared with angry blue fire.

"I don't think we should discuss this now," Becca interjected.

"I want to get to the bottom of it!" Brig insisted.

"What's to get to the bottom of? I was just protecting my sister, Chambers. If you can't remember what happened, I do!" Dean's lips curled in contempt and he pointed viciously at Brig. "You tried to ruin her," he accused. "You did everything in your power to see her disgraced before the entire racing establishment! Because of you Ian nearly lost his license!"

"What the devil—" Ian had returned to the kitchen and his stubbled chin frowned at the scene before him. "I thought we were through arguing about Sentimental Lady."

"We were—until Chambers came back."

Becca's anger got the better of her. "All right. That's enough! I don't want to discuss this any longer—"

"You'd better get used to it, sis. Once the word gets out that you've been seeing Chambers again, the lid is going to come off this pressure cooker and explode in your face! The press will be on you quicker than a flea on a dog!"

Brig's eyes glittered like ice. "And who's going to tell the press?"

"It's not something that's easily hidden," Dean remarked. "Especially once Gypsy Wind starts racing—that is *if* you're still around by then."

"Oh, I'll be around," Brig confirmed. It sounded more like a threat than a promise. "And by the time Gypsy Wind starts, I hope to have all the mystery surrounding Sentimental Lady's death resolved." Brig was beginning to sound obsessed. His bright gray eyes never left the strained contours of Dean's ruddy face.

Becca ran her fingers through her hair and her green eyes clouded in confusion. She stared at Brig, hoping to understand the man she loved so desperately. "I don't know how you expect to find out what the horse racing board couldn't."

The muscle in the corner of Brig's jaw worked, though he attempted a grim smile. "Maybe the board didn't have the same gut feeling that I have."

"What feeling?" Becca asked.

Dean stiffened and rose from the fragile protection of the chair. "You've got a gut feeling—after all these years?" He laughed hollowly and the false sound echoed in the rafters. "It's been six years, man—forget it. It's not worth all the trouble and it would cost a fortune to dig up all that evidence again . . ." He reached for his hat, but Brig's next words made him hesitate.

"That's right, it's been six years . . . nearly seven. I'm not up on the statute of limitations. Are you?"

"What do you mean?" Becca asked, but Brig ignored the question.

"As for the cost of sifting through the evidence, I don't think money will be the problem. Any a-mount it might cost would be well worth the price to see justice served and Sentimental Lady re-venged."

Dean whirled on his boot heel and leveled his angry gaze at Brig. "Money's never the problem with guys like you, is it?" he inquired as he pushed his Stetson onto his head. His words reeked of unconcealed sarcasm as he opened the door and tossed his final words to Becca. "I'm going into town . . . don't hold dinner!" The screen door banged loudly behind him and within a few minutes the roar of the pickup's engine filled the kitchen.

"What was that all about?" Becca asked. The strain of emotions twisted her finely sculpted face. "Why did you intentionally pick a fight with Dean?"

"I wasn't trying to argue with him," Brig responded. "I just wanted to get some answers from him, that's all."

"That isn't all," Becca refuted, her green eyes snapping. "You nearly accused him of being responsible for Sentimental Lady's death—not in so many words, maybe, but the insinuation was there."

"Now, Missy," Ian interjected kindly, "don't be jumping to conclusions."

"I'm not!" Becca retorted. "Sometimes I don't think I understand you—any of you." She tried to force her attention back to the dinner she was preparing, but found it an impossible task. Too many unanswered questions hung in the air like unwelcome ghosts from the past. It made her shudder inwardly. "What were all those questions about Martha and her daughter? Good Lord, Brig, half of the argument didn't make any sense whatsoever!" She placed a pan of rice on the stove and added under her breath, "At least not to me."

She pulled off her apron and tossed it onto the counter as she turned to face Ian. The unmasked guilt on his crowlike features added to her suspicion of collusion. It was obvious that both he and Brig knew something she didn't. "Okay, what's going on?" she demanded. "This has something to do with Dean, unless I miss my guess." She folded her arms over her chest and waited for an explanation. Fear slowly gripped her heart as the men remained silent, but she ignored the apprehension, realizing that the truth, no matter how painful it might be, was far better than the doubts which had assailed her for the past few weeks. "What is it?" she asked in a low voice that betrayed none of her anxiety.

Ian couldn't meet Becca's exacting gaze. "I shouldn't have said anything," he mumbled to himself.

"About what?" Becca asked.

"About Jackie McDonnell," Brig supplied. Ian pursed his thin lips together impatiently.

"What does Martha's daughter have to do with anything? I don't see that the fact that she dated Dean a couple of times means anything."

"It was more than a few casual dates," Brig explained.

Ian interrupted, his wise eyes anxious. "Look, Chambers, I don't think that we should say anything. We'd be out of line. It's really none of our business—"

"What are you talking about, Ian?" Becca demanded.

"He's trying to protect you, Rebecca." Brig came closer to her and she could see the worry in his dark eyes. Was it for her? He placed a steadying hand on her shoulder, but she pulled away from him in defiant anger.

"*Protecting me?*" she repeated incredulously. "From what? The truth?" Ian avoided her indignant gaze. "Well, I'm sick and tired of people trying to *protect* me. Just because I'm a woman doesn't mean I fall apart under the least little bit of pressure. Dean caused a major misunderstanding by lying to me and refusing to let Brig's calls get through to me, all for the sake of *protecting* me. I would think that you of all people, Ian, could trust me with the truth!"

"It's not a matter of trust, Missy."

Becca's eyes grew softer as she gazed down at the worried ex-jockey. He wore his heart on his sleeve and his face clearly reflected his concern for her. "Ian, can't you explain to me what it is that's bothering you? It's not fair for you to carry the burden all by yourself."

His silver eyebrows pinched together. "As I said, it's none of my affair."

Brig took charge of the conversation and Ian dropped his small frame gratefully into the nearest chair. The grizzled old man removed his cap and rotated it nervously in his fingers as Brig spoke.

"You thought that Martha left the farm to take care of her daughter, who was ill—right?"

Becca nodded pensively. The stern tone of Brig's voice reinforced her fears. Nervously she rubbed her thumb over her forefinger. "I wasn't here when she left," Becca whispered, her gaze locking with Brig's. "I was visiting a friend in San Francisco at the time and when I got home she had gone . . . without even a note of explanation."

"Didn't you think that was odd?"

"For a little while, and then Dean explained that

Martha's daughter, Jackie, was seriously ill and Martha had taken Jackie to a specialist in L.A. They had relatives that lived in Diamond Bar, I think. Anyway, the only thing I considered strange was the fact that Martha never bothered to call or come back even for a short visit. What exactly are you saying here, anyway? That Dean lied? Wasn't his story the truth?" Her green eyes fixed on Ian.

"Partially," Brig allowed.

"Meaning what?"

"Meaning that Martha did leave to help her daughter."

"But?" she coaxed.

"But Jackie wasn't sick, not really." He paused for a moment and Becca's heart began to race.

"I don't understand . . ." Her voice was uncertain.

"The girl was pregnant."

Becca swallowed with difficulty and had to lean against the counter for support. Her voice was little more than a whisper. "And Dean was the father," she guessed. A sickening feeling of disgust rose in her stomach as Brig's dark eyes confirmed her unpleasant conjecture.

"That's right, Missy," Ian agreed in a hoarse voice. He stared at the table and coughed nervously.

"Someone should have told me . . ."

"Dean should have told you," Brig corrected.

"So what happened—to Jackie, and Martha and the baby?" Dean's baby. Why hadn't he confided in her? Had he ever seen his own child? What had he been thinking all these years?

Ian acted as if he didn't like talking about it, but he decided to finally let the truth come out. "Martha and Jackie moved to L.A."

"So that part wasn't a lie." It was little consolation.

"No."

"But that doesn't explain why Martha never wrote me." Becca's face was filled with genuine concern and it twisted Ian's old heart painfully.

"You have to understand, Missy, that Martha blames Dean for the pain he caused her daughter."

"Because Dean didn't marry her?"

Ian nodded. "In Martha's eyes, Dean disgraced Jackie, though heaven knows what kind of a marriage it would have been." He wiped the top of his balding head with his hand. "Jackie gave the baby up for adoption, and swore she'd never have another child. That's a pretty rough statement. Martha thought she might never have another grandchild—one she could claim as her own. She offered to adopt the baby herself, but Jackie wouldn't allow it. The girl claimed she hated the baby and wanted nothing to remind her of Dean."

"And so Martha feels the same about me."

Ian gritted his teeth. His faded blue eyes were cheerless as they held Becca's gaze. "There are too many unhappy memories here for Martha. I don't think she'll ever come back."

"Then you still hear from her?"

"Only once in a while. The missus, she sends Martha a Christmas card every year—that sort of thing."

"Does Jackie know who adopted the child?"

Ian shook his head. "Wouldn't even let the doctors tell her if it was a boy or a girl—refused to look at it when it was born. It was nearly the death of Martha. The child is better off with its adoptive parents," Ian allowed.

Becca's heart was heavy. "Didn't Dean want to know about the baby?"

Ian shook his head. "He wouldn't even talk to Jackie when she told him she was carrying his child."

"Nice guy—that brother of yours," Brig observed dryly.

When she ran her fingers over her forehead, Becca noticed that she had broken out in a sweat. She felt cold and empty inside. Why hadn't Dean confided in her? "How is Jackie now?"

Ian brightened. "She's fine, from what I understand. Married herself a young lawyer, she did."

A wistful smile curved Becca's lips. "Maybe Martha will get that grandchild yet."

"I hope so," Ian agreed.

"I'd like to call Martha or write to her. Do you have her number?"

Ian's weak smile faded. "I don't know if that would be wise," he commented, rubbing his hand over the back of his neck. "No use in stirring up hard feelings."

"Give it time," Brig suggested.

"It's been over five years!"

"Then a few more weeks won't matter, will they?" Brig asked rhetorically.

"I'll think about it—after I talk to Dean."

Ian pinched his bottom lip with his teeth. "I don't know if I'd go bringin' it up to your brother, miss. He might not like the idea that we were talkin' behind his back."

"And I don't like the idea that he didn't level with me."

"It was hard for him . . ." Ian insisted.

"Dean has a lot of explaining to do."

"Just don't do anything rash," Ian said.

An uneasy silence settled upon the room as Becca finished preparing the meal. Dean didn't return, though Becca had set him a place at the table. The conversation was stilted at first as Ian explained about his plans for racing Gypsy Wind, including the proposed move to Sequoia Park. Slowly the tension in the conversation ebbed as dinner was served and then eaten. The three of them talked about the coming racing season and the stiff competition

Gypsy Wind would have to face. Brig and Ian agreed that Gypsy Wind should be started as soon as the season opened, in order to establish a name for herself since she hadn't raced as a two-year-old. They felt that the sooner she became familiar with race regimen, the better.

By the time Ian left, some of Becca's misgivings had subsided. She promised to call Grace, Ian's wife, for Martha's address and telephone number. Although Ian soundly disapproved, he patted Becca firmly on the shoulder and told her to do what she thought best.

Brig's suitcase stood by the stairs, reminding Becca that he was leaving her. She found it imposibble to think of a future without him, or of the empty days when he wouldn't be by her side.

"I have to go," he admitted, checking his watch and setting aside his coffee cup.

"I know."

"I wish I could convince you to come with me."

Her green eyes were filled with sadness. "I have to stay here with Gypsy Wind."

They were sitting next to each other on the couch. His arm was draped lazily over her shoulders, his fingertips moving silently against her shoulder. "We could board Gypsy Wind at the Chambers Stables."

Becca smiled and set her cup next to Brig's. "I can't move to Kentucky. I don't fit in with the Eastern racing set . . . at least not anymore . . ." Her voice faded as she remembered a time when she felt at home anywhere—when the world was at her feet, before Sentimental Lady's tragic death.

"I would be with you," he stated softly as he moved her head to lay upon his shoulder. It felt so right.

She longed to say yes, to tell him that she would follow him to the ends of the earth if necessary, but she couldn't. There was too much yet to be done,

here at The Starlight Farm. "Nothing sounds better," she admitted honestly. "But I think it would be
best not to move Gypsy Wind until after the New
Year when Ian plans to stable her at Sequoia."

"I'd feel better if you were closer to me."

"Then why not move the corporate offices of
Chambers Oil out here," she teased.

"Just like that?"

"Why not?"

"Be serious."

"I am."

"And I'm nearly foolish enough to take you up on
your offer."

"I'd love it if you would stay with me," Becca
confided, hoping beyond hope that they could find a
way to be together. He kissed her gently on the
forehead.

"I'll work on it, if you promise to be careful."

"I'm always careful . . ."

The hand over her shoulder tightened. His voice
was low and threatening. "I don't trust your
brother."

"You never have."

"But I wasn't convinced that he was dangerous
before."

Becca laughed at the severity of Brig's features.
He really believed what he was saying. "Dean might
be a lot of things," she allowed. "And I admit that
I've called him more than a few myself, but he's not
dangerous. Irresponsible, wily, and maybe slightly
underhanded, yes, but dangerous, never!"

"You're taking this too lightly."

"And you're acting paranoid. Just because my
brother shirked his responsibility toward Jackie
doesn't necessarily mean that he's dangerous."

"Just be careful, okay . . . and don't go getting
him upset. Don't even mention that you know about
Jackie."

"That's going to be impossible . . ."

"Please, Rebecca. Don't say anything until I come back."

She saw the look of concern in his eyes. "You're really worried, aren't you?"

"I just want to know what we're up against, that's all. And I don't like leaving you here alone with him."

"Brig, Dean's my brother! He would never hurt me—"

"You don't know that, Becca!" For the first time, Brig's fear infected her.

"This is more than your concern because of Jackie's baby, isn't it? You really think Dean was involved in Sentimental Lady's death."

Brig's eyes narrowed and he held her more tightly to him. "I just want to know what we're up against, and I need a couple of days to sort out a few things. Why don't you come with me, for just a few days, until I can get to the source of all this?"

"I can't leave the farm right now."

"Ian can handle it. I've already spoken with him."

"Brig, this is my home, my responsibility, my *life*. I just can't pack up and leave because you're paranoid."

Roughly, he gave her shoulders a shake. "I'm not paranoid, Becca."

"Then trust me to be able to handle myself—with my brother or anyone else."

His smile was weak. "You always were a stubborn creature," he conceded. "Do you have a gun?"

Becca paled. "*No!* And I don't need one," she asserted, her lower lip trembling.

"How can you be sure?"

"Stop it, Brig, you're scaring the hell out of me."

"Good, you should be frightened."

Her voice was as tight as her grip on the arm of the

couch. "I hope this is a severe case of melodrama on your part," she whispered.

"So do I."

"Dean is my brother—"

He waved off her arguments with his open palm. "I just want you to be careful, Rebecca. You're important to me." He twined his fingers in her tawny hair and pulled her head closer to his in order to press a kiss against her lips, silently promising a shared future. "Take care of yourself, lady."

Her voice caught and she had trouble forming her response. "I will," she promised.

"There's one other thing," he said as he reluctantly rose and stepped away from her. Reaching into the pocket of his corduroy slacks, he extracted a yellowed piece of paper. Becca recognized it as the note she had signed to Jason Chambers. Brig handed the small document to her. "I've taken care of this."

She took the paper, but continued to stare into his eyes, as if she was attempting to memorize their steely gray depths. "What do you mean?"

"The note doesn't exist anymore."

"I'm sorry, Brig, but I don't quite follow you."

"It's simple. As far as anyone knows, this note was never signed. You don't owe me or Chambers Oil a bloody cent."

Becca smiled sadly. "I appreciate the offer, Brig, but I can't accept it. You don't have to buy my way out for me."

"And I couldn't live with myself if I took your money. Don't you see what I'm trying to say to you—that I love you and that what I have is yours. I don't want your money, Rebecca. I want you."

"Then stay with me," she pleaded, searching his face to try and understand him. If only she could believe that he loved her with the same intensity she felt for him.

He took her hands in his. "I'll be back," he promised. "As soon as I can . . ."

Their last embrace was a surrender to the doubts that kept surfacing in her mind. She held him as if she were afraid he would step into the dark night and never return.

Chapter 12

IT WAS THE SECOND DAY AFTER BRIG HAD DEPARTED that Becca's worries began to affect her work. The first night she had been anxious, but slowly her worry had developed into fear. Not only had she not heard from Brig in the last forty-eight hours, but also Dean hadn't returned, and she couldn't track him down. She had known that Dean was angry when he left the farm, but she had expected him to show up before now. This wasn't the first time he had taken off in an angry huff, but it was surprising that he hadn't come home with his tail tucked between his legs and a sheepish grin on his face after he had cooled off. This time it was different.

Ian O'Riley had shrugged off her concern with a dismissive shake of his balding head. Ian figured that Dean probably just needed to go somewhere and let off steam. He would return again, the old man assured Becca, like a bad penny. Becca wasn't so sure. In her anxiety, she had called Dean's favorite haunts in the nearby town. No one had seen him since the night he had driven into town like a madman.

She was working on the books when she heard the familiar sound of Dean's pickup rattling down the drive. A smile of relief curved her lips as the truck came to a halt near the stables. Dean was known for his theatrical entrances. She closed the general ledger and was about to head outside when she heard the clatter of his boots pounding on the stairs. He flew into the office at a dead run. Breathless from his sprint across the parking lot, wearing the same faded jeans and work shirt he had donned on Sunday, he looked tired and drawn. There was the faint smell of alcohol mingled with sour sweat on his clothes. A tender bruise blackened one of his cheeks.

Becca tried to make light of the situation, though her suspicion could not be denied. "You look like something the cat dragged in and then kicked back out again," she teased, though her green eyes reflected her concern for her brother. "But I'm glad you're back. I was really beginning to worry about you."

"I'll bet," Dean ground out caustically. It was then she noticed the look of contempt that darkened his icy blue eyes.

"Is something wrong? What happened to you? Where have you been? I called all over town, but no one knew where you were. I even thought about calling the police . . ." she tried to touch him on the shoulder, but he shrank away like a wounded animal.

"The police?" he echoed. "That would have been great. Jesus, Becca, you don't have to pretend any longer. I know how you feel about me."

The sarcasm in his voice made her smile disappear completely. What had gotten into him? He acted as if she intended to hurt him. "Dean, are you in some kind of trouble?"

"I'm not sure," he admitted, dropping his insolent attitude for a second. It was replaced immediately, as if he suddenly remembered that she was the enemy. "It doesn't matter," he said. "And if I am in trouble, I know who to blame."

"I'm not sure I understand what you're getting at . . ."

"Don't give me that line, Becca. You know as well as I do that Chambers isn't going to let up on me for a minute, is he?" He wiped the sweat from his forehead with the back of his grimy hand as if he were trying to erase a haunting memory.

"What has Brig got to do with any of this?" she asked, her voice tight, her mouth dry. Apprehension slowly began to grip her heart. Dean was in trouble —big trouble—and Brig was involved. The bloody memory of Sentimental Lady's last frantic hours kept surfacing in her mind. Dean couldn't meet her eyes.

"Ah, hell, Sis. I don't have time to sit around here and swap stories with you now. I just came back for a few of my things and a couple of bucks . . ."

"What are you talking about?" she demanded in a hoarse whisper filled with dread.

Dean looked at her as if he were seeing her for the first time since entering the room. He ran his hand against the corner of his mouth as he studied her. He was skeptical. "You mean you don't know?"

She shook her head, her green eyes beseeching him as she attempted to understand the brother who had once been so dear to her. He was a stranger . . . a frightened stranger carrying a heavy burden of guilt. She could read it in his eyes. *Good Lord, Dean must have known all along what had happened to Sentimental Lady!* The brother she had known had changed more than she had been willing to admit. Her heart froze.

"Then, I'll tell you. Chambers is responsible for this," Dean stated as he pointed angrily at his discolored cheek.

"Brig?" Becca mouthed the word. She was incredulous. It was then that she noticed the dried blood smeared on Dean's plaid shirt and the slight swelling of his lower lip.

"That's right! Your friend, Brig Chambers, champion of all that is good and right with the world," he snarled. "Defender of the little people and the big bucks. That's how you see him, isn't it? As some modern-day Prince Charming?"

"I . . . I see Brig as a man, a good man . . ."

"Ha!"

". . . and I find it difficult to believe that Brig got into a fistfight with you."

"Of course you do. Because it's not his style, right? How many times have I told you that you get crazy when you're around him? Well, you're right; Chambers didn't beat me up. He wouldn't dirty his hands. One of his goons got hold of me the other night and decided to teach me a lesson."

"Why didn't you come home?" she cried.

"Because this guy, he wouldn't let me . . ."

"Oh, Dean—"

"It's true!" Dean's fist pounded onto the top of the desk. Becca nearly jumped out of her skin.

She wavered for a moment, trying desperately to understand her brother, the brother she had once trusted with her life. The question faltered on her dry lips. "How . . . how do you know that this man . . . the one that hurt you . . . how do you know that he was connected with Brig?"

"Who else?"

"Someone who bears a grudge against you . . ."

she was thinking as fast as she could, hoping to find someone, anyone, other than Brig who might be responsible. ". . . like Jackie McDonnell. Maybe she was behind it."

Dean's eyes flared dangerously. "I *know* it was Chambers, Becca." He glanced around the room nervously. "Look, I don't have much time. I need a check for a couple of grand." The checkbook was lying open on the desk. Dean picked it up.

"You need two thousand dollars?" Becca repeated. Too much was happening. She needed time to think and understand what was happening. "Why?"

"Because I'm leaving, damn it!"

"*Leaving? Why?*" Becca felt her entire body beginning to shake.

"I just can't sit around here any longer and watch you make a fool of yourself over Brig Chambers—"

"That's not what's bothering you."

"The hell it isn't."

Becca watched her brother through new eyes, but she gave him one last chance, praying silently that her suspicions weren't founded. "This has something to do with Jackie McDonnell and her baby, doesn't it?"

Dean laughed mirthlessly before his eyes narrowed. "Leave her out of this. And as for that kid of hers . . . how do I know that it was mine? Jackie had been making it with half the guys in the county. I wasn't about to raise some other man's bastard."

"Dean!"

He shook an angry finger under her nose. "I told you not to tell Brig about Gypsy Wind, but you had to, didn't you? And he had to come back here and start digging everything up all over again. This is all your fault, Becca—"

"Oh, God, no," Becca whispered. Tears pooled in her round green eyes. "Sentimental Lady—"

"Shhh!" The sound of a car racing down the drive caught Dean's attention and he put a finger to his swollen lips to silence his sister. His eyes glittered dangerously when he glanced out the window and a bitter smile thinned his lips. "Damn!" A silver Mercedes was speeding on the gravel driveway. Dean recognized it as belonging to Brig Chambers. "I've got to get out of here, Becca, and now. Give me the money—"

"You can't run," she murmured, her trembling voice betraying her battered emotions.

Dean's eyes were filled with undisguised contempt. "That's where you're wrong."

"But I don't understand . . ."

"I just bet you don't. And you probably never will." He ripped a check out of the book and stuffed it into his pocket before grabbing the loose cash from the top desk drawer. "Just do me one last favor, will you, Becca?"

"What's that?"

"Give me a few minutes to get out of here," he requested. A small shadow of fear clouded his gaze for a split second. Becca felt her stomach begin to knot.

"What . . . what do you want me to do?"

He was undecided. "Hell, I don't know. Anything. Stall Brig. Do whatever you have to, tell him you think you saw me out in the far pasture . . . tell him anything to get him off my back and give me a running start."

Becca's hands were shaking as she stepped toward Dean and placed her palms against his shoulders. He stiffened while tears streamed down her cheeks. "I think I know what you're running from, Dean, and it's a mistake. You can't begin to hide—"

"You're a miserable excuse for a sister!" Dean screamed at her as he shook himself free of her grasp and knocked her to the floor. "I knew I couldn't

count on you!" He ran to the window and opened it.
Quickly he calculated the fall. It was only two
stories, less than twenty feet. Surely he could make
it. He poised on the window ledge and cast one last
insolent glance of hatred at his sister. For the first
time Becca noticed the shiny butt of a pistol peeking
out of his pocket. He wrapped one hand around the
gun while with the other he took hold of the ledge.

"Don't!" Becca shrieked hysterically from her
position on the floorboards. Her hair was tangled,
her face contorted in fear, and she sobbed uncon-
trollably when she witnessed Dean lower himself out
of the window and finally release his grip on the
ledge. "*No!*" She heard him drop, the hollow sound
of a body hitting unyielding earth.

Brig burst into the room. His eyes darted from the
open window to Becca's ashen face and the terror
reflected in her deep green eyes. The concern on his
face deepened. "Are you all right?" he asked as he
raced to her side and took her into the strong
security of his arms. "God, Becca, are you all
right?"

"I'm okay . . ."

"You're not hurt?" His dark eyes raked her body
as if he were searching for evidence to the contrary.

"Really . . . I'm . . . I'm fine," she managed to
say as she wiped her tears with the back of one hand.
The other was braced behind his neck, holding him
near. She needed to feel the strength of his body
against hers, the comfort of his arms holding her
fiercely. She had to know there was something
strong in the world that she could grasp.

He held her just as desperately. For the last two
hours he had feared her dead, lost to him forever,
and he vowed silently that he would never again let
her go, should he find her alive. He pressed his lips
to the top of her head. "Dear God, Rebecca," he

groaned, "I was afraid that I'd lost you." His voice was husky, his vision clouded by salty tears of relief.

The next few moments were quiet, the silence broken only by her quiet sobs and the rapid beating of his heart. From somewhere nearby, he thought he heard a painful moan, but he ignored it, concentrating only on the warmth of the woman in his arms.

Slowly her thoughts became coherent. "Where have you been?" she asked in the faintest of whispers.

"In L.A."

"Then you didn't return to Denver?"

His smile was grim. "No. It's a long story. Your brother—where is he?"

Becca nodded feebly toward the window, afraid that Dean might be injured or worse. Reluctantly Brig released her, but before he reached the ledge the thought of Dean's hidden pistol entered Becca's weary mind. "Watch out," she called after Brig. "He's got a gun." Her heart twisted at the thought.

The sound of a pickup coughing and sparking to life caught her attention. Brig stood watching silently as the truck roared down the winding lane. "Stupid fool," he muttered through clenched teeth.

"Why did you let him go?" Once again confusion took hold of her.

"He won't get far, and I didn't come here chasing him," Brig explained. "It was you I came to see. I was worried about you." He came back to her and pulled her to her feet, wrapping his arms tightly around her waist. His eyes were filled with genuine concern. "When I heard that Dean had gotten away from Charlie—"

"Then Dean was right. It was you. You were behind it!"

Brig nodded curtly. "But, as usual, your brother used less than sound judgment. He wouldn't accept

Charlie's hospitality and tried to knock him out by hitting him over the back of the head. Charlie reciprocated."

"But why did you try and hold him? I think that's called kidnapping in this state."

"No one kidnapped anyone. We just invited Dean to play poker—for forty-eight hours. I guess he didn't like the game."

"But, Brig, why?"

"Because I needed time and I had to be sure that he wouldn't hurt you while I was in L.A."

Becca shook her head, rubbing the soft golden wisps of her hair against Brig's chest. "You didn't need to worry. Dean would never hurt me."

"When it comes to you, I don't take any chances. Come on, let's go into the house and I'll pour you a drink. You look like you could use one."

"What I need is answers. I want to know what it was you were after in Los Angeles."

Becca's knees were weak and she had to lean on Brig as they walked through the gathering twilight toward the old farmhouse. Brig's arm was a steadying reinforcement on Becca's slumped shoulders. She tried to think rationally, but the headache that had begun to develop between her temples and the memory of the fear in Dean's eyes clouded her mind.

Once inside the farmhouse, Brig poured two shots of brandy. Becca accepted the drink gratefully and had to hold the small snifter in both of her hands in order not to spill any of the amber liquor. She looked small and frail as she sat on the couch cradling the glass between her fingers. Brig wondered how much of her vulnerability was the direct result of his carelessness. He silently cursed himself before draining his drink in one lengthy swallow.

Her soft green eyes searched his. "I don't understand, Brig, why aren't you chasing Dean?"

"Because I'd rather stay with you—you need me right now."

She smiled weakly despite her fears. "But I thought you wanted to capture him—oh God, will you listen to me. I'm talking about my *brother!*" She dropped her head into her palm and felt the tears beginning to rise once again in her throat.

"Shhh, it's all right." He sat beside her on the couch after refilling her drink.

"How can you even think that everything's okay?"

"Because for the last six years we've all been living a lie—I'm just angry with myself for not sensing it any earlier. I let my pride get in the way of my clear thinking."

"I think we all could say that. But what about Dean?"

"He's probably already in custody."

"*What?*"

"I called the police and explained everything to them. They were going to pick up Dean and question him. I told them that I suspected that he would try to make a run for it after he came here."

"But how did you know that he'd be back?"

Brig's lips curved into a thoughtful frown. "Because the poker game—the one he skipped out on. It was rigged. For a while he won and big, then he started losing. By the time he took off, he didn't have a dime on him—or a credit card. He was bound to come here for some cash when he smelled that I was on to him." Brig shook his head in self-mockery. "That was a bad move on my part. He could have hurt you . . ."

"He would never hurt me."

"You don't know your brother anymore."

Becca's eyes were clear when she looked into Brig's stormy gray gaze. "Nothing that has happened has convinced me that Dean would intention-

ally harm me, at least not physically." She swirled
the liquor in her glass and studied the small whirl-
pool. Her voice was hoarse when she spoke again.
"All of this has something to do with Sentimental
Lady, doesn't it?"

Brig set his empty glass on a side table. "Yes."

"And that was why you didn't go back to Denver?"

"I couldn't . . . not when I felt I was so close to
the truth."

"But why couldn't you tell me? Why didn't you let
me know what you were planning?"

Brig raked his fingers through his dark hair and his
eyes closed for a moment, as if he were searching for
just the right words to make her understand his
motives. "Because I wanted to be sure that I was on
the right track. For God's sake, Rebecca, Dean's
your brother! I couldn't accuse him without the
evidence backing me up."

"And now you've got it?" she asked quietly as she
absently rubbed her temple. Brig's arm across her
shoulder tensed and he nodded. "Oh, God," she
murmured desperately. She fought against the tears
threatening to spill.

"You knew, didn't you?" he asked gently.

She shook her long blond curls. "No. Not really.
I . . . I had vague suspicions . . . nothing founded
and I guess I really wanted to look the other way. I
didn't want to believe that Dean was a part of
it . . . I guess I hid my head in the sand." She turned
away from him and her next words were barely a
whisper. "It explains so much," she confided, taking
a sip from the brandy. "Tell me what you found."

There was a dead quality in her voice that made
him hesitate. "I should have known that Dean was
involved when I found out that he had intentionally
not told you about the phone calls. That didn't make
much sense to me. It was as if he wanted to keep us

apart. From what I could remember about him, he was always interested in Chambers Oil. He didn't object to your seeing me six years ago and I suspected he was secretly hoping that you and I would get married and he'd be that much closer to my father's wealth."

Becca felt that she should defend her brother, but Brig's assessment of the situation was so close to her own feelings, she couldn't deny his supposition. She silently nodded her agreement, trying to hold at bay the sickening feeling of betrayal taking hold of her. It was true. Before the tragedy, Dean had been more than pleased with her relationship with Brig.

"But something happened," Brig continued. "It had to have been the accident. At first, I thought like everyone else, that the reason for Dean's attitude toward me and the fact that he didn't let the phone calls through was because he blamed me for not supporting you during the investigation."

"What changed your mind?" she asked, though something inside her told her that she really didn't want to know.

"It was something you said."

"What?"

"You mentioned that Dean suggested you go to my father for the money to breed Gypsy Wind. That seemed a little out of character to me. If Dean wanted us apart, why would he risk getting the old man involved?"

"We had no choice," Becca reiterated. "There was nowhere else to turn and I really don't think Dean wanted me to contact Jason. When I decided to go, Dean objected."

"I think he was just blowing smoke . . ."

Becca leaned heavily against the cushions and closed her eyes. She remembered meeting with Jason Chambers in his cabin in the Rockies. He had insisted that she meet him there, away from the eyes in the office. The transaction was to be a private matter. No one would know about it except for himself and Becca. He had seemed pleased that she had come, or was it relief that had sparked in his cool brown eyes as he puffed on his pipe and let the smoke circle his head? His smile as they had shaken hands seemed vaguely triumphant and he had tucked the note away in the bottom drawer of his scarred oak desk. His response had been immediate and Becca had left the cabin feeling that if she had asked for a million dollars he would have given it to her without batting an eye. Yes, it had been strange, but she had been so elated that the oddity of the situation hadn't really taken hold of her. Until now, when Brig brought it all back to her.

"There was something else that bothered me," Brig continued. "Jason agreed to that loan . . . without any restrictions, right?" Becca opened her eyes and nodded her agreement. "He wasn't exactly the most philanthropic man around," Brig observed, tracing the line of her jaw with his fingertip, "especially when you consider his attitude after the match race. His remarks were so unfeeling and cruel. It just didn't make any sense that he would loan you the money to breed another horse like Sentimental Lady. The answer had to be in that final race, but I just didn't know what it was."

"So why did you decide to go to Los Angeles? I'm sorry, Brig, you've lost me."

"Because Ian O'Riley slipped up. When I asked him about Martha, he mentioned Jackie McDonnell and the child."

"So you went to L.A. to find Jackie," Becca surmised. "Did you locate her?"

Brig's expression remained grim. "Yeah. I found her and her mother . . ."

"Martha."

"Let me tell you, there's no love lost between Jackie and your brother."

"I know," Becca replied as she reflected on Dean's cruel statement about the girl. How had she been so blind to her own brother's deceit?

"Jackie was more than willing to tell me everything she knew about the situation, which was only that Dean had been doing a few things for my father. She couldn't, or wouldn't, admit that he had injected Sentimental Lady. Maybe she really doesn't know, or maybe she was protecting herself. If she knew about the crime, there's a chance that she could be considered an accomplice."

"So you're sure that Dean was involved," Becca whispered dryly. She held her tears at bay though they burned hotly behind her eyelids.

His fingers rubbed her shoulder. "The way I've got it figured is that Jason paid Dean to inject Sentimental Lady within the last hour before the race, after the racing soundness examination. Dean got a bundle of money from my father and Jason Chambers' horse, Winsome, kept his flawless record intact."

"Becoming all the more valuable at stud . . ."

"Exactly."

Becca tried one final, futile denial. "But Dean, he never had any money . . ."

Brig pressed a silencing finger to her lips. "Because he spent it—"

"On what?"

"According to Jackie, your brother gambles, and I can speak from personal experience to tell you he's a lousy gambler—at least at poker."

"Then how do you know that Dean got the payoff?"

"Somehow he managed to give Jackie five thousand dollars to help with the medical costs of having the baby and to give her enough money to establish herself somewhere else, to get her off his back."

"No wonder Martha never bothered to write."

Brig's voice was soothing. "She never blamed you, but couldn't stand the sight of your brother."

Becca slumped lower on the worn couch, as if the weight of Brig's explanation were too much for her slim shoulders to bear.

"So Jackie is willing to testify against my brother and tell the police that Jason and Dean were in this together."

"I'm not sure she's that strong."

Becca's green eyes urged him to continue. "Then what?"

"I think that Dean will make a full confession when he understands that the circumstantial evidence points at him and paints a rather grim picture. He'd be smarter to play his cards right and try and keep this as quiet as possible—for everyone's sake."

"They'll be back, won't they?" Becca asked. "The reporters will be back."

"As soon as they get wind of the story."

Becca sank her teeth into her knuckles as she thought about her brother and the frightened man he had become. "Dear God," she whispered, feeling suddenly chilled to the bone. "That's why he took care of me, because of his guilt."

"And so that you wouldn't find him out."

The pain in her heart was reflected in the tortured emotions on her face. "Sentimental Lady was so beautiful . . . and so innocent. I can't believe that he would intentionally—"

"Dean never intended to kill the horse, Rebecca. He only wanted to disqualify her. It was the misstep and her temperament that finally killed her."

"But if he hadn't injected her—"

"We'll never know, will we?"

A shuddering sigh passed Rebecca's lips. "It doesn't matter; Sentimental Lady is dead."

"And you took the blame for that. You and Ian O'Riley."

"It's over now."

"And you can start fresh with Gypsy Wind."

"I don't even want to think about racing right now," Becca confided. "I'm so tired, and confused. I don't think I'll ever want to race again."

"You will."

"I'm not sure, Brig." She looked at him with eyes filled with agony and remorse. "If it weren't for my stubborn pride and the fact that I had to prove myself to the world as a horse breeder, none of this tragedy would have taken place . . . and my brother wouldn't be on the run—"

"Don't blame yourself, Becca."

She wrapped her arms about her abdomen and rocked on the couch. "Hold me, Brig," she pleaded. "Hold me until it's over . . ."

Chapter 13

THE POLICE HAD TAKEN DEAN INTO CUSTODY THAT same afternoon, and when pressed with the evidence stacked against him, Dean had confessed that he had been responsible for drugging Sentimental Lady in her stall six years before.

Injecting Sentimental Lady with Dexamethasone had been Jason Chambers' idea. He had dealt with Dean in the past and knew that Becca's brother was always in debt, so he offered to pay him twenty-five thousand dollars to drug the horse. It was beneficial to both parties. Dean would be able to pay off several mounting gambling debts and an impatient loan shark. The last five thousand he would give to Jackie for the baby. The deal was sealed and Jason Chambers didn't have to worry about his horse.

According to Dean, Jason had considered Sentimental Lady strong competition and he was unsure of Winsome's ability when it came to racing against the fleet filly. To withdraw Winsome from the race was out of the question because it would be obvious that the colt was demurring to the filly. Jason couldn't take a chance on losing the race. He had to keep Winsome's racing record intact because he planned to put him out to stud and wanted to demand the highest possible fee for Winsome's services. He knew that no matter what the outcome of the race, Sentimental Lady would be disqualified when traces of the steroid were found in her test sample taken immediately after the race.

Twice Rebecca had tried to see her brother, but he had refused, preferring not to face her or the fact that he had let her shoulder the blame for his crime. It was difficult for her, but she realized that if and when Dean wanted to see her, he would contact her. She left the police station feeling drained and exhausted and was met by a bevy of reporters who had gotten wind of the story. She was grateful for Brig's strong arms and calm sense of responsibility. After a firm "no comment" to the eager press, he had whisked her away from the throng and into his car. Within minutes they had left the inquisitive reporters on the steps of the station house.

"They're not going to leave you alone," Brig pointed out, gently smoothing her hair away from her face.

"I know," she murmured, her misty eyes darkened with pain. "But I just can't face them . . . not yet." She turned her head and tried to focus on the passing landscape, but she couldn't think of anything other than her brother's lies. For six years he had hidden the truth. It was ironic, she thought quietly to herself, that six years ago, when she thought Brig had betrayed her, Dean had helped her through that rough period. As it turned out, Dean had been the culprit, and now Brig was helping pull her life back together.

She felt safe once back at Starlight Breeding

Farm, but her dreams were tormented with haunting images of her brother behind bars and a terrorized Sentimental Lady rearing against the pain in her bloodied foreleg. When Becca woke in the middle of the night, still trembling from the frightening images, Brig was beside her. His strong arms surrounded her and helped comfort her. "It's all right," he whispered against the tangled strands of her hair. "Everything's all right now. You're with me, darling Becca." And she believed him. In the desperate hours of the night, with the shadowed fragments of the dream still fresh, she believed him.

It was dawn which brought reality thundering back to her and forced her to rebuild her life. Two days after Dean's arrest, there was a sharp rap on the front door. As Becca raced down the stairs to answer it, she could hear a car idling in the drive. Since it was only seven in the morning, Becca knew it had to be someone with news of her brother. Her heart hammered fearfully as she conjured reasons for the unexpected visit. Had Dean decided to see her after all, or had he attempted to escape? Or was it worse? In his confused state of depression, could he have tried to harm himself?

She yanked open the door, expecting to face a grim police officer. Instead she stood face to face with a slim, attractive woman of about thirty-five, whose well-manicured appearance and practiced smile were neatly in place as her brown gaze swept over Becca's slightly disheveled appearance.

"Ms. Peters?" the woman inquired with a flash of near-perfect teeth and inviting smile.

Becca was instantly wary. She ran her fingers through her long golden hair, attempting to restore it to some kind of order. "Yes?"

"My name is Marian Gordon. I'm with the *Stateside Review*." She paused for a moment, waiting for the desired effect, and then extended her hand.

Becca forced a wan smile onto her face, hoping not to appear overly alarmed. The *Stateside Review* was little more than a cheap scandal sheet which boasted a healthy nationwide circulation. The stories it covered were usually the most bizarre imaginable and Becca realized that there was probably no way to put off the inevitable. One way or the other, Marian Gordon would get her story. Becca took the slim woman's hand grudgingly, and then released it.

"What can I do for you, Ms. Gordon?" she asked coolly. Her elegant dark brows arched instinctively upward.

"Your brother is Dean Peters?" Becca drew in a long, steadying breath before nodding. "I thought so." Marian Gordon seemed pleased. Her poised smile became smug. "Mr. Peters has agreed to give me an exclusive interview concerning his arrest and alleged part in the scandal concerning Sentimental Lady's death."

"He did what?" Becca replied, stunned. Then, collecting herself, she retaliated. "Is this with or without his attorney's knowledge?"

Marian shrugged, obviously not interested in minor details. "I was hoping that I would get your cooperation, Ms. Peters. It would give the story more depth and perspective if I could hear your side of it. Don't you agree?"

"I wasn't aware there were sides."

"Obviously you haven't spoken to your brother lately."

"Obviously." Becca bit back the hot retort that hovered anxiously on the tip of her tongue. "I don't think I can comment on anything at the moment," Becca hedged with a lofty arch of her brows. It took all of her control to be polite to the sharply dressed woman.

Marian Gordon smelled a story—a big story. This could be the story that would give her career the shot in the arm it so desperately needed. Rather than be taken aback by Rebecca Peters' cool reception, she pursued that elusive big story. "Your brother claims that you've . . . been keeping company with Brig Chambers again. True or false?"

"It's true that I see Mr. Chambers," Becca admitted after an initial moment of hesitation. "What does that have to do with my brother or his case?"

"Are you living with him?"

"Pardon me?"

Marian smiled sweetly. "I asked you if you were living with him." This was turning out better than the wily reporter had expected and she switched on her pocket tape recorder. She was right. The story was hot.

"Mr. Chambers has visited the farm," Becca replied evasively.

"Is he here now?"

Becca paused slightly. It was useless to lie. The Mercedes was visible in the driveway. No other vehicle on the farm compared to its luxury. It wouldn't take this reporter long to figure out that it belonged to Brig. "Yes. As a matter of fact, he is."

The woman's eyes lighted with unexpected pleasure. "Good. Then maybe I'll get a chance to have a word with him. This story involves him, too. You know, what with his father being involved and all." Marian couldn't believe her good fortune.

"I don't think so."

"But surely he has some thoughts about your brother and his father and why they drugged that poor horse."

Becca nodded her head and smiled. "I'm sure he does," she agreed. "And I'm sure that I can convince him to give you a call when he decides to make an official comment."

Marian was cagey. She tried another, more subtle tack. "Is there any truth to the rumor that you borrowed money from Jason Chambers in order to breed nearly a carbon-copy of Sentimental Lady. What was that horse's name—Gypsy Wind?"

Becca's suppressed temper began to flare. "I'm not sure I understand what you're insinuating."

The reporter looked appalled. *"Insinuating?"* she echoed. "Why, nothing, dear. According to your brother, you borrowed a rather large sum of money to produce a horse which would be a full sister to Sentimental Lady. Jason Chambers loaned you that money . . . privately of course. True?"

Forcing her fingers to unclench, Becca replied. "I bred Night Dancer to Gypsy Lady a second time. I had no idea that the offspring would be a filly, but it was. Gypsy Lady gave birth to Gypsy Wind. Now, if you'll excuse me, that's all I have to say on the subject . . . make that any subject."

"Well, one last thing. Can I see her?"

"What?" Becca had begun to turn, but spun back to face the tenacious reporter.

"I'd like a picture of Gypsy Wind for the paper. Surely you wouldn't mind a little free publicity for your horse. After all, she never raced as a two-year-old. The public will want to see if she's all she's cracked up to be."

Becca's thin patience shattered. "What she is, Ms. Gordon, is a fine racing Thoroughbred. She'll prove herself on the racetrack. And I don't want any photographs of her to be taken, not yet. She's very high-strung and there's no reason to upset her."

"You said she'll prove herself on the racetrack. What will she prove? That Rebecca Peters is still a qualified horse breeder?"

"That Gypsy Wind is a great filly."

"Prove it. Let me get a picture of her."

"No."

"The horse, *if* she is a champion, will have to get used to it sooner or later—"

"When the time comes. Not now." Becca's voice was stronger and filled with more determination than she had thought possible. The reporter had made her angry and she felt an impassioned need to protect Gypsy Wind.

Marian realized that she had blown whatever chance she had for a more in-depth interview, and she cast a hungry glance at Brig Chambers' car in the drive. Beyond the car were the barns. If only she could get one peek inside. Rebecca Peters was still lingering at the door and her expression was more than slightly perturbed, but Marian couldn't resist the chance for a final question. Why not? She had gotten far more than she had expected from the fiery blond woman.

"Well—no pictures. But tell me this, do you think your horse can duplicate Sentimental Lady's racing career?"

"That remains to be seen."

"Something bothers me, Ms. Peters."

"Just one thing?"

Marian let the pointed remark run off her back. "Why did you take a chance like that?"

"I'm sorry—like what?"

"Why would you borrow fifty thousand dollars to breed a horse so much like one who ended in such a tragedy? Was it for the horse—or the man? Did you really want another racing Thoroughbred, or was this one last desperate attempt to reunite with Brig Chambers?"

Becca's green eyes grew deadly. "I think that's about enough questions. Good day." Refraining from slamming the door in Marian's pleasant face, she watched the reporter step into her waiting car, make a full circle and drive down the lane. "And good riddance," Becca mumbled under her breath once she was assured that the reporter had left the farm. Becca wanted to make certain that Marian didn't try to snoop around the barns looking for Gypsy Wind.

"Bravo," a strong male voice asserted from somewhere in the house.

Becca closed the door behind her and noticed Brig leaning against the staircase, just out of Marian's range of vision from the front porch. "Have you been lurking there, listening to the entire conversation?"

Brig's grin wasn't the least bit sheepish. "Most of it," he admitted.

"Then why didn't you add your two cents?"

"With that vulture? Not on your life."

"Chicken," she accused with a laugh.

He came up to her and put his hands on her waist as he looked deeply into her mocking green eyes. "You did an eloquent job," he insisted.

"And you could have helped me out."

He touched her lightly on the nose. "Not true, beautiful lady. I think my presence here would only add fuel to the rampant fires of gossip."

"I wouldn't worry too much about that. It seems as if those fires are blazing pretty well with or without you."

Brig laughed and his eyes twinkled. "It's good to see you smile again," he whispered. "You handled yourself very well and I'm proud of you. What brought about your sudden change of heart?"

"Marian Gordon's holier-than-thou attitude might have had a lot to do with it. I suddenly realized that I had to put my life back in order with or without Dean."

"Are you sure you can do that?" he asked, serious concern clouding his sharp features.

"I hope so. I can't believe that he would sell out to a cheap scandal sheet like the *Stateside Review*," she fumed.

"There were quite a few things you couldn't believe about your brother," he whispered, folding her into his arms. She sighed as she leaned against him.

"The worst is that I was so easily duped. God, what a fool I've been."

"Becca, we've all made mistakes. This whole thing about Sentimental Lady colored everyone's judgment. Besides, it's not stupid to love someone or care about them the way you did with Dean."

"Unless you become blind to their flaws."

Once again he smiled. Dear God, she thought she could die looking at the warmth of his smile. "Are you blind to mine?"

"I don't know," she whispered against his chest. "Do you have any?"

"Why don't you tell me . . ." His finger touched the gentle pout of her lips, forcing them apart so he could run it along the serrated edge of her lower teeth. She touched the tip of it with her tongue and the salty impression started a yearning deep within her.

He groaned and his hand lowered to the neck of her sweater. "You're the one who's perfect, lovely lady," he stated in a rough whisper. His hands gently cupped a breast through the lightly ribbed fabric of her sweater, while he softly kissed her eyelids. Feeling the weight of her breast in his palm, his throat went dry with sudden arousal. "Marry me," he pleaded. "We've run out of excuses and out of time."

His voice was as persuasive as the tips of his fingers running lightly over her nipples. He gently lifted the sweater over her head and let her naked torso crush him. "Marry me and end this torment," he coaxed.

"You're right," she agreed with an acquiescent

sigh. "We have run out of time. I need you." She let her fingers twine in the coarse strands of his dark hair. His gray eyes held her bound. "We've waited much too long . . . let too many things come between us. I was just too stupid to understand that I have to be with you."

"The one thing you're not, Rebecca, is stupid." He cocked his head as if to study her. "Strong-willed and determined, yes. Stupid? Never!"

His lips found hers in a kiss that was savage with passion yet gentle with promise. His hands slid lightly over her body as he undressed her in the unhurried time of a patient lover. His fingers caressed her breasts as if they were new to him. They explored and demanded, creating restless yearnings that made her impatient in her hunger for him.

Warm blood ran in her veins until she could think of nothing but the quiet mastery of his hands on her body and the unyielding desire building within the most feminine depths of her being. She burned for him, ached for his touch.

His movements were slow as he gently pushed her onto the burgundy carpet and savored the sight of her white body stretched against the dark pile. His palms rubbed against her breasts until they tightened in anticipation of the warmth of his mouth covering her nipples. She was not disappointed and gasped in pleasure when she felt the gentle bite of his teeth against her supple breast.

She duplicated his movements. After removing his shirt, she traced the hard line of his muscles with the tip of her finger, past his shoulders, down his chest to stop at the waistband of his jeans. He encouraged her by moving over her and pressing his abdomen closer to her fingers. "Undress me," he commanded, the ache within him burning to be released.

Deftly she removed his pants and let her fingers

and gaze touch all of him, delighting in the feel and the sight of all of his lean, hard length. She quivered at the feel of his firm flesh against hers.

"It's your turn," he announced in a voice thickened with awakened passion. "Make love to me." Quickly he reversed their positions, pulling her over him.

A slow smile crept over her lips as she kicked off the rest of her clothes and lay the length of her body over his. She let him guide her with his hands, while slowly she pressed against him, coaxing the fires within him to burn wildly in his loins.

"I love you," he murmured, letting his impassioned gaze rove restlessly while he watched her eyes glaze with the desire flooding her veins. He watched her stiffen over him and knew the moment she really wanted him, needed the fulfillment. Then he let go, giving into the rising tide of passion roaring in his blood.

Brig arched up to meet Becca, while his hands pushed her tightly against him. They erupted together in a heated flow of molten lava that began in their souls and ran into each other as their combined heartbeats echoed the thrill of spent love. Spent, they collapsed together.

Becca lay quivering in his arms, exhausted and refreshed at the same time. After a few moments of silence broken only by her shuddering sighs, Brig spoke. "I meant it, Rebecca," he reaffirmed. His grip on her tightened. "I want to marry you and I won't take no for an answer."

"I'm not foolish enough to deny you, my love," she whispered into his ear. "I think I've wanted to marry you from the first moment I met you."

He grinned at the memory. "Then let's not wait. Get up and get going." He gave her a playful slap on the buttocks to reinforce his impatience.

"Today? Right now? Are you crazy? I'm not ready—"

"Idle excuses, woman," he joked with a mock scowl. "We've waited too long to stand on ceremony. Neither one of us has any family to speak of—not close, anyway. Reno is only a few hours' drive. We could be married by this evening."

She held her hands up, palms stretched outward. "Wait. Everything's moving too fast for me. What about the farm? Your business? Gypsy Wind?"

"I've considered everything," he confirmed, tossing her the slightly wrinkled clothes. She caught them along with the satisfied twinkle in Brig's dark eyes. "The first few months will be rough. There's no denying that much. I'll have to spend some of the time in Denver. But I've already decided that I can work just as well from the San Francisco office."

She wasn't convinced. "But that's still a three-hour drive from here—"

"A lot closer than Denver. Anyway, it will have to do until we can fix this place up properly. Then I'll have an office in the house and only make the trip into the city a couple of times a week. If I'm needed in Denver—really needed—I can fly there." He jerked his jeans on and buckled the belt with authority. "Any other questions?"

Becca struggled into her clothes. "Sounds like you have it all worked out," she observed with more than a trace of awe in her voice.

"It's something I've been thinking about for a long time."

"Since when?"

"Since the night I found you on the doorstep to my father's cabin," he admitted roughly and Becca felt a wayward pull on her heart. He seemed so genuinely earnest. "I just didn't think I could convince you."

She had begun to slip into her sweater, but stopped. A wanton smile pulled at the corners of her mouth and she dropped her eyelids suggestively over misty green eyes. "Why don't you try convincing me again?" she suggested smoothly.

His dark eyes sparked at the game. "You *can* be a capricious little thing can't you?" He crossed the room and stood over her, daring her to respond.

She rose to her full height, and then stretched to her toes in order that she could whisper into his ear. "Only with you, love. Only with you."

Chapter 14

THE CEREMONY UNITING BRIG AND BECCA AS HUSBAND and wife was simple and to the point. A dour-faced justice of the peace and his round sister performed the rite in Reno. Rebecca had never been happier than she was that day, holding onto Brig's strong hand and unashamedly letting the tears of joy run down her face. Although she had always envisioned a large church wedding complete with an elegant white lace dress, Becca felt resplendent in her pale pink suit and ivory silk blouse. Brig stood proudly beside her, wearing his crisp navy suit and slightly crooked smile with ease. For the first time in years, Becca knew that everything in her life had finally come together. She had even managed to push aside her lingering doubts about her brother for the time being. These few precious moments belonged to Brig alone. In the glittery town of Reno, Nevada, tucked in a valley rimmed by dusty hills, she had become Brig's wife.

Smiling contentedly to herself, she leaned against Brig's shoulder as he drove westward. A lazy sun had sunk below the horizon and twilight descended as they headed through the mountains. Aside from the soft hum of the car engine, the quiet of the oncoming night remained undisturbed. In the purple sky, shimmering stars winked in the dusk. Time seemed to have stopped and Becca was only conscious of the strong man who was now her husband. For years she had dreamed of marrying Brig, and determinedly pushed those dreams into the darkest corners of her mind. Now the marriage had become reality and she sighed contentedly with the realization that nothing could ever drive Brig away from her.

Their time together was much too short. After spending a carefree week making love to Becca at Starlight Breeding Farm, Brig was forced to return to Denver. He couldn't put off his responsibilities as the head of Chambers Oil.

Days on the farm without Brig seemed long and empty to Becca. She was restless and the pleasure she usually derived by immersing herself in work was missing. She couldn't help but wonder what Brig was doing or when he would return to her. She lived for the short telephone conversations that bound them together. Though there was more than enough work to keep her busy at the farm, she felt a deep loneliness envelop her and she impatiently counted the hours until his return.

For the most part, Brig's time was spent on airplanes between Denver and San Francisco. The challenge of moving the headquarters of a corporation the size of Chambers Oil was monumental. Though Brig had originally hoped that the transfer would take only a few weeks, he soon discovered that it would take months to accomplish his goal of resettling Chambers Oil on the West Coast. His impatience grew each day he was separated from Becca.

Becca and Ian continued to work daily with Gypsy Wind. Slowly the temperamental filly seemed to be settling into a routine of early morning workouts. When Brig was on the farm, he, too, would add his hand at trying to shape the skittish horse into the finest racing filly ever to set foot on a California racetrack. It was a slow and tedious job as Gypsy Wind had her own opinions about racing. Without Ian O'Riley's patience and love for the filly, Becca would have given up. But the feisty trainer continued to insist that Gypsy Wind was born to run in the sport of kings.

The remodeling of the buildings around the farm had started and Brig insisted that a security guard be posted round the clock to watch the barns. Becca had argued against the need for the guard, but had finally agreed when she was forced to consider Gypsy Wind's welfare. Brig convinced Becca that Gypsy Wind was a celebrity who needed all the protection available. The horse could be an easy target of a malicious attack aimed at anyone involved with Chambers Oil or Sentimental Lady. Ian O'Riley concurred with Brig, and Becca was forced to go along with his decision.

After the first few uneasy days, Becca recognized the worth of the security guard. The press had been hounding Becca day and night, and with the patient but insistent aid of the guard, Becca was able to keep the hungry reporters at bay. It was hard for Becca to retain her composure all of the time, and the press seemed adamant for a story, especially Marian Gordon. The cool reporter for the *Stateside Review* returned to Starlight Breeding Farm in search of a new angle on Gypsy Wind. The perfectly groomed Marian unnerved Becca, but she managed to hide her unease. Becca reminded herself that she was partially to blame for the furor. Not only had Dean's confession brought Sentimental Lady's tragedy back into the public eye, but the fact that Becca had married Brig Chambers had fanned the already raging fires of gossip concerning Gypsy Wind. Brig Chambers was one of the wealthiest men in the country, his father and a beautiful young model had recently perished in a traumatic plane crash, and Brig had once denounced Becca publicly—or at the very least refused to come to her defense. Everything touching Brig Chambers was hot copy for the scandal sheets and the press was frantic for any insight, real or fabricated, into the relationship between Brig and his wife. Gypsy Wind and her famous owners were suddenly the hottest story of the year. It was no wonder that the eager reporters weren't easily discouraged. Dean had been right when he had predicted that Becca was begging for trouble by breeding Gypsy Wind.

Throughout most of the ordeal, including Dean's trial, Becca had managed to appear outwardly calm and only slightly perturbed. Though she smiled rarely in public, the security of Brig's love had given her the strength to deal with both the reporters and their insensitive questions. It was only when someone would ask too personal a question about her brother that her green eyes would darken dangerously and she would refuse to answer. Dean still refused to see her and it would take years to heal the bitter sting of his rejection.

Gypsy Wind's first race was held in Sequoia Park. Brig had arranged his schedule in order to witness the running. Though the race was a little-publicized maiden, the crowd was expectant, largely due to the well-publicized fact that Gypsy Wind, a full sister to the tragic Sentimental Lady, was entered. If Brig's confidence wavered, it wasn't apparent in his casual stance or the fire of determination in his eyes. He held Becca's trembling hand in the warm strength of his palms as he watched Gypsy Wind being led to the starting gate. Gypsy Wind's moment of truth was at hand and it seemed to Becca that the entire world was watching and holding its breath. Even Ian appeared nervous. His face remained stern and lined with concentration as he shifted a match from one corner of his mouth to the other.

Gypsy Wind entered the gate without too much trouble and Becca sighed in relief when the nervous filly finally settled into the metal enclosure. Within minutes all of the stalls in the gate were filled with anxious fillies. Suddenly the gates clanged open. Gypsy Wind leaped forward and a big chestnut filly slammed into her so hard that Gypsy Wind nearly stumbled. Becca's heart dropped to her stomach as she watched her game horse adjust her stride and rally, only to be bumped at the three-eighths pole by another filly.

"Dear God," Becca murmured, squeezing Brig's hand with her clenched fingers.

Gypsy Wind was now hopelessly behind the leaders, but found it in her heart to make up some of the distance and finish a mediocre fifth in a field of seven. "Thank God it's over," Becca thought aloud, slowly releasing Brig's hand. She couldn't hide her disappointment.

Brig's smile slowly spread across his handsome features. "Well, Mrs. Peters," he announced. "I think you've got yourself a racehorse."

Becca shook her head, but the color was slowly coming back to her face. "Do you?"

Ian O'Riley cracked a pleased grin. "That you do, Missy," he replied, as if the question were directed at him. He took off his cap and rubbed his grizzled chin. "That y'do."

Ian was assured of the filly's potential, and al-

though the press crucified the dark horse for her first
run, the wily trainer was eventually proven right.

Gypsy Wind's unfortunate experiences during her
first race affected her running style for the remainder
of her career. After leaving the gate with the field,
the fleet filly would drop back to avoid the heavy
traffic and possibility of being bumped. With her
new strategy, Gypsy Wind managed to win her next
race by two lengths and the next seven starts by an
ever-increasing margin over her opponents. She
followed in her famous sister's footsteps and won all
three jewels of the filly Triple Crown with ease.
Reporters began to compare her to some of the
fastest horses of the century.

Becca was ecstatic about Gypsy Wind's success.
Everything seemed to be going her way. The breeding farm was being expensively remodeled, her
career as a Thoroughbred horse breeder was rees-
tablished, Gypsy Wind was winning, effortlessly,
and most important, Becca was married to Brig. The
only dark spot on her life was her brother, Dean. He
had been found guilty of criminally tampering with
Sentimental Lady and still refused to see Becca.
Even during the trial, Dean had refused to look
across the courtroom at Becca or even acknowledge
her presence. When she had spoken with Dean's
attorney, the man had suggested that she forget
about her brother until he was willing to face her
again. The attorney had promised to inform Becca
the minute that Dean wanted to see her.

It was when the fans and the press began demanding a match race that Becca balked. Although she
had half-expected it, the thought of a match race and
reliving the nightmare of Sentimental Lady's death
unnerved her. She couldn't find it in her heart to put

the additional strain on herself and her horse. Already there were rumors of Gypsy Wind challenging the colts and settling the arguments concerning which horse was the finest three-year-old of the year.

In a normal racing year, one or two of the best horses prove themselves in regularly scheduled stakes races. But this year the Triple Crown races were inconclusive. Three different colts ran away with the separate events. Added to the colt dilemma was Gypsy Wind, the undisputed filly of the year. Several tracks had made offers for a match race, supposedly a race which would settle, once and for all, the arguments surrounding the favored horses.

Rebecca remained adamant. She wasn't about to race Gypsy Wind, though the other owners pressured her and the various race tracks were offering phenomenal amounts of money to field the event. The bidding by the tracks for the race was incredible, and added to that cash were offers from sponsors and television networks. With an attraction such as Gypsy Wind and the notoriety which followed her career, the sky was the limit in the bidding game, and the American public demanded the race!

Lon Jacobs, a prominent California promoter, couldn't be pushed aside. He called Becca Chambers each week, hoping to entice her into entering Gypsy Wind in a match race.

"Neither I nor Gypsy Wind have anything to gain from the race," Becca explained to Lon Jacobs for what seemed the tenth time in as many days.

"What do you mean?" the California promoter asked incredulously. "What have you been working for all of your life, Mrs. Chambers? All those years of breeding champions certainly add up. You may well have the horse of the century on your hands, but no one's going to buy it until she stands up to the colts."

Becca closed her eyes and her fingers whitened around the receiver. "I'm just not interested."

"What about what the racing public demands? You have a certain obligation to the American people, don't you?"

Becca ran her fingers through her blond hair. "I have a responsibility to my horse and my family."

Lon Jacobs coaxed her. "I realize that the money isn't important to you. Not now. But what about the fame? With this one race you could establish yourself as one of the premier breeders in the country."

"I don't know if the race is necessary for that. The entire world knows the potential of Gypsy Wind."

"Potential, yes," he agreed smoothly. "But she hasn't really proved herself."

"I think she has."

There was an impatient edge to the promoter's voice. "Well, then think about Ian O'Riley, will you? He was the one who really bore the guilt for your brother's crime six years ago. He was the trainer who was brought before the board. His reputation was scarred irreparably when it turned out that Sentimental Lady was drugged while in his care."

Becca was silent and intuitively Lon knew he'd hit a sensitive nerve.

"Look, Mrs. Chambers, I think I can convince the owners of the other horses to agree to a race nearby. That way you wouldn't have to ship your horse all over the country. You could prove to all those people who watched Sentimental Lady run that you knew what you were doing—that Ian O'Riley is still a damned good trainer. And Gypsy Wind would have the home-court advantage, so to speak."

"She doesn't need any advantage."

Lon laughed jovially. "Of course she doesn't. She's a winner, that filly of yours." Becca wondered if she were being conned. "So what do you say—do we have a horse race?"

"I don't know . . ."

"You would be doing Ian O'Riley a big favor, Mrs. Chambers. I think he's done a few for you."

Becca's decision was quick. "Okay, Mr. Jacobs. I'm willing to race Gypsy Wind one last time, against the colts, as long as it's here, at Sequoia. And after that she'll retire. I don't want to hear anything more about racing my filly."

"Wonderful," Lon cooed as he hung up the phone. Becca was left with the uncanny feeling that she might have made the worst decision of her life.

She couldn't hide her unease when Brig entered the room. "Who was on the phone?" he asked.

"It was Lon Jacobs." She managed to meet Brig's wary gaze squarely. "He wants a match race at Sequoia. I agreed."

"You did what?" Brig was astounded and an angry gleam of fire lighted his eyes. "Becca, love, why?"

"It was a weak moment," she confessed, explaining about Lon's arguments for the race.

Brig's jaw hardened in suppressed anger. "I don't think Ian O'Riley thinks you owe him any favors. You've always stood up for him, and Gypsy Wind's career added luster to his. Dean confessed to drugging Sentimental Lady. Ian was absolved of the crime."

"I suppose you're right," she said wearily.

"You know I am!" He shook his head and looked up at the ceiling as if he could find some way to understand her. When his eyes returned to hers they were as cold as stone. "Why don't you face up to the real reason you're racing Gypsy Wind?"

"The real reason?" she echoed, surprised by his sudden outburst.

"This is what you wanted all along, wasn't it? To prove that your horse could handle the colts. Six years ago, Sentimental Lady was beaten, and you've never gotten over it. You still have some goddamn burning desire to prove yourself!"

"Not true, Brig," she argued. "I told Lon Jacobs that Gypsy Wind would retire."

"Right after she races against the colts," he surmised. "What is it with you, Rebecca? Are you a glutton for punishment? Wasn't once enough"—his eyes narrowed savagely—"or don't you give a damn about that horse of yours?"

His biting words slashed her heart. "You don't think she can do it, do you?"

"I don't care if she can win or not. I'm only concerned about you and Gypsy Wind, and I don't like the fact that you were manipulated by the likes of Lon Jacobs!" Rage blazed in his gray eyes and his jaw clenched. Before she could defend herself, he continued with his tirade. "Why take the chance, Becca? You know that match races are hard on any horse . . . whether she wins or loses." His anger began to ebb and he looked incredibly tired. Becca's heart turned over. "Oh, Becca, why?"

"I told you why," she whispered.

"And I told you that you're not being honest with me . . . or yourself."

He reached for the decanter on the bar and poured himself a stiff shot of bourbon before turning back to his den. Becca felt alone and depressed. The reconstruction of the house and the barns was finished, the grounds were once again well tended, but there was a black void within her because she had disappointed Brig. Was he right? Did she still feel the need to purge herself of Sentimental Lady's unfortunate death, prove to the world that her filly could outdistance the colts? She felt the bitter sting of tears burn in her throat. Why had she been so foolish?

In the month it took to arrange the race, Brig and Becca avoided the subject of the event. Perhaps if they chose to ignore the argument, it would disappear. Brig reluctantly agreed to go with her to the track, but he advised her in no uncertain terms how he felt about the race. He was against it from the start and considered it a monumental risk on her part. Even Ian O'Riley, the trainer who had predicted Gypsy Wind's supremacy over the colts, seemed unusually pensive and out of sorts as the day of the race drew near.

From the moment she arrived at Sequoia Park, Becca was enveloped by an eerie feeling. The doubts she had pushed into the darkest corners of her mind resurfaced. She should never have agreed to the race, or she should have insisted upon another track instead of the very same place where Sentimental Lady had run her last horrifying race. Though Gypsy Wind had raced before at Sequoia, a thousand doubts, plus Brig's fears, came to rest on Becca's slim shoulders. She attempted to tell herself that it was her imagination, that she shouldn't let the feeling of *déjà vu* take hold of her, but the noise of the crowd, the hype of the race, and the poised television cameras added to her overwhelming sense of unease.

Ian O'Riley was concerned. The tension in the air had affected Gypsy Wind. Though she had never been as nervous as Sentimental Lady, in the last two days Gypsy Wind had appeared distressed and off her feed. The veterinarian hadn't found anything physically ailing the horse and yet something wasn't right. Ian O'Riley wrestled with the decision of scratching her from the race. In the end, he decided against it. This was the filly's last chance to flaunt her speed and grace.

The day had dawned muggy, with the promise of rain clinging heavily to the air. It seemed difficult to breathe and Becca felt a light layer of perspiration begin to soak her clothes. Storm clouds threatened in the sky and the shower of light rain started just as the horses were being led to the gate. Becca prayed silently to herself. Gypsy Wind seemed to handle the adverse weather and entered the starting gate without her usual fuss. That fact alone disturbed Becca. The filly wasn't acting normally—not for her. Brig took Becca's sweaty palm in his and for a moment their worried gazes locked. *Dear God, what am I doing,* Becca wondered in silent concern.

The starting gate opened with a clang and the four horses escaped from the metal enclosure. Becca's heart leaped to her throat as she watched Gypsy Wind run gallantly, stride for stride, with the colts. Instead of hanging back as was her usual custom, the blood-bay filly galloped with the colts, meeting the competition head-on. Determination gleamed in her proud dark eyes and her legs propelled her forward as her hooves dug into the turf.

In the back stretch, two of the colts pulled away from her, their thundering strides carrying them away from the filly and the final horse, who was sadly trailing and seemed spent. Becca's concern increased and her stomach knotted painfully, although she knew she was watching Ian O'Riley's strategy at work. The ex-jockey had decided to let the two front runners battle it out, while his horse hugged the rail. Gypsy Wind had plenty of staying power, and Ian knew that she would be able to catch them in the final quarter.

The dark filly ran easily and Becca noticed the slight movement of the jockey's hands as he urged Gypsy Wind forward. Becca's throat tightened as the courageous horse responded, her long strides eating up the turf separating her from the leaders.

As Gypsy Wind made her bid for the lead, the outside colt bumped against the black colt running close to the rail, jostling the ebony horse against the short white fence. Gypsy Wind, caught behind the two colts, stumbled as she pulled up short in order to avoid a collision.

The crowd witnessed the accident and filled the stands with noise, only to quiet as it watched a replay of the tragedy of seven years past. The jockey attempted to rein in Gypsy Wind, but she continued to race, plunging forward as she vainly attempted to catch the colts.

Becca's face drained of color. Seven years of her life rolled backward in time. "No!" she screamed, her voice lost in the noise from the stands and the address system. "Stop her, stop her," Becca begged as she pulled away from Brig's grip. A horrified expression of remorse distorted Becca's even features and tears flooded her eyes. "It can't be . . . it can't be!" she cried, stumbling after her horse.

One horse was disqualified, and Gypsy Wind had finished a courageous third. Becca felt Brig's strong hands on her shoulders as he guided her toward Gypsy Wind. The jockey had dismounted and Ian O'Riley was running practiced hands over the filly's forelegs. Cameras clicked and reporters threw questions toward Rebecca. She ignored the press and was thankful for Brig's strength throughout the ordeal.

Ian nodded toward Becca as she came close enough to touch the filly. "I think we might have a problem here," he admitted in a rough whisper.

"Oh, God, not again . . . not again," Becca prayed.

"Excuse me!" The veterinarian was at the horse's side within a minute after the race was over. Quickly he examined Gypsy Wind's leg and issued terse directives that the horse was to be taken to the nearby veterinary hospital. The horse attempted to prance away from the noise and confusion, but was finally taken away amid the shouts and oaths of racing officials, attendants, and the television crews.

Brig tried to comfort Becca, but was unable to. Guilt, like a dull knife, twisted in her heart. It was her fault that Gypsy Wind had raced. Likewise Becca was to blame for the horse's injury.

The waiting was excruciating, but didn't take long. It was quickly determined that Gypsy Wind would recover.

"It even looks like she'll be able to race again," the veterinarian admitted with a relieved smile. "She pulled a ligament in her left foreleg. It's only a slight injury and she'll be as good as new," the kindly man predicted with a sigh. "But she won't be able to race for the rest of the season."

"Or ever," Becca vowed, tears of gratitude filling her eyes. "She's retiring—for good."

"That's a shame," the veterinarian observed.

"I don't think so." She took the vet's hand and shook it fondly. "Thanks."

Brig put his arm over her shoulders. "Let's get out of here," he suggested. "Ian's staying here and there's no reason for us to stick around. If he needs us, he can call."

"Are you sure?" Becca didn't seem certain.

"Aren't you? You're the one who always had faith in Ian. He'll take care of the Gypsy."

They walked out of the hospital together and were greeted by a throng of reporters.

"Mrs. Chambers . . . how is Gypsy Wind?" a dark-haired man asked as he thrust a microphone in Becca's direction.

"She'll be fine," Becca replied with more conviction than she thought possible.

"But the injury?" the man persisted.

"A pulled ligament—the vet assured me it's nothing too serious."

"Then you do plan to race her again?"

Becca paused and her green eyes looked into Brig's before she turned her self-assured smile back to the reporter. "Not a chance!"

Slowly, Brig was guiding her to the car. The thick crowd of reporters followed closely in their wake, shouting questions at them. When they finally made it to the Mercedes, Brig turned on the crowd, and the irritation in his eyes was only partially hidden. "Perhaps if you asked your questions one at a time," he suggested.

It was a strong female voice that caught Becca's attention and she found herself looking into the knowing eyes of Marian Gordon.

"Mrs. Chambers," Marian greeted coldly. "How do you feel now that you know you almost killed Sentimental Lady's sister the way you killed her?"

Becca bristled, but felt Brig's strong hand on her arm.

"No one killed Sentimental Lady, Ms. Gordon. It was an unfortunate accident."

"Not an accident—your brother drugged that horse," Marian responded. "Was that with or without your knowledge?"

Brig took a step forward, but Becca held him back with the gleam of determination in her eyes. "What happened with my brother is very unfortunate, Ms. Gordon, and has nothing to do with me, or Gypsy Wind. It's also old news. I suggest that you try writing something a little more topical."

"Such as how Gypsy Wind almost went to her grave today?"

"Such as how that brave filly stood up against the colts."

Before Marian could respond, another reporter edged forward and smiled fondly at Becca. "Mrs.

Chambers, do you plan on breeding a sibling to Gypsy Wind?"

"No."

"But you still will be breeding Thoroughbreds— for the future?" the young man insisted. Becca cast a speculative glance in Brig's direction. His eyes were riveted to her face.

"I'm not sure—not right now."

"How do you feel about it, Mr. Chambers?" the young reporter asked, turning his attention to Brig. A smile tugged at the corners of Brig's mouth.

"I think my wife will make her own decision. She's a very . . . independent woman," he observed with a twinkle in his eye. "Now, if that's all—"

The reporters realized that they had gotten as much of a story as they could and reluctantly backed away from Brig's car. Once inside the Mercedes, Becca managed a weak laugh. "So you think I'm independent?"

"Not totally, I hope."

"What's that supposed to mean?"

Brig maneuvered the car away from the racetrack and drove toward the hills surrounding Starlight Breeding Farm. "That means that I'd like to think that you depend on me—some of the time."

"You know that I do." She paused slightly. "What about you, Brig? Do you depend on me?"

His smile turned into a frown of disgust. "More than you would ever imagine," he admitted. "I don't know how I got along without you for the last six and a half years. I must have been out of my mind."

The rest of the journey was finished in silence. Becca bathed in the warm glow of Brig's love. When they pulled through the gates guarding Starlight Breeding Farm, Becca felt her heart swell in her chest. The new buildings, freshly painted a gleaming white, stood out against the surrounding green of the hills.

Brig helped Becca out of the car and they walked to the closest paddock. Two mares were grazing peacefully while young colts scampered nearby. The horses raised their inquiring heads at Becca and Brigg, flicked their dark ears and turned their attention back to the grass. The colts ran down the length of the fence, glad for an audience. As ungainly as they appeared, there was a grace in the sweep of the colts' legs.

Becca leaned her head on the top rail of the fence. "I don't know if I can give this up," she sighed, studying the graceful lines of the colts' bodies.

"I haven't asked you to."

"But I can see it in your eyes." She turned to face him and caught the look of tenderness in his eyes. "I do love you," she admitted, throwing her arms around his neck.

"No more than I love you."

"But you want me to quit breeding horses and racing them," she accused, smiling sadly.

"Not at all, Becca. I just want you to slow down. You've proved yourself today and purged yourself of Sentimental Lady's tragedy. Go ahead and breed your horses—race them, if you want. But slow down and enjoy the rest of what life has to offer."

Slowly his words began to sink into her tired mind. She cocked her head coquettishly to the side and her shimmering honey-colored hair fell away from her face. "Just what do you have in mind?" she asked as she observed him with an interested smile.

His eyes darkened mysteriously. "I thought I might be able to convince you to forget about breeding horses long enough to consider having a child."

Her dark brows arched. "Oh you did, did you?" she returned, touching his chin lightly with her fingertips.

"We've waited too long already."

"I might agree . . . but tell me, just how do you propose to convince me?"

"With my incredible powers of persuasion, Mrs. Chambers—" His head lowered and his lips captured hers in a kiss filled with passion and promise. She closed her eyes and sighed as she felt her bones melt with his gentle touch.

"Persuade away, Mr. Chambers," she invited, her eyes filled with her overwhelming love. "Persuade away."

"Dear God, lady, I love you," he whispered as he scooped her into his arms, straightened, and carried her toward the house. "And I'm never going to let you get away from me again."

With his final vow, he opened the door, carried her inside, and turned the lock.

If you enjoyed this book...

Thrill to 4 more Silhouette Intimate Moments novels (a $9.00 value)— ABSOLUTELY FREE!

If you want more passionate sensual romance, then Silhouette Intimate Moments novels are for you!

In every 256-page book, you'll find romance that's electrifying...involving... and intense. And now, these larger-than-life romances can come into your home every month!

4 FREE books as your introduction.

Act now and we'll send you four thrilling Silhouette Intimate Moments novels. They're our gift to introduce you to our convenient home subscription service. Every month, we'll send you four new Silhouette Intimate Moments books. Look them over for 15 days. If you keep them, pay just $9.00 for all four. Or return them at no charge.

We'll mail your books to you *as soon as they are published.* Plus, with every shipment, you'll receive the Silhouette Books Newsletter absolutely free. *And Silhouette Intimate Moments is delivered free.*

Mail the coupon today and start receiving Silhouette Intimate Moments. Romance novels for women...not girls.

Silhouette Intimate Moments

Silhouette Intimate Moments

──── Coming Next Month ────

A WOMAN WITHOUT LIES
by Elizabeth Lowell

•

DISTANT WORLDS
by Monica Barrie

•

SCOUNDREL
by Pamela Wallace

•

DEMON LOVER
by Kathleen Creighton

Silhouette
Intimate Moments

more romance, more excitement

---------------------------------- **$2.25 each** ----------------------------------

Silhouette
Intimate 🖤 *Moments*
more romance, more excitement

SILHOUETTE INTIMATE MOMENTS, Department IM/5
1230 Avenue of the Americas, New York, NY 10020

Please send me the books I have checked above. I am enclosing
$_____ (please add 75¢ to cover postage and handling. NYS and
NYC residents please add appropriate sales tax). Send check or money
order—no cash or C.O.D.'s please. Allow six weeks for delivery.

NAME _____

ADDRESS _____

CITY _____ STATE/ZIP _____

MAIL THIS COUPON
and get 4 thrilling
Silhouette Desire®
novels <u>FREE</u> (a $7.80 value)

Silhouette Desire books may not be for everyone. They *are* for readers who want a sensual, provocative romance. These are modern love stories that are charged with emotion from the first page to the thrilling happy ending—about women who discover the extremes of fiery passion. Confident women who face the challenge of today's world and overcome all obstacles to attain their dreams—*and their desires.*

We believe you'll be so delighted with Silhouette Desire romance novels that you'll want to receive them regularly through our home subscription service. Your books will be *shipped to you two months before they're available anywhere else*—so you'll never miss a new title. Each month we'll send you 6 new books to look over for 15 days, without obligation. If not delighted, simply return them and owe nothing. Or keep them and pay only $1.95 each. There's no charge for postage or handling. And there's no obligation to buy anything at any time. You'll also receive a subscription to the Silhouette Books Newsletter *absolutely free!*

So don't wait. To receive your four FREE books, fill out and mail the coupon below *today!*